Cover designed by: GetCovers

Formatting designed with Atticus

Jaded Wears the Crown

Chronicles of Radelea
Samara Saward

To teenage me:
You are not alone.

Content Warning

Jaded Wears the Crown contains content that may be triggering to some readers, including, but not limited to, abuse of power, torture, asphyxiation, gaslighting, depictions of and references to death, unknown heritage, misogyny, war, suicidal ideation, PTSD, trauma, vivid imagery, murder (including decapitation), and sexually explicit scenes.

Your mental health matters.
Beyond Blue (1300 224 636) provides information and support to help everyone in Australia achieve their best possible mental health, whatever their age and wherever they live.
If you have any concerns, my inbox is always open.

A Guide
to Radelea

Radelea — *Rah-dell-ia*

AUTUMN COURT

Bria — *BREE-ah* — Daughter of the High Lord

Kerym — *keh-RHYME* — High Lord

Fayeth — *FAY-eth* — Kerym's mate; Rennyn's mother

Rennyn — *WREN-en* — Prince; Bria's half-brother

SPRING COURT

Nyana — *NIGH-ar-na* — High Lady

SUMMER COURT

Ad'Starrag — *ADD-stah-rag* — Summer Court keep

Iker — *EYE-kerr* — High Lord

Yaryn — *ya-REN (i.e Karen)* — Tohminic's mother

Tohminic — *TOM-in-ick* — Prince; High Lord

Chlora — *CLAW-rah* — Tohminic's lover

Xaler — *ZAY-ler* — Selkie leader; Tohminic's second

WINTER COURT

Ruith — *ROO-ith* — High Lord

Tarathiel — *ta-RATH-eel* — Prospective mate

NIGHT COURT

Maude — *MORD* — High Lady
Bim — *BIM* — Prospective mate

DAY COURT

Warakoris — *WAR-rack-oar-iss* — Zentha's home
Zentha — *ZEN-thuh* — High Lady
Elmon — *ell-MON* — Zentha's son
Kyra — *KIE-rah* — Betrothed to Elmon
Nikolai — *NICK-oh-lie* — Bria's lover

DAWN COURT

Jonik — *JOHN-ick* — High Lord
Tasar — *t-SAR* — one of the triplets; Prince
Ulakas — *YOU-lah-cuss* — one of the triplets; Prince
Larrad — *Lah-RAHD* — one of the triplets; Prince

DUSK COURT

Vander — *VAN-dah* — High Lord
Wynetta — *WIN-et-tah* — Vander's sister
Torin — *toh-RIN* — Vander's second
Nyree — *nigh-REE* — Leader of the Ill-fated
Penna — *PEN-nah* — Healer

1

REBELLIOUS.

It is a word my father often uses to describe me, and tonight, I am stepping into the shoes he believes I wear. I dislike proving Father right, but what am I supposed to do when his guards watch my every move, when the crown I ignore grows heavy, and title I detest determines every aspect of my life?

I slink through the silent halls, the swish of my satin slippers a whisper against the marble floor as I fight the urge to run. My breath catches in my chest in a pointless moment of panic as I pass too close to Father's study. He will remain there until long after the moon has reached its zenith, when he will succumb to the copious amount of wine he indulged in today, then stagger into bed. It is a routine I know as well as the lines of my palm.

As High Lord of the Autumn Court — where the fae are renowned for their control of the earth and animals — he mostly shoulders his burden with poise and ardour. On days like today, when he is stuck in meetings with demanding nobles arguing over what is best for our court, that burden is heavy. When the stars we love so much glitter from above, and his subjects have flitted from the court to their village homes, Father retreats to his study to drown his problems with wine.

The nobles only visit the court when the moon is full.

It is both a blessing and a curse.

Greeting the nobles as if I am pleased to see them, my cheeks aching from the demure smile Father forces me to wear all day, and holding court with the rest of the unmated females are all curses I endure for my father's sake. And the blessing, my reward for behaving, is so very worth it.

With Father too inebriated to bother himself with my whereabouts, my brother entertaining the fae males in the eastern village, and Father's mate otherwise distracted, the full moon is my only opportunity to see Nikolai.

The son of a fishmonger who spends many moons at sea and the rest of his time scraping barnacles from the ship's hull is — according to Father and Fayeth and likely every noble within our lands — beneath the likes of me, Princess Bria Sutherland of the Autumn Court. Blessed Mother Star, what a mouthful.

I fist my hands in the rough material of my borrowed gown, hiking it up so I do not trip on my way down the marble stairs. The grey fabric scratches against my skin, a far cry from the satins and silks I am accustomed to, whispering against my shins with every step. But the maid's gown is essential if I wish to venture into the western village without the guards realising who passes beneath them.

A balmy breeze filters in through the open doors, caressing my skin with the scents of spices and figs and a crisp woodsy note I have loved since I was a youngling. I glance outside to the inner bailey to ensure no one lingers, then hold my breath as I slip into the shadows and dash across the bedewed grass and into the stables.

I snatch a travelling cloak from its hook by the door and drape it over my shoulders, pulling the hood over my head and ensuring it hides every strand of copper. As the distinguishing feature of the Spring Court, my hair is evidence of who I am — the illegitimate daughter of our High Lord.

I cast a longing glance at the horses. It is easy to venture to the village for a few hours unnoticed, but creatures as magnificent as these are sure to be missed by the ever-diligent stable hands. I have snuck from the court under twelve full moons, and I am yet to find the courage to ride to the west village. One day, I will find the courage. On that day, I will never return.

I reach a hand out and run my palm over the closest horse's neck, a gorgeous chestnut with a wild obsidian mane. "Soon, my beauties. Soon, we will run through the fields and feast on apples until our stomachs are full to bursting."

The horse nickers in response.

With a sigh, I turn from the horses and their shining coats, inhaling their musky scent once more before slipping outside.

My pace is brisk as I cross to the drawbridge that leads to the viaduct and outpost. Not because I am afraid the guards will lift it soon — in my five and seventy years, I have yet to see it raised — but because once I pass under the portcullis, there is nothing to hide me from view. If I am not careful, the sentry in the gatehouse above will see me disappear into the night.

That is the last thing anyone needs.

Spending so much time within the walls is a hindrance. But this, knowing when the sentries will be watching, is one of the rare advantages of being confined in the marble and stone castle.

I bunch the skirt of my gown in my hands, lifting it to knee height while listening for the telltale sound of the sentry turning north. The moment his feet scuff against the stone overhead, I make my escape.

The soft grass of the viaduct mutes the thud of my feet against the ground as I race towards the outpost. Stone walls border the path on either side, their shadows stretching over the grass like menacing claws. Though the path is wide enough for four horses to trot side-by-side, I keep to the left, the dark fabric of my borrowed cloak blending with the welcoming shadows. My heart sings as the darkness surrounds me, fluttering at the thought of making it out of the castle undetected.

I know if I keep running, the sentries ahead will not see me; my pace does not falter until I am under the towering outpost and hidden from view. Arches on every wall open the outpost to the elements, the wooden ladder in the corner worn and brittle from exposure, somehow still clinging to the hatch that leads to the watchtower overhead.

I push aside the earthy scent of Autumn, close my eyes, and focus on the sounds from the two sentries above. Three heartbeats later, my enhanced hearing detects one turning west while the other turns east, and I take my chance.

The meagre magic swirling within my fae body rushes to the surface as I dart into the open. Warding the court against folding is essential — the ability to fold the realm and jump from one place to another in the blink of an eye is a gift every fae wields — but on nights like this, I wish I could fold from within my chambers. It would save a lot of hassle.

The ripple of the ward's magic washes over me not three steps from the castle walls, crisp and prickling as I dart beyond the barrier and fold the western village towards me. Space and time and stars blur as I step from the outpost and into the bustling street of the village, the earthy scents of the court replaced by the salt of the ocean and the briny scent of fish.

I make sure the hood still covers my hair before setting off towards the docks. The castle was silent, with my family otherwise engaged and the nobles having left for their own homes. In contrast, the village is bustling.

Each building is a mirror of the others, their panelled walls and burgundy roofs identical to the last tile. Trails of smoke stretch for the night sky, the bitter odour tainting the ocean's scent. Beyond the main road, where most of the village's stores are closed, rows of houses climb the hill, growing larger as they near the summit. At the highest point, several manors of brick and dark tile — the homes of the nobles, forever looking down on the working class fae, those they refer to as *lesser*.

Fishmongers shout from my right, claiming their wares are the best in the village. I beg to differ. If they caught the best fish or sold the best crab, they would not be bartering their goods well into the night. I lower the hood further over my face, hiding my emerald eyes from view in the hopes they will leave me be. I am not interested in purchasing day-old salmon.

Cheers and raucous laughter sound from the nearby tavern, causing me to pause and smile. We host balls and feasts at the castle often, but none are as fun as I imagine the tavern to be. As much as I would love to enjoy a night with the anglers, I know if I enter, I will have to remove my hood. Then everyone would know who I am. No, it is best I continue to the docks.

The paved road splits in two, the left dipping towards the docks and the right inclining towards the houses. I do not cast my eyes to the right as I step towards the docks. My slippers are not sturdy enough for the uneven boardwalk, and I am careful where to place my feet, not fond of the idea of a nail sticking into my foot. Wide posts provide a safety net as I steady myself against them, placing my hands between barnacles and scaring the occasional small crab.

It is darker down here, the shadows from the hewn cliff beside me growing denser the farther I walk. I do not mind the darkness. Still, I bring an orb of fae light to my palm, the amber glow illuminating the path ahead, shining on thick coils of rope and mounds of rusted chains. It is times like this when I wish I hailed from the Dawn Court. If I could manipulate light the way they do, I would not have to bother with an inadequate fae light. Or even the Summer Court, with their fire magic. A shiver prickles down my spine. The Summer fae also wield one of the three dark arts — necromancy is the second most despised magic in Radelea — and I go to great lengths to avoid dealing with them.

My gown rustles as it grazes the wooden boards, the sound quiet compared to the barking squawk of a nearby night heron. The hem will be stained with salt residue by the time I return to the castle. There is nothing I can do about that, shy of staying home like the good little princess I am supposed to be. But where is the fun in that?

I slow as I approach the first row of ships. The vessels belong to the Day Court, their lack of sails and masts revealing their home court. The water wielders have the fastest boats in Radelea. Their advantage over the other six courts sees them catching the biggest fish and making the most profit from trades.

I see him then, on the second ship. His flaxen hair shines under the glowing fae lights as he hauls a woven trap across the deck. My stomach flutters as I lean against a wooden post, the base securing a thick rope, and watch him for a moment. Sneaking from the castle is worth it, if even for a moment, to watch Nikolai while he works.

As if he senses my appraisal of the firm muscles beneath his smock — though the sleeves are loose, the damp material clings to his muscular arms — Nikolai turns towards me, those golden brown eyes shining.

"Ria!" he calls, raising a hand.

He does not know my real name or where I am from. I cannot risk word spreading that I dally with an angler every full moon. Hearing the name I chose for myself makes my heart beat harder and my mouth curves into a smile.

I peel away from the post, shoving my responsibilities, my true identity, and my reservations to the back of my mind as I cross to the plank that leads to the ship. The timber is slick beneath my slippers, and my hand shoots out to grip the wooden railing so I do not fall into the gently lapping water below.

Nikolai rushes over as I step onto the main deck, gripping my hand and keeping me steady. "Well met, Ria."

I slip on the mask I always wear with him. An essential lie, but a lie nonetheless. According to him, I am but a lowly, magicless servant to the Spring Court, permitted this freedom by my High Lady every full moon. It is not so far from the truth. My hair is sign enough my mother — whoever she is — is a Spring fae, and for as long as I can remember, I cannot control anything more than folding, shields, and fae lights. Not the earth magic of my father's court, not the nature power from my mother's, and nothing in between.

Something flickers on the horizon, way out to sea where I know there to be nothing but waves and salt and coral. The twinkling lights of a city, or a blanket of stars having fallen from the sky. It is gone before I can put a name to it, and I shake the thought away.

"Well met. I trust the sea is treating you well?"

Nik leads me towards the quarterdeck, stating the sea has been rough of late. Five crew fell ill. He is worried about the rare occurrence, though my appearance eases his tension.

We descend a wooden ladder into the depths of the ship. It is huge, twenty long swords or more — I have never understood why the Day Court prefers such large ships over the usual fishing vessels — but it takes mere heartbeats to enter Nikolai's cabin, our small talk forgotten.

As soon as the heavy door thuds closed, I hike my gown up to my hips, the cool air washing over my exposed legs and caressing the most intimate part of my body. "The Mother Star knows I have missed you, Nik."

He smiles as he pulls the string of his pants loose. "I will pray every night that your High Lady finds it in her heart to allow you more freedom." He slides his pants down his legs, freeing his erection. "Until then, every full moon will have to do."

I fist my hand in his smock and drag him closer, wrapping my free hand around his length and angling him at my entrance. I lift my leg, and he grips me below the knee, holding me steady as I lower myself onto him.

We moan in unison.

"The moon has waxed and waned," he says through gritted teeth, "and I do not think I can restrain myself."

"I am not here for pleasantries or sweet nothings. I am here to lose myself, to forget the realm around us and bask in the glory of my body unravelling at your hands. Just for a moment."

He hardens further, and I clench around him. "At least let me see your face. Just this once."

I angle my hips, taking him deeper. It is all I need for his thoughts to change direction.

With a groan, Nikolai slowly pulls back before thrusting into me, seating himself to the hilt. Delicious tingles spread from my core throughout my body, and I throw my head forward, resting my brow on his shoulder as he slides in and out with barely restrained slowness.

This is why I risk Father's wrath. This bliss, this small slice of freedom and excitement, it is unlike anything I have felt before.

Our bodies work together to pick up a steady rhythm, the melody of our joining a background to my moans and his harsh pants. It does not take long for a wave of ecstasy to churn low in my belly. It builds and builds, spinning faster and harder with every thrust, until it crashes through me like a tsunami.

"Ah, Mother Star!" I cry out, throbbing around him as he jerks twice more.

He growls his release, his seed spilling into me and dribbling down my legs when he pulls away too soon.

At this moment, I am not Princess Bria of Autumn. I have no responsibilities, no one watching my every move, and no tainted history. I am no one. This moment is what I came for.

Rebellious, indeed.

I clean myself up with the tattered cloth Nik hands me, feeling more unlike the female I am supposed to be than ever. My chest lightens at the thrilling experience, and a small smile pulls at the corners of my lips. Perhaps if my family had treated me fairly throughout my life, I would feel differently about the role I was born into.

"Do you have time for a drink?" he asks, hoisting his pants up and pulling the string tight. "The ale at the tavern is always cold, and always delicious."

I make sure my hood is still in place before turning towards him. "Not tonight. I have to get back."

His face falls. For twelve full moons, we have met at the docks. Twelve full moons, and he is yet to see my face, yet to gain more than a greeting out of me before we rush to his cabin. I know it is not fair to him. But if anyone were to recognise me and realise an angler has been frolicking with the High Lord's daughter... he would be dead by morning.

"Shall I return next full moon?" My tone is hopeful. Without my adventures to the village, I think I would lose my mind; if I have nothing to look forward to, nothing to distract me while I endure life at the castle, I will wither away and die. Immortality be damned.

He sighs, running a calloused hand through his hair. "Very well."

I see myself out, worry clenching my stomach. It is rare for him to push like that. Next time, I will need to alleviate his worries. I will have to give him *something*, or I risk losing him forever.

The ship's deck remains empty as I cross the slick surface to the plank that joins the vessel to the land. The crew are likely enjoying several tankards of ale at the tavern. The pewter handles would feel foreign in their rough hands, so used to rope and wood as they are.

I have always wanted to meld into the wild crowd at the tavern, tankard in hand and a smile on my face as the anglers and captains tell story after story about life at sea. But the nobles of Autumn believe ale is improper, that it is the drink of the lesser fae in the village. If I am to drink anything, it is plum wine or warmed mead. Sometimes I will enjoy a brandy if I am so lucky.

I make my way back through the village, studiously ignoring the sound of enjoyment from within the tavern, and like with every full moon, struggle up the hill on the outskirts of town where I will fold back to the castle. The air pressure changes, the crispness of night making way for something more sinister.

A ripple of awareness washes over me, and I look over my shoulder towards the village. The lights twinkle below, a mix of flame and fae light, stretching through the streets and disappearing at the docks. And beyond the ships and sails and ropes as thick as my arms, the ocean churns with ominous darkness. Waves crash against the shore as if a lone gust of wind is pushing them forward.

My eyes lift, settling on a hazy image in the distance, and my body turns of its own accord. The same glittering lights from before shine from atop the water, an undulating landscape filling the expanse of darkness. A landscape that I know does not exist, yet it calls to my very soul. I take one step forward.

Like when I saw the strange land from the ship, it disappears as quickly as it came, leaving nothing but dark seas and the blanket of night in its wake.

I stay for longer than normal, watching and waiting for the land to reappear. I am not worried about being found out here. No harm will come to me; Radelea is a peaceful realm. Most of the courts are amicable since the civil war in the north-east when members of the Day Court fought for the right to form a court of their own. It was the birth of the Dawn Court, the first new court in millennia.

Over the past four hundred years, Dawn has remained neutral. Their light magic is a passive power, and those who are born with the ability to heal others travel throughout Radelea and settle in courts not of their own, spreading kindness and peace wherever they go. I always marvel at how calm and serene the Dawn healers are. On the few times my wounds were bad enough my rapid healing was not adequate, I enjoyed the company of the court healer, Cataleya.

The strange vanishing land does not resurface. My ribs seem to shrink into my body, constricting my chest as an overwhelming sense of disappointment courses through me. My breath hitches, and I wince at the pain in my chest.

Before my body reacts further, before I can wonder where this feeling of melancholy has come from, I draw on my fae magic and fold the Autumn castle towards me, stepping through the void with the same ease as walking across the marble entrance in the castle. The small seaside village disappears, replaced by an imposing castle at my back and rolling hills of soft grass at my front. The colour reminds me of pea soup during the day, but at night, I cannot tell if the grass is yellow or green.

I duck into the shadow of the outpost before either sentry can spot me, my eyes travelling the length of the wooden ladder and peeking into the chamber above at the males watching over the land. One faces north while the other faces west. Five beats of my rebel heart, and the sentries change positions, leaving the path to the castle free from their watchful eyes.

I grip the travelling cloak tighter and race across the grass, keeping to the shadows on my right. They were long and clawing when I left. Now, they are short and stubby, like the horns of an ogre. The monstrous creatures keep to their lairs — deep in the forest to our south — never venturing into our territory. They know Father will have their heads if they step beyond their wards. Just as he will have mine if I do not return to my chambers soon.

I slow my pace halfway along the viaduct, waiting for the guard in the gatehouse to turn the other way. This is the most perilous part of my night, when the sentries change direction more often and the chance of being seen is greater. Fortunately, the sentry ahead turns, and my feet pound against the grass as I silently dart over the drawbridge and under the portcullis.

Ten heartbeats later, I am slipping from beneath the gatehouse and into the stables. I unclasp the cloak and return it to the hook by the door, bid the horses goodnight — they are all sleeping, and I receive nothing but a wheeze or two in response — and sneak towards the washhouse, where I approach one of the large wooden tubs, strip the grey gown from my body, and poke it into the water, all evidence of my night disappearing with the suds.

In nothing but my nightgown, I dash into the castle, up the marble stairs, and slink through the hallways until I enter the west wing. I pause at Father's study, listening for signs of activity within.

Certain he has staggered to bed by now, I move to the next set of chambers. My brother — Rennyn is five and twenty years my senior — should still be enjoying himself in the east village. True to tradition, no sounds come from within.

With a breath of relief, I walk away at a brisk pace. It could be coincidence Father gave me these chambers, or it could be his way of ensuring I behave, but I have always hated the proximity to Father and Fayeth.

As if the thought has called her through time and space, Fayeth appears at the end of the hallway. Standing before the double doors that lead to the chambers she shares with Father, she glares at me, her golden-hazel eyes narrowing. Her light brown waves are loose, curling at the ends and tickling her ribs.

"Good night." My voice does not betray the edge of tension thrumming through me. "Sleep well."

I duck into my chambers before she can question me. A princess wandering the court at night — what a scandal.

2

I AM ASSAULTED BY a rush of cool air as my hand maiden yanks the quilt to the end of the bed. "Up," she commands. "The High Lord is waiting."

I groan and roll over. "A little longer, Lymsia."

"If you cannot rise when your father demands it, I suggest retiring earlier." I peek at her from beneath my arm. She rests her hands on her hips, and her brown eyes narrow to slits. "Instead of disappearing to the Mother Star knows where in the middle of the night."

"You know how I feel about threats first thing in the morning. At least let me eat first." I clamber from the bed, missing the warmth of the blankets the moment I am free of their soft embrace, and stagger to the seat by the window in the main chamber.

Lymsia tames my wild copper locks while I stare out at the land and sea, watching the Mother Star rise to yet another dull day in the Autumn Court. In the distance, the sleepy western village begins to wake, and beyond that, the glittering ocean on the horizon is calm. There is no sign of the veiled land I saw last night.

I tap my foot against the stone floor as I contemplate telling Father what I saw. On one hand, he will be furious to hear I ventured into the village. On the other, it may pique his interest and a little excitement may fall upon the court for once.

"What is on the agenda for today?" Lymsia asks, setting the brush down.

"Nothing. I will likely wander the court looking for someone to taunt. Maybe harass Rennyn for a little while. If I have time, I will head to the metal bender and make sure Ren's born day gift is as I imagined."

She gathers some hair and pulls it away from my face, revealing the point of my ears. "Then there is no need to tie your hair back. Perhaps a half-crown of braids, with the bulk of your hair loose?"

I shrug. "Whatever you want. It is not like I have anyone to impress."

By the time she has finished, there is a thick braid wrapping around the top of my head like a crown and soft waves falling down my back.

I stand, resigning myself to endure the next few moments.

She helps me step into a silk gown. It is such a dark indigo, it appears black until the fae lights hit it right. Next, she wraps a corset around my waist, cinching it tight and stealing the breath from my lungs before sliding lavender slippers onto my feet.

With my breasts swelling, my ribs creaking, and my hair glimmering, I am ready to face my family for breakfast. Why I have to look so presentable when it is only Father, Fayeth, and Rennyn is beyond me. If I could wear nothing but a night robe and fur-lined boots, I would.

Before I slip out the door, Lymsia pokes a sprig of lavender into my hair. "You reek of the sea. This will distort the scent. Next time, may I suggest you bathe before retiring?"

I smirk. "You have my thanks, Lymsia." I startle when I open the door, my hand flying to my chest. "Bless the Mother Star. Ren, you scared me."

"Father sent me to find you." He rests a hand on the shining hilt of his short sword, a gift from our father on Ren's fiftieth born day. He is wearing a beige gambeson today, the leather buckles snaking from his left shoulder to his right hip. He looks every bit the prince.

"Are you off to war, brother?" I ask as I join him in the hallway. "Why the armoured coat?"

He smiles, and the golden tint to his brown eyes grows brighter. His face is all harsh angles and high cheekbones until he smiles, then his entire demeanour changes. He turns soft, his angles disappearing behind a youthful glee. "Father has asked me to instruct the younglings on how to correctly wield a sword. I am not due at the training grounds until after noontime, but changing is such a waste of time, do you not think so?"

"At least you do not have to wrangle a corset when you change," I mutter, jumping the last three steps into the entrance hall. "Do you think Father will let me join you for once?"

He opens the large door to the dining hall, waving me ahead of him. "It may be worth asking. He is in a pleasant mood today." At my raised brow, he adds, "His meetings went well yesterday. The nobles have agreed to collect the taxes from their regions on his behalf."

Father's magic washes over me when I step into the dining hall. Dense, like thick clay. Suffocating clouds of dust. Calm, like a humble mare. I relish in it, allowing the power to ravage my creamy skin. It is the feeling of home, of comfort, and of safety. But not of love. Never love.

With control over the earth and everything that encompasses — dirt and gems and everything between — as well as being a tier one animalist, Father is the strongest fae in the Autumn Court. I have always coveted his ability to see through the eyes of any creature and control their bodies from afar. I hope the Mother Star will grant me the gift of magic one day, something more than shielding and folding and fae lights.

"That is excellent news, Father." I grace him with a wide smile as I approach the long table. "The castle is dreadfully boring when you leave to collect the taxes."

His eyes crease at the sides, the emerald shining brighter as he slices into a fat sausage. "Two moons wasted travelling. Instead, I will remain here. Old age has its benefits."

"You are not old, Kerym," says Fayeth. "You may have silver hair, but two hundred is considered middle-aged."

"You say that because you are nearing two hundred yourself," Father says.

I lower into my seat beside Rennyn, who is at Father's right, and stab my fork into a sausage, not bothering to cut it before biting a chunk from the end. It is a move I make every morning with the sole purpose of enraging Father's mate.

Rennyn ruffles his brown hair, a few shades lighter than his mother's. "Must you anger her today?" he whispers from the corner of his mouth.

I smirk and take another bite, looking Fayeth directly in the eye.

She leans forward, her Day magic roiling with Father's. Her power is a cool drop of water, and wispy like smoke. "Tell me, Bria. Where were you last night?"

Father pauses, his fork halting between his plate and mouth.

The few moments I lingered on that hill may have cost me my freedom, but there is one thing I can say to turn the tide in my favour. I lunge for the opportunity. "Visiting the west village."

"Bria," Father warns.

"Father. I saw something. An... An island or some other land mass that I know does not belong there. It appeared at sea before disappearing once more. I think it is worth looking into."

He clasps his hands on the table. "Then we will ride to the village at once."

My mouth pops open, and I lower my fork to the table. "Truly?"

"Finish your breakfast and collect your cloak." His eyes flash, and I know not to argue, but...

I had not considered investigating with him. Never in my wildest dreams did I think Father would allow me this shred of excitement. Any other day, I would jump at the opportunity to be free of the castle walls. "Father, if I may remain here —"

"You saw the strange land. I did not. This is not up for debate."

Fayeth smirks, as if she knows I do not wish to venture into the village so soon after last night.

Mother Star, have mercy. My world is about to come crashing down around me if Nikolai is there... If he somehow recognises me.

It takes an hour for the stable hands to have our horses ready. We could fold to the west village if Father did not demand a handful of guards accompany us. He does not know what to make of the mystery island and is reluctant to take chances where his family is concerned. Pity Fayeth counts as family.

While waiting for my beautiful mare to be ready, I swap my satin slippers for leather riding boots — Father refuses when I beg for the chance to wear pants for the first time in my life — and don a heavy riding cloak in a blue-grey that compliments my gown. I have always thought it dull when my clothes match. I sigh as I cross the inner bailey courtyard to the stables. It would not surprise me if Lymsia has instructed the stable hands to select a saddle that matches, too.

My mare is ready and waiting when I enter, her coppery-brown coat shining in the low light as a stable hand walks her towards the door. I stop him in the hey-strewn aisle, the stalls on either side empty of geldings. The guards are already astride their horses, likely waiting at the gatehouse for us.

"Hi, beautiful." I caress my mare's jowls and nose. "We are going to the village today. You need to be on your best behaviour. We both do."

She sighs, blowing hot breath from her nostrils, which encompasses my face with the scent of hay.

I chuckle. "I know the feeling, Solana. But Fayeth is coming, and if she suspects I have a... friend in the village, she will have him detained."

Solana nickers and I gesture for the stable hand to lead her outside, where Father, Fayeth, and Rennyn wait with their own horses. Father's stallion is a gorgeous dark brown, so dark he is almost black. I have always loved the strip of white running from Tycho's nostrils to between his ears.

The stable hands line the horses along the edge of the inner bailey, placing foot stools beside them. Fayeth's gelding, Saber, throws his head back and snorts — he is only calm around his rider — his black mane whipping in the breeze.

Ames, Rennyn's pure black stallion, snaps his teeth at Saber before stilling, ever the role model when other horses are around. Though he looks intimidating with his assessing eyes and colossal frame, Ames has a gentle soul and yearns to please his master.

I brace a foot on the stirrup before swinging a leg over the seat and settling into the saddle on Solana's back. The long skirt of my gown bunches at my thighs, and I cannot help but feel robbed of the chance to ride in comfort like Father and Rennyn. Even Fayeth looks a little put out, with her scarlet skirt creasing around her knees.

Autumn denizens cast glances our way, no doubt wondering where the royal family is going, before averting their gazes and returning to their morning tasks. Babes and younglings race through the bailey with wooden swords, laughing as their makeshift weapons clash. Their excitement increases when they see us, and they pause mid-duel to wave and watch us leave.

I am the only one to acknowledge them with a smile.

Leaning forward, I run my hand along the length of Solana's neck and pat her shoulder. "Are you ready?"

Father snaps his reins and Tycho lurches forward with a whinny. Rennyn follows, then Fayeth and her golden-brown gelding, and then me. Always last, always the least important. Being the High Lord's bastard daughter will do that.

We carve a line through the lesser fae gathered in the inner and outer baileys, then pass under the gatehouse, where four guards on geldings mount their horses and walk in pairs behind us. Four more guards join us as we pass through the outpost, taking the lead and protecting Father from any head-on attacks. Each of our eight guards carries twin broad swords, the weapons of our court shining from their backs in warning.

I feel free out in the open — regardless of the guards and my family — and relish in the tickle of air across my face, the scents of Autumn filtering over Solana's sweet musk. The fields of grass and chirp of birds are comforting, and the lack of stone walls makes my hands itch with the need to explore.

It is a short distance from the castle to the west village and should only take an hour if the horses behave. We trot along a dirt path which has been worn into the grass by millennia of use. The grass ripples all around us, the pea-green blades whipping back and forth as the wind picks up.

It is not unusual for the Autumn Court to experience harsh winds, but during the eleventh moon, it is rare. The winds carry a hint of something foreboding, like a warning that Radelea is about to change, and not necessarily for the better. I wonder if it has anything to do with the island I saw.

Rennyn pulls back, guiding Ames until he is trotting beside me. "So, little sister, tell me about your adventures to the village." I do not miss his smirk, as much as he tries to hide it. "What reason does a High Lord's daughter have to leave the castle under the darkness of night?"

"You know how I feel about being locked up, Ren. I need adventure in life. The thrill I get from sneaking through the castle and disappearing beyond the wards is worth the risk of Father's wrath."

"You have done this more than once?" he asks, arching an eyebrow. When I do not answer, he probes further. "How long?"

Being the High Lord's eldest and only son, he is well above me in rank. And the tone he is using — though it is rare he uses such authority with me — leaves no room for argument, not with the four guards at my back.

I sigh. "Twelve full moons."

"Bria," he groans. "If Father discovers the extent..."

"I know, I know. He will lock me in my chambers until I see sense. While Father's fury is intimidating, it is your mother I am worried about. May I speak freely?"

He arches an eyebrow again.

I huff a laugh. "I have been seeing somebody in the village. An angler. I think... I think I love him."

"Nonsense," he growls. "You love the idea of him. You love how being with him angers Father, how the refusal to conform irks my mother, and how bedding a lesser fae goes against everything we stand for."

I keep my face forward, but my eyes flick towards him. Perhaps he is right, and it is not Nikolai I love, but the knowledge I am rebelling against everything I have endured during my five and seventy years. I have always despised life at court, resented the role I must play for Father's sake.

"I love you, little sister. You know I would offer my last breath to the Mother Star if it ensured your happiness. However, the path you are walking only leads to despair. I cannot allow you to continue seeing him." A quick flash of his golden-brown eyes, and he adds, "I am sorry." He snaps Ames's reins, the stallion galloping towards Father.

"Ren, wait!" I call. A groan slips free when he ignores me.

I have made this mistake more times than I care to admit in my short life. Telling Ren my deepest secrets when he is such a stickler for the rules is something I am slowly learning to avoid. No matter what he tells Father, I will never, *never* reveal Nikolai's identity.

My father and brother talk in whispers, both males casting frustrated glances in my direction. I lift my chin and ignore them, instead focusing on the coastline ahead. It is where my gaze remains until we enter the village.

If we wished for our arrival to go unnoticed, our prayers would not be answered. The hooves of our horses clack against the paved road, drawing the attention of those within the stores to our right. The fae press their faces against salt-stained windows, their mouths popping open in awe.

It is seldom the High Lord and his family visit the seaside village. We prefer to spend our time in the eastern village, where cliffs curve around the town like a crown and towering trees border the western edge. It is safer there. Not to mention Father is not too fond of water.

Funny how he tied his life to a fae from the Day Court, who has the power to manipulate water. They are not true mates, couples brought together by the will of the Mother Star — she has not blessed Radelea with a truly mated pair in millennia — but merely mated before the glimmer of stars. Chosen mates.

I turn to her now. The Mother Star is the only star to shine during the day. The sun, some call her, is bright and golden in her perch high in the sky, almost at her zenith. I offer her a prayer of sympathy, beg her to have mercy on my rebellious and jaded soul. She is yet to listen to any of my prayers, but I am determined to earn her favour one day.

I am sure the first fae thought the same when the land of darkness turned to one of light and colour, when the Mother Star rose for the first time after the courts negotiated a treaty. I wonder if they marvelled at her brilliance after so many eons spent in the dark.

No one knows why she rose. No one knows why the stars appeared. It is one of those mysteries in life we will never understand. What we understand, though, is the importance of pleasing the Mother Star. For if we fail, if we somehow corrupt this land of fae and magic, what is to stop her from sinking beyond the horizon, never to return? A chill runs down my spine at the thought. Only the dark fae of the Night Court would appreciate a world so bleak.

"Bria!" Father calls from ahead.

I whip my face towards him, wondering how many times he has called my name while thoughts of the sun consumed my mind. My hands grip the reins tighter as I trot closer, pulling up beside Tycho. "Yes, Father?"

"Wipe the grimace off your face. We will discuss your wanderings upon our return to the castle." His arched eyebrows sink lower, the only sign of his displeasure he will offer. "Where were you when you first saw the island you spoke of?"

I point towards the docks. "Near the largest ship. The one belonging to the Day Court. I was... I was admiring the lack of sails." Although I should not lie to my father, my words are technically the truth. I did marvel at the lack of sails.

"Your lies anger me." He pulls Tycho away, commanding the guards ahead to take the left fork. The one which leads to the docks. The one which leads to the ship Nikolai works on.

Father's power pulses around us in thick waves, warning the village folk to stay clear of our entourage. For the most part, he keeps his magic firmly within his body, but today, he is in no mood for peddlers or praise.

Regardless of Father's threat, fishmongers and other merchants scurry forward, offering samples of their wares. One of the rear guards collects each item, storing them in the leather pouch hanging from his saddle. None of us will see them again; experience tells me the guard will discard them as soon as we are home.

Luck is not on my side — I knew the Mother Star was not listening — and I spot Nikolai scraping barnacles from the hull of his ship as we approach. He turns his head upon hearing the clack of hooves, his golden-brown eyes skimming over each of us.

I breathe a sigh of relief when he skips over me, showing no sign of recognition. If I can refrain from speaking, I might come out of this unscathed. Rather, Nikolai will remain unscathed.

"You!" Father shouts to Nikolai. "Approach."

Nikolai drops his metal scraper to the wooden plank he is balancing on, wipes his hands on his beige pants, and jumps onto the dock, bowing low. "Well met, High Lord Kerym."

"Rise." Father's voice is stern, as if he already suspects Nik clamped his calloused hand around my leg last night, gripping tight while he slid inside me. I shake the thought away, willing the blush creeping over my cheeks to retract.

"What can I do for you, Lord Kerym?" Nikolai looks Father in the eye. "Is it fish you are after? A day on the water? I am happy and able to provide either or both."

Father slides from Tycho's back, swishing his travelling cloak behind him and resting a hand on the long sword at his hip. "I have received reports of a land mass appearing on your seas. What do you know of it?"

Four guards dismount and flank Father, each of them looking in different directions, waiting for a threat that will not come.

I click my fingers at a guard and hold my hand out in a request for help to dismount. It is not normal for me to be so rude, but Nikolai will recognise me if he hears my voice after hearing it only last night.

The guard grips my hand, bracing his other just above my elbow, and helps me slide down. I thank him with a nod of my head before rounding Solana, using her large body to hide me from view while I listen to the males converse.

Nikolai has not seen the island for himself, but several of the males who work the ship with him have, including the captain. "If it pleases you, Lord Kerym, I can call for the captain. I am certain he can give you more information."

"No need," says Father. "Bria witnessed the enigma herself."

I stiffen, my hands curling into fists as they fall to my sides. Solana turns her head towards me, nipping at my arm in the hope I will keep patting her. I do not have it in me to pay her any mind.

"Bria?" Father calls, adopting a pleasant tone for the sake of appearances. If any of our denizens believe there is turmoil at the castle, they may take advantage.

I cannot prevent the frustrated sigh which huffs from my lips as I straighten my skirt and move to stand beside him. "Yes, Father?"

Fayeth's cruel smile sends warning bells tinkling through my thoughts, and I realise she has been watching me this entire time. If she used her spirit magic without my knowing, it is likely she knows Nikolai and I... She knows our spirits have met.

"Where did you see this land mass?" asks Father. "Where were you at the time?"

I flick Nik a glance, apology shining from my eyes, before turning back to Father. "The land appeared while I was on the main deck of the Day Court's ship. I can show you if you are willing?"

While Father mutters about requiring permission to board another high fae's ship — in the case of the Day Court, Father needs permission from High Lady Zentha — I risk a second glance at Nik.

As soon as our eyes collide, he breathes, "Ria?"

I widen my eyes, my head shaking frantically before he can say anything more. I beg him with my eyes, the emerald dripping with fear. Fear for both my sanity and his safety.

Thankfully, he understands. He turns away from me and focuses on Father. A small crease forms between his straight eyebrows and his lips curl down.

I can only hope no one has witnessed our small interaction.

3

AFTER A QUICK LUNCHEON at the village inn, we wait on the docks for Nikolai's captain to send a messenger to the High Lady of the Day Court. Father intends to use their ship to investigate the waters around the strange island I saw. We would take our own ships — which are hidden beyond a sheer cliff away from the view of every court in Radelea — if it would not take an entire day to ready them.

Father sends a guard back to the court with orders to prepare our ships, anyway. If we find anything out in those churning waters, he wants to be the first to bear witness. His claim over the new territory will hold more weight with the other courts, and depending on the size of the island, we may end up holding the most land in Radelea, ahead of the Summer Court and Night Islands.

The Night Court, a chain of several islands of all shapes and sizes, was once part of mainland Radelea. Three hundred years ago, the land broke away, and the Night Islands were born. No one knows why the land did what it did, or if the phenomenon can be reversed. Like many things in our world, it just *is*. I have always assumed the Mother Star deemed the Night fae too dark with their ability to manipulate blood and bone or believed them too powerful with their mind control powers, so she sent them as far away from the rest of us as possible.

"You wanted adventure, Bria," says Rennyn, leaning against the hewn rock beside me, giving his back to the village. "Now you have it. You know, I am surprised Father agreed to investigate your claims so readily. You hold more sway with him than you believe."

"Do you believe he would have bothered with this if Fayeth had expressed concern or dislike for the idea?"

His earth magic roils at being so close to the water, his very essence rebelling at the proximity as he looks out to sea, his brown hair fluttering in the salty breeze. "Mother does not hate you. This notion you have is both ridiculous and unwarranted."

My eyes roll so hard I fear losing them entirely. "Love blinds you. If Fayeth did not despise me to her core, why would she go out of her way to make my life miserable? Why refuse me the friendships I so yearn? Why deny me the freedom I am entitled to?"

Rennyn and I have had this argument too many times. He cannot acknowledge his mother's pain and see it for what it is. Jealousy, bitter and consuming.

Not that I blame her. Any sane female would feel the same if their mate bedded another, and the joining resulted in a babe. But I am not responsible for Father's actions. I am a product of his betrayal, not the cause of it.

Before Ren can refute my claim, several fae fold onto the docks, all of them lithe, with golden-hazel eyes. Members of the Day Court.

Their High Lady, Zentha, wears a beautiful gown the colour of a shy blush. It compliments her warm brown skin beautifully and makes her honey-coloured eyes shine brighter. She approaches Father, the tight coils of her hair bouncing on her shoulders.

"Well met, High Lady Zentha," says Father, his chin dipping.

"Well met, High Lord Kerym." She lowers into a minuscule curtsey. "How curious I was to hear of your interest in my ships. I am, of course, glad to offer you this vessel."

Father smiles. "You have my gratitude. Please, sail with us today."

"I had hoped you would be so kind." Zentha smirks before throwing her arms around Father's waist. "How are you, old friend?"

I chuckle at the loss of formality. Autumn and Day are old allies, and our courts have worked together without issue for millennia. When Day's civil war broke out, we sent an infantry to hold the lines. In the end, Zentha's tranquil nature won out over her need to keep her court whole, and she allowed the Dawn Court to form.

Father returns her embrace. "I am well. Thank you for this. Are you aware of our reasons?"

Zentha pulls back but keeps her hands on Father's arms. "Indeed. I intend to witness your claim to this mysterious land. Once you have established the island, I will visit with my family." She gestures to the plank joining her ship to the docks. "After you, Kerym."

With the way Father helps Zentha onto the ship, the two of them always touching, always smiling, I wonder if Zentha could be my mother. I shake the thought away before it can take root. I am nothing like the High Lady of Day. While she is calm and kind, I am restless and a little defiant. Not to mention copper hair is a trait of the Spring fae.

Zentha orders the ship's captain to remain but sends the rest of the crew — who stumbled from the inn and tavern to help prepare the ship — home for a well-earned rest. Zentha's private crew will commandeer the vessel.

I cannot say I am upset Nikolai will not be joining us for a day-long sail, but if I had hoped for a chance to pull him aside and explain... There will be time for that when I am back on land, I decide as I step onto the ship's deck beside Fayeth.

There is something brewing within her eyes, a cunning glint that shines through the hazel. For five and seventy years, she has lorded my existence over Father's head. For five and seventy years she has done everything in her power to make my life miserable, from sending a friend from my youth to another court to making sure Rennyn and I never had the chance to grow too close.

And though I am the daughter of the High Lord, I know my Father will continue to try atoning for his sins. I know if it comes to a choice between me and Fayeth, he will choose her. It is clear I am nothing but a reminder of his mistakes, nothing but a responsibility he did not ask for. I have no true place in this world.

The thought is sobering, and all of a sudden, I wish for nothing more than the privacy of my chambers. Seeking Father in the crowd of guards and royals on the ship's main deck, I hurry over to him.

Zentha's crew bustle about, heaving ropes and crates and shouting orders back and forth. They have no sails to prepare, instead relying on their magic, and I have little to no time to beg Father to allow me to return home.

As soon as the word slips from my lips, though, Father shuts me down.

"I need you here today." He barely spares me a glance, too focused on Zentha. "You are the only one here — other than the captain — who saw the island. I forbid you from leaving this ship without my permission."

"Very well." My cloak flares around me as I spin on my heel and disappear below deck, seeking solace in the only place I can. Nikolai's cabin.

While I am walking along the narrow hallway, the ship lurches forward. The gentle bob of the ocean is soothing as the ship rocks from side to side, but we are close to land. Once we are far enough out, the waves will crash against the hull and threaten to send me careening into the walls.

I duck into the familiar cabin, closing the door softly behind me. Just last night, I pressed my back against this same timber, Nikolai keeping me balanced. The memory is tainted now, my only form of escape and freedom shadowed by the fear of what Father will do when he discovers Nik's identity. What Fayeth will make Father do.

Already tiring of the ship's swaying, I sink onto Nik's firm mattress, burying my head in my hands. I thought Rennyn would keep my secret, even though he has proven time and again his only wish is for Father's respect. He can tell me he loves me until he is blue in the face, but it means little when his own reputation is on the line. As the prince of the Autumn Court, Ren has his own battles to face. He will rule these lands one day, just as Father does now.

Perhaps telling Ren about Nikolai was my way of seeking some kind of connection with my half-brother. Perhaps, deep down, I had hoped for someone to share this with. Knowing Ren did not hesitate to inform Father of my adventures makes my heart twist with sadness.

I move to lie down, sliding my hand under the duck-feather pillow. My fingers graze against something soft but hard, and I pull a journal free from its resting place, along with a stick of charcoal.

An idea springs to mind, and I rifle through the pages until I find one that is blank. I scribble an apology and an explanation, my letters long and looping. Nikolai will find the note next time he feels the urge to jot down his thoughts.

Closing the journal without reading the entries takes more effort than I will admit. It is not my place to pry into the mind of an angler. I slide the leather-bound book and charcoal back under the pillow, feeling a little lighter knowing Nik will understand once he reads it.

"There you are," says Rennyn, hurrying across the deck when I resurface somewhere around dusk. "Where have you been?"

"Exploring." I grip my cloak tighter around me. The chill of night is settling over Radelea, and out here in the open sea, the air is bitter with cold.

He arches an eyebrow. "Father has been looking for you. Zentha's crew have prepared a light dinner."

He leads me along the main deck to where servants have prepared a table with plates of steaming food. Grilled fish, tossed salads, steamed vegetables, carafes of sauces, and piles of crab weigh the table down.

"Join us, younglings," says Father, waving to the two empty seats beside Fayeth.

"We were just discussing Rennyn's upcoming born day," says Zentha. "One hundred is a sacred celebration in our court. It is when maturity has its claws sinking into us, the last vestiges of youth giving way to wisdom and responsibility."

"Shame, the responsibilities of growing old." I smile. "If I could remain five and seventy forever, I would."

Zentha laughs as I take my seat beside Rennyn and accept a goblet of sparkling wine from Father. Strangely, the wine is the colour of straw. My first sip surprises me, and I nod my appreciation at the fruity flavour.

Conversation flows with ease while we eat. Zentha and Father discuss our trade agreements — we supply Day with meat and furs while they supply us with fish and salt — Fayeth scowling at the two from beside Father, the lines of her brow growing more pronounced with every word.

She has pinned her hair back since we left the docks, having ordered Father to retrieve her hand maiden before we embarked on this journey. As always, appearances are everything. Although, not having to chew on my hair as well as the grilled fish would be a welcome reprieve.

Rennyn is deep in conversation with Zentha's son, Elmon. The willowy male is at least a head taller than me, with intense amber eyes and brown skin so golden, he almost shimmers. There is something about him, though, something... mysterious. I wonder if he wields more spirit magic than water.

A chill brings gooseflesh to my arms. There is something harrowing about dealing with souls.

One of Zentha's crew approaches the long table, his hands clasped behind his back. It is clear he has waited for our plates to be empty before approaching, a sign of respect that makes my skin crawl. I have always hated the divide between fae nobility and those deemed lesser. Some courts are better than others, and I am proud to say Autumn is one of the more forgiving courts, though we still have a long way to go to bridge the gap.

"It is time," says the Day male, "to prepare to anchor. If you could navigate us to a specific location, we would be ever so grateful."

"Allow me a moment to confirm," says Zentha, standing.

We all follow suit as the water fae bows and steps aside.

Zentha leads us to the bow of the ship, where we approach the low wooden railing meant to prevent us from falling. Maybe it would if it were higher than our knees.

"Show me where you saw the land, Bria," says Father. "Zentha's crew believe we are near. We cannot risk moving closer if there are wards in place."

"I am certain it was resting on the horizon, far enough from the docks that I could not see the details clearly, though I believe there were hills of some kind." My hand stretches above the water, a lone finger pointing to the west. "It was there, I am sure of it. I —"

A gust of wind ravages the ship, cutting my words short. My cloak and gown whip behind me, snapping with the force of the gale. An agonised cry flows on the wind, the sound heavy with sorrow.

Closer than I thought able, the island appears, larger than I assumed and imposing in the low light. Beyond the wind and the view and the salt of the ocean, something calls to me. A whisper on that same breeze. It does not call me by name, but I know there is something on that island waiting for me, yearning for me as I yearn for it. If only I could discover what it is.

The ship shudders to a halt, and the Day fae who are using their water magic to urge the ship forward collapse to their knees, grunting with the effort of trying to remain upright. Magic ripples from the ward protecting this place. Its strength is frightening. The power needed... Whoever set the ward is someone not to be trifled with. I have never felt such a thing.

My eyes devour the island, drinking in every detail, as if afraid the sight will vanish once more. I wonder if it would, if given the chance. Though something tells me that is not the case. Something deep in my bones is screaming that this island is here to stay, for better or for worse.

I am not the only one to notice the sweeping hills and swaying trees. Nor am I the only one to realise those are not stars shining from the valley in the centre of the island.

Rennyn stills, his golden-brown eyes pinned on the twinkle of lights before us. "There is life on this island. Inhabitants. That is a building of some sort, I am sure of it."

Indeed, as I watch the curling coastline, several fae dressed in black step from the shadows. They watch us as we watch them, each party curious about the other. The whispering in my ears grows more determined, and I step forward, my legs hitting the low railing around the deck.

Before I can so much as scream, I am plummeting to the icy waters below.

Fear steals my breath as I plunge into the icy depths, water sucking me down until I cannot tell which way is up. I thrash, flailing in every direction and fighting the weight of my soaking cloak as it tightens around my throat. Panic like nothing I have ever felt seeps into my bones, constricts my chest, and seizes my limbs.

Even through the panic, I am aware it is quite beautiful below the surface. Specks of glittering... something float past, shooting in every direction every time I move. The darkness is so penetrating, so soothing, that I wonder why more fae do not dive deep below the water. If I could witness the beauty of the ocean during the day, I am certain I would be just as awed.

My thrashing ceases, my mind numbing at the realisation this is my penance for the lies, my punishment for disobeying Father. The Mother Star listened when I spoke. She listened and decided I am not worthy of this life. Shame for her I am not ready to leave this world.

A dull ache throbs in my chest as my lungs beg me to take a breath. I try to ease the discomfort by releasing the last of my air, sending bubbles rushing past my torso and legs towards the surface. I flip my body around, instinct urging me to kick my legs.

The water churns around me, groping and reaching as if controlled by hands. When a tendril of icy water wraps around my waist, I fight the battle with my lungs and drag air through my mouth in preparation for a scream.

Water scorches my throat and lungs, my body heaving as the tendril tightens. Although I can see nothing but the ocean's dark depths, I know my vision is tunnelling. In the back of my mind, I am aware of the water tendril dragging me to safety, barrelling for the surface. The sting of cold against my face is piercing as I am thrown into the air, the tendril whipping me towards the boat like the curling tentacle of a kraken.

I am aware of all of it, but also I am not. A flutter of fear clenches my stomach as frustration clenches my jaw. Though my body does not react to it. It is like they are the emotions of another fae, filtering into my mind unbidden.

By the time the water tentacle places me on the ship's deck — Zentha's arms are outstretched, as if she is the one controlling the water — my own emotions replace those of the stranger, the curious occurrence slipping from my mind as I cough and splutter.

"Bria!" Father shouts, falling to his knees beside me. He smacks a hand onto my back as I continue to spew water over the wooden deck. "Get it out, darling. Get it all out."

I look up at him with fear and understanding in my eyes. Too long. I was in the water for too long. It is the only reason he would be so panicked. That, and the crowd of fae around us witnessing how he cares for his daughter.

Black encroaches on my vision and my chest refuses to co-operate, instead jerking with vicious movements as I struggle to draw breath. Everything blurs, and as if I am moving too fast, the images distorted at the edges as I take in the sea of concerned faces.

The darkness wins, and I tilt sideways, the world disappearing as I crash to the deck.

4

"Blessed Mother Star, she is waking up," says a soft, feminine voice.

I turn towards it, my eyes heavy as I peel them open and croak, "What happened?"

Zentha leans over me, her brown coils forming a halo around her face. Her eyes crinkle at the sides, her full lips pulling down. "You almost drowned. I apologise for the delay in retrieving you from the water. I only made progress when I realised the wind was not fighting me. Rather, it was helping."

The wood-panelled room we are in is not a large space. The mattress beneath me is too soft, as if whoever lies here at night needs to sink into the duck feather lest they fall to the floor when the seas grow rough. There is a desk in the middle littered with maps and journals, splatters of ebony ink marring what I can see of the dull wooden surface. Zentha and another — who can only be a healer from the Dawn Court with his golden skin and eyes — fill the only standing space available.

"Where am I?" I push myself up and rest my back against the walls. "Captain's quarters?"

"Quartermaster's," says the Dawn fae. "The captain is busy finding a way for our ship to turn around and had use of his quarters."

"We cannot leave?" I ask, running a hand down my face. My voice is scratchy, as if I spent an entire moon screaming. But beneath the pain, beneath the ache in my lungs and the burning of my throat, there is something wild. A burning need to see the island once more. The feeling is both foreign and familiar, and a memory tugs at my thoughts, slipping away before I can grasp it.

A flicker of concern crosses Zentha's face. "It would seem that way. Unfortunately, this ship is warded against folding, a measure I put in place to prevent the crew leaving the ship stranded. If you are feeling up to it, I would like to speak with the captain."

"I do not know what I can offer that he cannot, but I will escort you, if you wish."

She cups my face, forcing me to look into her honey eyes. "My dear, you are more connected to the island than you believe. I see your spirit. I see the tether binding you to this place."

My head shakes of its own accord. "Do you think that is why I fell overboard? When the land appeared, I felt this... this need to be closer. I stepped forward without considering my actions."

Icy air stings my entire body as I allow her to pull me to my feet. I was comfortable on the bed, cocooned in its warmth. Now I am standing, the chill in the air is sinking deep into my bones.

"Your spirit yearns for the island," says Zentha as we navigate the narrow hallway towards the main deck. "I am not surprised by your actions."

I do not want to think about some part of me longing for a mystical land, so I change the subject and ask where my father is. Surely, he wishes to see his only daughter after she almost drowned.

"Kerym and Rennyn have taken the rowboat to shore. I believe they intend to prepare their own ships and approach the island tomorrow when the Mother Star shines bright. I am under strict instruction to ensure you do nothing reckless while they are gone."

"And Fayeth?"

Zentha snorts. "Locked herself in a cabin and refuses to show herself until we reach land. She looked a little green the last I saw her. Though she was born into my court, the ocean does not call to her like it does to the rest of us. It is no wonder she agreed to mate with your father."

"And have you told any of them about my spirit? About the... tether, did you call it?"

She rests a hand on the door to the quartermaster's cabin. "Bria, I may enjoy your father's company, but divulging something so sacred is not my place. If you wish for him to know, you may tell him. Until then, I will not utter a word to anyone."

"Thank you," I breathe as she opens the door.

Our meeting with the captain passes quickly. According to him, the crew has done everything they can think of to get the ship moving. They have used their water magic to push at the ship from the side, from the rear, and from the front, and we have not moved at all.

We step onto to the main deck, night having well and truly fallen, and wrap our cloaks tighter around our bodies when a fierce wind nips at our skin. Waves crash against the ship's hull, the salty spray peppering the already slick timber boards. The wind wants us gone, but there is something buried deep within the tongues of air, something akin to desire and intrigue.

I lean against the low railing, careful not to put too much weight on the only barrier between me and the ocean, casting my eyes over the shore of the island. The same cloaked figures stand on the sandy beach watching us. The four of them, dressed in all black, are unmoving as they watch the ship bobbing in the water.

I do not know why I do it, but I lift a hand in a wave. As soon as the tips of my fingers curl back down, the ship lurches backwards and the wind dies down. The four fae turn and leave, seeming to disappear into the shadows.

The crew, startled by the sudden freedom, launch into action after a moment of quiet. They shout commands and race for their stations, ripples of water magic bringing a hint of freshness to the already frigid air.

"How curious. They were waiting for you," Zentha murmurs. She turns to face me, wonder staining the amber in her eyes. "And how your spirit sings, knowing it is wanted."

I flick my eyes to Fayeth for the ninth time. She looks ill after our time on the churning seas. The wind that battered the ship did not make for a comfortable journey home, and even safely on Solana's back, I feel as if the ground is tilting from side to side.

It is a welcome reprieve that Fayeth does not have energy enough to scold me. We ride in silence towards our castle home, both of us wondering if Father and Rennyn have set sail yet. A quick glance to the south and I am certain they are still on land. There are no ships dotting the glittering ocean, no burgundy sails and mahogany masts poking from the horizon.

If they wait much longer, they will not be the only court to have ships surrounding the island. I wonder what the others make of the phenomenon, whether the fae of the Night Islands are as curious as we are, whether the Winter fae with their snow and ice and shadows have sent an armada to the new land, seeking to claim it as part of their territory.

Perhaps war is on the horizon. We fae have fought over less.

It is common knowledge I find life at the castle beyond dull. Unless I wish to spend my free time — and there is a lot of it — cross stitching or walking in the gardens with the other court nobles, I must fill that free time with something else. And what better way to kill time than to delve into the mind of another? Books.

They are the backbone of society and the bridge between the past and present, all the while providing a sounding board for the future. The court archives are home to many a tome on war and battles, long-lost traditions, and recounts of heroics. And the stories I love the most? Tales of true mate bonds, pairings chosen by destiny. I claim my love of reading is because of a strong desire to know our history, but really, I like to envision myself in times of old.

Bria, soldier and defender of the innocent. Bria, finding her true mate in a faraway court, leaving the old behind. I sigh. Father is always telling me that losing myself to Radelea's history is not such a wise pastime. He says I must live in the present, think of the future, and that the past holds nothing but stale memories.

Father took four guards with him, leaving the remaining four to escort Fayeth and me home, though I know he will have dragged several more from their beds the moment he stepped foot on land, ordering them to prepare our ships. He may be at sea for weeks or months. Those guards will be away from their families for so long their hearts will ache.

As will mine if I am forced to endure Fayeth without Rennyn or Father acting as mediator. I look at her again as we pass under the outpost, worry churning inside me at the thought of her toppling sideways from her horse. Saber does not seem to notice his rider's condition, walking with his head held high. He would just keep walking if she slid from his back. The thought makes me chuckle.

Fayeth whips her face towards me. "What is so amusing?"

"I was just wondering what life will be like with Father and Rennyn at sea, whether you and I will come to verbal blows if left to our own devices for too long."

Her face sours. "You will keep your distance. Unless you wish for me to tell Kerym exactly *who* you were seeing in the village?"

My face pales. I had hoped she did not notice my interaction with Nikolai. Instead of playing into her games, I turn my attention to dismounting Solana and handing her over to the stable hand. If distance is what she wants to keep that information to herself, distance is just what she will get.

My mind is so full of everything that has happened of late that I am surprised when I find myself standing in the middle of my bedchamber. I do not remember leaving the stables, let alone making my way through the castle.

Fayeth's threat against Nikolai was subtle, yes, but a threat all the same. I have no doubt in my mind she will ensure his demise if I give her reason enough. So I will play by her rules, and I will remain well away from Father's mate while he is away. I will lock myself in these damn chambers if I must.

Seclusion. I can think of nothing worse.

Mere heartbeats after arriving, Lymsia calls for the court mender, Cataleya. The spritely female, who hails from Dawn, assesses me from head to toe before ordering me to take a day of rest. She claims if I am seen outside my chambers, she will restrain me in the infirmary.

She owes nothing to any court and works within the walls of Autumn from the goodness of her heart; I cannot scold her or threaten her with Father. I have no choice but to adhere to her rules and hope to never scorch my lungs with water again.

When she leaves, after offering one last warning to remain here, Lymsia orders me into the bath to wash away the salt clinging to my skin before scurrying away to find some kind of scented oil. I hope it is lavender at such a late hour.

Alone in my bathing chamber, the panic sets in. I peer into the copper tub, my eyes crossing, and fear sinks its ugly talons into my heart. I gulp down a breath, my shoulders tight as a cold sweat beads at my hairline. It does not matter that I have always enjoyed soaking in the tub, does not matter this is a small amount of water. This is a meagre drop compared to the ocean. Even thinking about dipping a toe into the steaming water makes my knees weak.

I am still standing beside the copper tub when Lymsia returns.

She clicks her tongue, setting the vial of oil to the side before beginning to unlace my salt-stained corset. "Nothing will happen to you here, Bria. I know you are afraid. Just know you are also safe."

"I keep seeing the ocean pressing in on me, the last bubbles of air from my lungs wobbling towards the surface. Water can trap a soul as easily as it can breathe life into the land."

She turns me to face her, those deep olive eyes penetrating. "When water drips, it wears away at stone. You are born of the court of earth. If you allow the water to drip into your fear, drip into your very being, it will wear away at you, just as it does to stone."

I take a shuddering breath. "You are right. You are always right, Lymsia. But tonight, it is too soon. Perhaps tomorrow I will fight the fear."

She dips her chin and returns to freeing me from my clothes. The entire time she is undressing me, I keep one eye on the still water in the tub, watching it until I see nothing but water and the copper tub, no longer envisioning the depths of the ocean.

It is not enough to keep the nightmares at bay.

When I wake in the morning, my body is slick with sweat and my bedding drenched. I feel as though I did not sleep a wink, my night plagued by the memory of drowning.

I spend the day doing nothing but staring out the window at the western sea. The island seems small from so far away, a tiny blip on the horizon. Ships of all shapes and sizes surround the land, bobbing in the waves. I marvel at how far we fae can see and wonder if every creature roaming the realm can see as far as us, or if this is a gift from the Mother Star.

She has moved past her apex, well on her way to meeting the horizon, when boredom sets in. The longer I stare out the bay window, the greater a need inside me grows. A need to be doing something, anything, to get to that strange land. It is as if my heart and soul cannot be whole without it, as if I cannot possibly go on without stepping foot on the sandy shore.

I retire sometime around dusk, when the light is bending in strange ways and the sun and moon are battling for a stronghold over the realm. I toss and turn all night, my dreams haunted by waves and tendrils of water. Except tonight, gusts of air join the sea, whipping at my clothes and pulling at my hair.

5

"I WILL TAKE MY breakfast on the balcony," I tell Lymsia when she finishes pulling my hair back into a romantic tuck.

I stand and brush my hands over the sea-green silk draping over my body before clasping an emerald velvet cloak around my shoulders. The breeze is cool today, the weather doing what it pleases without Father's mood to influence it.

As High Lord of the Autumn Court, he has sway over the wind and rain and temperature. Mostly, our climate is tepid with a slight breeze. When Father is feeling particularly enraged, the wind turns icy, bringing heavy rain and thunderstorms. My favourite days are the ones where Father is relaxed. When the weather is neither warm nor cold, the breeze settles to a caress, and white clouds streak across the sky.

"As you wish," says Lymsia, dipping to a courtesy. I have told her time and again to treat me like a friend, but she refuses out of fear for her position. If Father or Fayeth were to discover her acting anything less than respectful, she would be relieved of her duties before she could so much as argue the point.

I push open the double doors in the main chamber and step into the cool breeze, my eyes darting straight to the mysterious land and the ships surrounding it. Every time I am near the windows, my eyes find the island, as if drawn to it by fate or the stars or whoever determines such things.

Radelea looks so small from up here. Although my chambers face west, towards the Night Islands, and there is not much more than ocean for me to see, I know my father's northern view offers a vast landscape of mountains and plains and forests. But I love my view. I love watching the Mother Star retire for the night, dusk chasing away the last remnants of light. There is something about the day's end that soothes my jaded soul.

As I sit down to pick at my eggs and toasted bread, I wonder if I can return to normal life here at the castle. Now I know there is a mysterious land out there calling my name, I do not believe I can handle something as monotonous as the court expectations. My entire being screams for adventure, for something wild and unexpected, and like the plain eggs on my plate, life here is not all that exciting.

I spend the day doing everything I would normally do on a day where I am not besieged with thoughts of strange islands. I begin by visiting the court younglings — at just one and twenty, they are a raucous bunch — teaching them all I know about the courts of Radelea, which of them are allies and which are enemies. They pepper me with questions of truces and wars, preferring the gritty details to the drab ones.

The study hall we occupy is a grand space with cream walls adorned with gold embellishments. It is gaudy and unnecessary, and I like to pretend the walls do not exist and focus on the seven youths in front of me.

I tuck my feet beneath my chair, crossing my ankles. "What have we learned from the Winter Court?"

"That living inside a mountain makes you crave solitude. It makes you boring," says Hamon.

The others laugh.

Dey swipes their long chestnut locks over one shoulder. "We know they have the greatest protections known in Radelea. Their enemies, the Night Court, could not penetrate their mountain court for centuries. This is why Summer deemed the ice fae worthy allies."

"Very good, Dey." I gesture to the tapestry behind me. The map of Radelea and its courts has frayed edges from millennia of use. "Winter is in the north-west corner. With only the Spring Court at their border, the court has been peaceful since Radelea broke apart."

"Why did the Night Islands form?" asks Dillon, the most inquisitive of the bunch.

I smirk, knowing the younglings will hate what I am about to say. "I will leave it to you to discover. Next time we meet, bring me an essay on the history of the Night Court with emphasis on how their High Lady, Maude, came into power."

Dey is the only one who does not groan. Their love of knowledge knows no bounds, and they often request extra work. It is an effort to find topics difficult enough for them.

Mitah groans the hardest and says, "We have an upcoming assessment in combat. Can you be lenient? Just this once?"

I look each of them in the eye. The twins, Rhett and Orli, wither under my scrutiny. "Prince Rennyn and High Lord

Kerym are at sea. What else are you to do with your time until their return?"

"Why the spontaneous voyage?" asks Mykaela. "Is there something we should know?"

"They are investigating the new island. As the first court to witness the phenomenon, Father is hoping to claim the land as ours. Imagine exploring such a new and exciting place." When they look a little too eager, I add, "Imagine the essays you could write about it."

They groan again.

I chuckle. "Now, who can tell me about our intangible powers?"

Dey's hand shoots into the air. "Unlike our physical powers — think fire, water, and earth — each court specialises in an intangible power. They are ordered by tiers, with tier one being the strongest."

"Good." I smile at Dey. To Mitah, I ask, "How many tiers in the animalistic magic of the Autumn Court?"

"Three. Depending on our tier, we can talk to all creatures, control them from afar, or see through the eyes of any animal. The rarest animalist known to the court was a male who could control animals from within."

"Like, his soul entered the animal?" asks Mykaela, shuddering.

Before the conversation turns sour — which is likely with this group — I ask them for information on each of the other six courts and their intangible gifts.

Each has a preferred type of magic, with none of them favouring the Summer Court's necromancy magic. There is a definite preference for the mind powers of the Night Court and the psychic nature of Spring, with only Dey interested in Winter's shadow magic, Day's ability to speak with spirits, and Dawn's healing power.

After wrapping up the lesson, I enjoy a light luncheon in the gardens surrounded by blooming cyclamen and petunia. The zinnia at my back is budding, and soon the gardens will be thriving. I have always loved flowers, but today, they feel wrong. They do nothing to abate the need swirling in my chest, and I sweep from the gardens without finishing my meal.

After noontime, I visit the court metal bender and inspect the progress on Rennyn's born day gift.

The master forger greets me with enthusiasm. "Well met, Princess Bria. How wonderful to see you again."

"Well met, Fylson. I was hoping for an update on Prince Rennyn's gift. There are few moons remaining until his born day."

He brushes his dark hair away from his eyes, leaving a smear of black across his forehead, before leading me to the back of the forging chamber. "The sword is coming along nicely. I am quite proud of this piece."

Swords and blades of every description cover the rear wall. From axes and daggers to long swords and even the occasional trident. The work table in the centre is host to several tools, none of which I have any inkling of their purpose.

The fire blazing from the side wall throws a suffocating blanket of heat over the space, and I wonder how Fylson and his apprentice work under such conditions. I make a mental note to bring it up with Father upon his return. How can we expect the best quality steel when the forgers risk their health?

The bridge between the wealthy and poor is becoming larger the older I get, the more I see and realise. Even someone as gifted as Fylson, who wields a rare power, is treated like scum. The ability to manipulate metal is both feared and revered in the Autumn Court. Less than one metal bender is born every one thousand suns.

"Here she is," says Fylson, balancing a raw-looking sword in one hand. "The atryxium steel was an excellent choice by you. Such beauty."

The blue-grey metal — a difficult metal to mine and the strongest known to fae — is dull, not yet polished by the apprentice's blistered hands, but no less beautiful. The cross-guard curves away from the hand, providing a stable base for the grip which is yet to be bound in leather.

The pommel, the focal point of the sword, has been forged into the shape of a diamond. It is the only thing I could think of. Rennyn is strong, yet beautiful. Stubborn, yet caring. That, and I hope the sword brings my brother strength and courage in battle.

"It is gorgeous," I breathe.

When I move to caress the near complete long sword, Fylson snatches it away. "The first to touch the blade will be the bearer," he says, apology dripping in his muddy brown eyes. "Other than myself and my apprentice, of course."

"Then how will I gift it to him?" I ask, clasping my hands together behind my back to suppress the urge to caress the metal.

"It will be sheathed. Now, which leather do you prefer for the grip? I have black, brown, beige… Is there a colour you are fond of?"

I ask to see samples, then spend too long contemplating which to use. Brown and tan are common among the Autumn fae, but I want Rennyn's sword to be unique in a sea of replicas. The beige and white leathers will only stain over time, and the black screams of the Night Court, sending a shiver down my spine.

"Do you have anything in a reddish amber?" I am growing frustrated that nothing is calling to me.

Fylson's face falls. "I do not. However, I can procure something. It will take a moon or two."

"We have the time." Relief fills my veins. "I would appreciate your subtlety in your search. The sword is a surprise gift for my brother. You understand."

"Of course, of course." He sets the weapon back on the wall rack. "I will send word when it is ready. Two moons or thereabouts."

I thank him and exit the stifling chamber, taking a deep breath of fresh air once in the outer bailey, ignoring the two guards trailing behind me. They have been following me everywhere — on Fayeth's orders or Father's, I am not sure — like twin shadows refusing to part.

The rest of my day, I read through history tomes, looking for something more exciting to teach the younglings. I skim over the civil war between Day and Dawn, skip the making of the Night Islands altogether — the younglings are already researching this, not that they will find much — and move onto the history of the Spring Court.

We often call it the Court of Blooms. With the power to control all plant life, from flowers and vines to the roots of trees, they are our allies. Honestly, I think Father is a little frightened of Spring's ability to see the future. His reasons are valid. I too have always believed the future is not ours to see, that everything happens for a reason, and we should not interfere with the Mother Star's plans.

I set the tome aside and scribble notes on a length of parchment, soon losing myself to the world that once was.

My days continue much the same. For six moons, I wander the castle halls, boredom threatening to overcome me, while avoiding Fayeth as best I can. Every time I see her, she is carrying a wicked smirk and a malicious glint in her cunning eyes. She is planning something, that much is clear. Just what that is, I doubt I will know until it is too late.

Too late comes in the form of my brother and my father, back from sea after eight moons.

I watch them from the stained-glass window in the archives, the coloured glass giving them an otherworldly feel. Twelve guards accompany them, six leading the way under the gatehouse and six trailing behind. They are a large party, especially with the dozen sailors bringing up the rear. From my perch in the archives, it is hard to determine what is occurring — especially with the way the coloured glass distorts the view — but I swear on the Mother Star my father is furious. The clouds overhead churn, turning a menacing grey which grows darker with every breath.

They bring their horses all the way to the inner bailey, the smaller courtyard before our family home, leaving the stable hands rushing after them. It is so out of the ordinary that dread settles inside me and I have the sudden urge to hide in an alcove.

My hands tremble as I pack away the tomes and scrolls I was pouring over, creating more than one crease in the otherwise pristine parchment. I leave them on the table, deciding ruining the rare texts is not worth it.

I snatch the skirt of my cobalt gown in my hands, freeing my feet from the trap of the six layers of chiffon, and dart for the stairs. If Father is enraged, something ominous is coming. If he is so furious his emotions are affecting the weather... What happened at sea?

The memory of those four fae standing on the island flashes in my mind, and I wonder if something happened between our fleet and the natives. Or, more likely, the other courts of Radelea had the same idea as Father. If there is some kind of fight for the land — regardless of those already inhabiting it — we may be on the cusp of war.

My silk slippers are silent as I race through the halls towards the grand foyer, my panicked breaths the only sound. The silence is deceiving. When I rapidly descend the grand staircase to see Fayeth waiting by the doors, my heart sinks.

Her ever-present scowl deepens when she notices me walking towards her. "Leave, Bria. Kerym does not need your antics upon his arrival."

Five and seventy years is a long time to hold a grudge. Fayeth has spent my entire life pushing Father and me apart, and this is just one of her little games. I am sick of it and I deserve better.

Father's wandering eye is not my doing. I am not to blame for his deception.

"Is it Father you are worried about, or yourself?" I stand beside her, letting my skirts fall around my feet. "The only reason you do not want me here is so you can claim Father's attention for yourself."

"Watch your tongue."

I have mere heartbeats to get my point across. Few moments until the foyer is full of castle staff, arriving to greet their High Lord and Prince. I make the time count.

My face is a mask of calm as I face her and say, "It must be tiring, forever fighting for Father's attention. How your heart must ache knowing he bedded another female because you are not enough."

Pink creeps up her neck and over her cheeks. "You overstep."

The large double doors swing open, chased by a bitter gust of wind and a clap of thunder. Father and Rennyn, dressed in full regalia, do not pause on the threshold like they would on a normal day, but storm through the foyer towards the rear wall.

My stomach sinks. There is only one chamber back there, behind the staircase.

The war chamber.

"Bria," growls Father. "My study. Now."

Ice tracks down my spine and sinks low into my stomach. In antagonising Fayeth, I did not keep her bond with Father in mind. No doubt she used their mind link to inform my father of my harsh words the moment I said them.

On his way to the war chamber, Rennyn offers me a grimace, mouthing words I am not sure I understand. Be good or do not push, whatever his advice, I am not sure I will come out of this meeting with Father unscathed.

6

M Y KNEE BOUNCES IN time with the rapid beating of my heart as I wait for Father. The wooden chair feels wrong against my rigid back, the timber digging into my shoulder blades as if to warn me of approaching heartache.

I turn my attention to the details of the room in one last attempt to distract my spiralling thoughts. The russet walls make it feel small. It is anything but. With a stone fireplace, floor-to-ceiling shelves stacked with books and scrolls and other bits and pieces, and an imposing mahogany desk, Father's study is both practical and opulent.

My eyes linger on the details, on the oil paintings hanging on the walls — landscapes of the Autumn Court, family portraits, and a lone abstract with splashes of brown and red that reminds me of a dying animal — on the sword above the fireplace, and on the gleaming timber of the furniture. None of it is enough to hold my attention.

My thoughts drift, the past few moons tumbling through my mind on repeat, and I wonder why I was foolish enough to tell Rennyn of my adventures to the western village. Had I kept those details to myself, I would not be in such a predicament. If I kept the knowledge of the mysterious island to myself, none of this would have happened. If I wielded the power to go back in time and reverse the damage, I would not hesitate to do it. Instead, I am left with the common powers of fae, the folding and fae lights and shields which do little to protect me.

I often beg Father to allow me to visit the Night Court and have them search my mind for a reason, any reason, why I cannot wield magic. He has always refused, claiming a female of my standing does not need to defend herself when she has guards and sentries to do it for her.

"It is necessary, Kerym." Fayeth's voice filters in, an edge of urgency and determination to her words that makes fear prickle over my scalp. "If only to keep war at bay. New alliances are essential during such times. Look how you benefited from our joining."

Father's voice is strained when he says, "You may be right. She will not like it. In fact, she will fight with vigour against it."

The door swings open, my father and Fayeth filing into the study without a greeting. I do not turn to face them, knowing Father prefers to greet his subjects from behind his desk. It is a show of intimidation, a way for him to feel more important.

It does not work on me.

Fayeth takes the empty seat beside me, smoothing the burgundy skirt of her gown with practiced motions. She spares me a look when Father is not watching, a conniving, evil tilt of the lips.

Father unbuckles his cloak and hangs it on the stand by the door, running a hand through his silvery-white hair as he rounds the desk. He sinks into the cushioned chair, crossing an ankle over a knee and steepling his fingers beneath his chin.

"Tell me, Bria. What must I do for you to cease this infantile behaviour?"

"What do you mean, Father?"

He leans forward. "Sneaking into the village under the cover of darkness, fraternising with an angler, tarnishing the family's reputation, and flouting the rules. You have shown me time and again you are too reckless for the responsibility you crave. Your proclivity for defiance bores me. I have had enough."

"You keep me locked in this castle day in and day out, yet expect me to obey every command? I am not a youngling, Father. I can make my own choices." I sit straighter, steeling my spine. "You have always been stricter on me than Rennyn. You allow him leniency to visit the villages. Why am I forced to endure the monotony of remaining here while he lives a life of excitement and glory?"

"You are a female," he says simply. "As such, you are expected to mate and birth heirs."

My breath hitches. "I will do no such thing."

"You will do as I command!" he shouts before tempering his volume. "War is brewing. Every court except Dawn has claimed the new land. You will mate a male of *my* choosing, to strengthen old alliances or form new ones through your joining. Refuse to do so, and my guards will pay your village lover a visit."

"I am not some possession to be bought or sold. My life is not something to barter with."

"You are my flesh and blood, and you will do your part for this court. You begged for more responsibility and less monotony. This is my answer. It is not up for discussion." His magic roils, drenching me in the choking scent of moss and tilled dirt. "On the subject of responsibility, you have a new hand maiden. I have disposed of Lymsia."

I bolt upright, springing to my feet. "Why?"

"I questioned her this morning," drawls Fayeth. "While I admire her dedication to you, her duty is to the court. She should have come to me or your father the moment she realised where you were sneaking off to."

I spin back to Father. "You cannot be serious? Lymsia has been my hand maiden since before I could walk."

She has been there for me through every heartbreak, every struggle. She is more of a mother to me than Fayeth has ever been, certainly more than my real mother is. Lymsia is my friend and confidant. She is the only good thing in this wretched place.

"I will have no one in this court who does not wish to answer to me and me alone," says Father. "End of discussion. You may leave."

And leave, I do. I do not bother with a travelling cloak, do not bother with riding shoes. I dash for the stables, hoisting myself onto Solana's back without saddling her first.

The stable hands protest, but wither under the glacial glare I shoot their way as I guide Solana from her stall and into the cool afternoon air. Are they afraid of my wrath, or is it the tears streaking down my face making them uncomfortable? Either way, they do not hinder me as I urge Solana into a canter.

The sentries in both the gatehouse and outpost watch me flee. I have no doubt one of them is racing to inform Father of my departure, yet I cannot find it within myself to care.

Solana picks up speed as we cross the field separating the court from the western village, clouds of dust churning with every thud of her hooves.

A lone drop of rain plummets from the sky, landing on my cheek and merging with my tears. The realm shudders as a crack of thunder booms overhead, a torrential downpour falling immediately after. Father knows I left.

Let him rage and stew.

I urge Solana faster still, clinging to her flaxen mane for dear life as she navigates a sloping hill. If I can just make it to the docks before Father sends guards chasing after me... The village swims into view, blurred through the rain. By the time I am moving along the paved road, it is quiet, the fae dwellers having found shelter in their homes or in the tavern.

The docks, though, are still bustling with activity. The courts have ordered every ship they own to prepare for war, to return to their home court to ready for battle. I never thought I would live to see a war, and I cannot say I am looking forward to it. War only leads to death and destruction, to broken alliances and bittersweet reunions.

I guide Solana towards Nikolai's ship. She tosses her head, grunting. I do not blame her for not wanting to venture close to the water — I am not too fond of the idea myself — but leaving her alone on the road is not an option.

"Nik!" I shout over the pouring rain and cracks of thunder.

The sky flashes, as if Father has heard my call.

A figure on the docks turns towards me, pausing before rushing over. He pulls his hood from his head and says, "What are you doing here, Ria? Or should I bow and call you by your title, Princess Bria of the Autumn Court?"

I slide from Solana's back, keeping a hand on her shoulder to keep her calm. "I am so sorry. It was never my intention for you to suffer for my actions. I left you a note explaining everything."

He scoffs. "And a note is supposed to make everything right? I have guards watching my every move."

"Are they watching now?" I ask as I turn my face towards the tavern.

"No." He swipes a hand over his golden hair, brushing the growing strands from his eyes. "They disappeared when the storm rolled in."

I huff a sigh of relief. "Good. I have immensely enjoyed our time together. And you know I care about you." My eyes meet his, emerald-green clashing with golden-brown. "Run away with me, Nik. Run away and never look back. We can make a life for ourselves in a different court. Zentha would host us for a time."

He staggers back. "You want me to leave the life I have built for myself? For what? For you?"

I reach out to him, but he evades my groping fingers and I let my hand fall to my side. "I thought you cared for me, too? We can be together. Please, just think about it."

I want to beg him. If getting to my knees and fisting my hands in his cloak would make him agree, I would do it without question. But the look on his face tells me nothing will make Nikolai wish to flee with me. Not even the promise of love, a sure future if we continue to see one another.

He shakes his head. "I will not spend my life running from your father. My answer is no. Our friendship has been a lie. Nothing I know about you is the truth. You are nothing but a sad, lonely female looking for a way to gain your father's attention."

His words sting more than I care to admit.

"Nik..."

"Do not return here. If I see you on these docks again, I will call for your father's guards and have them drag you back to the castle kicking and screaming." He pulls his hood over his head, then does the last thing I thought he would do. He turns his back on me.

My heart sinks, all but splattering on the wooden boards at my feet. I watch Nikolai until he is nothing but a blurred outline in the pouring rain.

"Come on, Solana, let us leave this place." I run my hand over her belly, the fine hairs sticking to my damp hand, before using a discarded barrel as a step and hoisting myself onto her back. "Take it slow, beautiful. We are in no rush."

We walk in the rain — which has let up a little, but still torrential — for hours. I let Solana choose our path, trusting her to keep us close enough to home that, should we encounter trouble of any kind, we can easily reach the safety of the castle walls.

She takes us along the southern border of our territory, across the many creeks and rivers that snake through the land like twisting veins, and settles beside one of the largest, south-east from the castle walls.

The redwood forest to the west is a dark and dangerous place that overlooks Father's private port. Autumn's land is as far south as Radelea goes, with a mixture of steep cliffs and sandy beaches marking the edge of the land. To our north, the Summer Court's vast desert and steep hills.

I have always liked it here, with the forest and the creek and the view of the distant ships, though many of them remain at sea, defending the land Father wishes to claim as ours. I believe that is why Solana brought me here. She knows how to calm me down, how to soothe my aching heart.

I slide from her back and slip down the hill towards the gurgling creek almost overflowing with Father's downpour, and collapse to the soggy ground. I allow my head to droop, my chin resting on my bent knees as I consider my options.

I could run. Right now, I am alone with no guards to stop me. It would be easy for Solana and me to slip away unnoticed, to find a home in a new court. I will have to fake my way into earning a living, since I do not think a keen interest in history will pay for food or shelter.

Or I could return home. I could go through the motions like I always do and let Fayeth win. Although Father said I will mate a male of his choosing, he will allow me some say.

There is zero chance I will mate with a fae from the Night Court. Father will agree with me. I am unaware of any eligible males within the Day Court now that Zentha's son is promised to another. The rest of them, though, are all options I would consider. Although, I have reservations about the Summer Court. And I doubt Father will allow me to join the Spring Court. Mother Star forbid I learn who my mother is.

That leaves me with Winter or Dawn. Snow or light. Shadow or healing. I do not know enough about either court to decide right now.

My third option is to convince Father that sending me away is not the best course of action. He is stubborn — I had to inherit it from someone — and with Fayeth in his ear, my fight will be a long and difficult one. But I am as determined as they come.

I can run, obey, or fight.

I have never been one to hide from hardship.

Playing by the rules has never been my thing.

The rain lessens as I uncurl to my feet, my mind made up. Father will see sense, and if he does not, I still have option one to fall back on.

Walking Solana home takes two hours. Two hours of second-guessing and internal debate. By the time I lead her through the gatehouse, I am happy with my decision to fight.

7

"WHO ARE YOU?" I ask, pulling to a stop in the door to my chambers.

The female, with warm tawny skin and impossibly shiny black hair, dips into a rough courtesy. "Your new hand maiden."

The door clicks shut as I enter. "Do you have a name?"

Her whole face lights up when she smiles. "My parents named me Wynetta, but it's such a mouthful. Everyone calls me Wyn."

Although she is not Lymsia, and Father relieved my previous hand maiden of her duties because of my actions, I like her. She is tall and muscular, as if she has spent many hours training — something Father has always denied me — and gives off an air of confidence I wish I had. Her steel-grey eyes are piercing, and when she smiles, they blaze with silver.

"Okay, Wyn," I say, turning my back to her, "help me get out of this damn thing."

"You're soaking," she says, pulling the string free on my corset.

I bunch my still dripping hair at my nape to make things easier for her. "You might as well know what you are in for with me. I... thought about running away. In fact, I begged my lover to run with me, but he refused."

"Seems an interesting story." She unlaces the corset, moving to my front to unclasp the busk. "Will you tell me about it while I run you a bath?"

There is something about Wyn that makes me trust her. Something different in the way she speaks and holds herself, as if she has piles and piles of confidence. I tell her about Nikolai, and how I would sneak out every full moon to meet him. Then I tell her how I confided in Rennyn, and how that backfired, before moving onto Father demanding I find a mate. By the time I have finished, the bath is full, steaming, and smelling of the sweetest rose. I do not so much as balk at the water.

"Where I'm from, females choose their own mates. We're not beneath the males in court, but equal to them," she says, helping me out of the cobalt gown. "I think you'd like it there."

"I have never heard of such a place. What court are you from?" I ask, sinking into the comfort of the warm water.

She looks uncomfortable in the grey maid's gown, which is belted at the waist with a length of dark leather tied in a knot, as she sits on the wooden seat beside the tub. It is almost as if she does not wear gowns often. She crosses one leg over the other, foot bouncing. Her silvery eyes seem to glow in the dim light. "The Dusk Court."

I scoff. "There is no such place."

She leans on the edge of the copper tub. "I assure you there is. I'm trusting you here, Bria. Can you assure me this will stay between us?"

I rub a bar of soap over my arms, considering. If there is such a place as the Dusk Court, I am certain I would have heard about it or read about it in the history texts I love so much. But the way Wyn talks, the way she holds herself, and the slight accent she is trying to hide... If she is speaking the truth, and she is indeed from a hidden court no one knows about, can I keep that information to myself?

I face her once more. "Yes. What you tell me stays in this chamber."

She tilts her head to the side, her silky locks falling over her shoulder. "In your bathroom?"

For the first time in many moons, I chuckle. It is husky, my voice not accustomed to making such a sound. "We will only speak of it in this very chamber."

She leans back once more, the fingers of her right hand trailing over a tarnished grey bangle in the shape of a coiled snake. "Three hundred years ago, there was a terrible war —"

"That is when the Night Islands formed."

"Do you want to hear my story or not?" she asks, those steel-grey eyes narrowing.

I move onto scrubbing my legs and apologise.

"There was a war in the Night Court. The last battle was so devastating, the land broke into many pieces. What was once a whole is now many. The original court occupies four of the five largest islands."

"And the fifth? The island I do not believe to exist?"

"Is home to the Dusk Court, fae with the ability to control the wind and weave illusions who fought for their freedom against the High Lady of Night. For decades, Maude believed we died on the battlefield. But my father, who was High Lord for three hundred years, weaved such a powerful illusion over our island that we have lived in peace since the war, even after Maude eventually discovered our existence. The illusion fell when he died and our home was unveiled for all to see." She blinks a few times, forcing back tears that are surely fighting to be free. "As his firstborn, the Dusk fae expected me to become High Lady. I did not want the responsibility."

My hand has not moved since she began to speak, the soap resting against my shin as I listen. I resume my scrubbing. "Who took the role?"

"My brother, Vander. He's more suited to leadership than I am."

"So the island which appeared to the west... that is the Dusk Court?" She nods as I set the soap aside. Turning back to her, I say, "I am sorry for your loss, Wyn. But you must know, the courts of Radelea are at war. Seven courts, all wishing to lay claim to your home."

She pulls the bangle free and twirls it between her fingers. "Which is why I'm here, spying on the court closest to us. Well, that, and Vander has taken a liking to you."

I jerk upright, and water sloshes over the side of the tub. "What do you mean?"

She huffs a laugh. "Oh, come on. You were the first to see us, according to our intel. Then you fell into the damn ocean."

"So Vander thinks I am what, leading the charge against your court?"

She smirks. "Something like that."

"I do not have magic. How can you expect me to lead an army into battle and claim an unclaimed land? Which, as it turns out, is an established court. No matter that Father is sending me away soon, off to mate whoever he deems best."

"You forget that Dusk will not kneel without a fight. We may be the smallest court in Radelea, but we are fierce. If the High Lords and Ladies wish to claim our land as their own, they're going to have a fight on their hands."

⁂

"There is something I have been wondering," I say to Wyn two days later as she helps me into a flowing gown of blush pink. "If Vander is your new High Lord, why not just put the illusion back in place to protect the Dusk Court? Why go to the effort of sending fae to infiltrate every court and spy?"

"Because it was too late. By the time we worked through the immediate grief of losing our father and realised the illusion had fallen, you were already there on your damn ship. Well, you and the Winter Court."

I startle at that. "High Lord Ruith was there?"

She hums. "He was to our north-west while you were to our south-east. It didn't take long for the Night and Spring Courts to send ships, either. After two moons, we were surrounded. I believe the respective leaders met on the Dawn Court's ship and called a cease-fire until after the celebrations."

"What celebrations?"

She spins me until I am facing her. "Your brother's one hundredth born day, which is *tonight*. Mother Star, Bria. When did you become so dense?"

"But why is that such a big deal?" I ask, smoothing the gauzy skirt. "Why would the courts agree to put war on hold for a ball?"

"It gives them time to assess the situation. Time to make their own plans, gather their armies, and figure out their next move. With the bonus of free food and drink, of course."

My face falls. "I still do not understand why Father invited the nobles of every court tonight. It makes little sense."

"Maybe he wants to make a show of power?" She shoves me into the wooden seat by the window and begins working on my hair. "Maybe he's hoping to form new alliances during the ball. The world of politics is delicate, and easier to control when wine fills the bellies of those in charge."

A most unladylike snort escapes me. "This is true." After a moment of hesitation, I ask, "Why me? Why did you choose to spy on me?"

"When you were watching us from that ship, the wind carried your thoughts and emotions. It was obvious then — and it's obvious now — that you're not happy. The wind sighed with your pain." She snatches a metal rod from the table. "We are not saviours by any means, but we decided then and there to save you."

"How?"

"We aren't sure yet. Give us time."

"I wish you would hurry and figure it out," I say, watching as she holds the rod in the fire, heating it to curl my hair. It is a technique I have never seen before, and I am in awe of her ingenuity. Even if I am a little afraid she will burn the hair straight from my head. Actually, perhaps I should ask her to. If I were bald, no noble male would want me, and Father's plan would evaporate.

I decide against going bald and by the time she has finished, my copper locks are falling in soft waves around my shoulders, draping down to tickle the swell of my breasts.

8

F YLSON WARNS ME YET again to keep my hands off the blade, demanding I carry it by the scabbard. The weapon is as beautiful as they come, with blue-grey atryxium steel and reddish-brown leather. In fact, I am a little envious of my brother, and yearn to wield such a glorious sword myself.

I drape a length of red velvet over it, hiding it from view as I carry it through the inner bailey and the castle. Excitement surges through me as I imagine Ren's reaction to my gift. Even my grumbling stomach cannot distract me from the happiness threatening to burst free.

Over the past two moons, I have avoided my father. I have let him stew in his thoughts, waited for his anger to abate enough to broach the subject of sending me off to mate and breed. This morning at breakfast, I have every intention of making my thoughts known.

I arrive in the dining hall before everyone else, and stow Rennyn's born day gift under the table, resurfacing just as the kitchen staff enter with their arms laden.

They try to give me a wide berth, perhaps understanding I am the reason for the two-days-long storm Father's emotions caused. Either that or they truly do not appreciate it when we arrive early.

Every dish they place on the long, rectangular table is something Ren enjoys. His favourite fat sausages, potatoes the head cook has shredded and squeezed back together before the cooking them in butter, and bowl upon bowl of juicy red grapes.

It is a stark difference from my born day celebrations, when the kitchen staff do not make the extra effort, instead serving up a typical breakfast. I understand why Rennyn is the favourite. It just hurts sometimes, knowing I am unwanted, even by the staff.

Nikolai does not want me, that much is clear.

Fayeth certainly wishes I did not exist.

Rennyn will always choose duty over me — though I have not given him a reason to dislike me — as has been ingrained into him by his mother and our father.

The court staff avoid me, too scared of father's mate to treat me with the respect my position demands.

And Father... He took me in out of responsibility and nothing more. He tries to treat me with fairness, but I see the shadow cross his eyes, the reminder that he betrayed his mate.

All of a sudden, I hate it here.

I have never been fond of the Autumn Court, never felt like I belonged here, but I have always persevered. I have always settled. Now I know about the Dusk Court, and I have seen Wyn's confidence and the spark of life in her silver eyes, I know I cannot remain here. Perhaps mating the Prince of Winter or falling for the Prince of Dawn is worth it after all.

I thank the kitchen staff when they are done.

One of them offers me a half-hearted smile before darting through one of the side doors. That is it. No one bows or curtseys or nods. No one so much as utters a word of welcome. I should be used to it, but it still stings.

Father, Rennyn, and Fayeth arrive together, chatting about Ren's special day — one hundred years is a remarkable achievement — as they take their seats.

Fayeth's icy stare lingers on my curled hair. "Mother Star," she says, pressing a hand to her chest. "What have you done?"

"It is a new style I am trying. My hand maiden learned it somewhere along the way. Do you like it?"

Her nose crinkles as she lifts her chin, refusing to answer.

"Good morning," says Father, spearing a sausage. "I trust you slept well?"

I accept a serving spoon from Rennyn, keeping my eyes on Father to gauge his mood. "Yes, I did, thank you. Father, I was hoping to talk to you about your plan to find me a mate. I —"

"Today is not about you." Father does not peel his eyes away from the fried eggs on his plate. "You will not ruin this day with your defiance."

"That is not what I —"

He slams his hand down on the table. "Enough!"

I catch Fayeth's smirk from the corner of my eye.

Maybe I have been blind for the past five and seventy years, or maybe I just did not want to see it. This is not a home. It is not a loving family. The Autumn Court is ruthless, and I honestly believe this was Father's plan all along. In fact, I am surprised he has not tried to find me a mate before now.

I spend the rest of breakfast in silence, observing the three fae around me. I cannot help but think of life here a few full moons from now.

Fayeth will have a cruel smile on her face, relishing in the sight of my empty seat.

Father will be relieved I am no longer a burden.

Rennyn will think nothing of my absence, too focused on his new role as Lieutenant, a gift from Father for his born day. He will work his way up the ranks from there, climbing the army ladder until such a time as Father steps down from his position.

Father and Fayeth finish within moments of one another, and flit away to their respective duties — Father to command the guards and sentries, Fayeth to attend the final details for tonight's ball — leaving me alone with Rennyn.

"You should not push him," he says as soon as the doors close behind Father.

I sigh. "That was not my intention. I merely wished to voice my preference for Winter and Dawn."

He places another of those buttery potato pancakes on his plate. "Do not rock the boat, sister. It is not worth it. You already escaped punishment for running two moons ago."

"You cannot blame me for not wanting to end up in the hands of the Summer Court, or by the Mother Star's grace, the Night Islands."

He arches an eyebrow. "An alliance with either of those courts would benefit Autumn. You should be eager to further our prospects."

"You are a fool if you think joining with Summer would benefit us. Their court runs the length of our northern border.

High Lord Iker would love nothing more than to extend his land into ours."

"Perhaps you are right."

"Enough talk about politics and arranged mates." I push away from the table and collect the sword hidden beneath. I hand it to my half-brother, leaving the red velvet over the scabbard, my heart fluttering with nerves. "Happy born day, Ren."

He wipes his hands on a silk napkin before accepting the gift. "What have you done?" His jaw slackens, his golden-brown eyes widening as he unwraps the velvet.

"Fylson has been working on this for three full moons. I did not know what to gift somebody who has no need for possessions and no hobbies, so I asked Father his thoughts. When he mentioned gifting you the rank of lieutenant, I begged him for permission to have this made."

He unsheathes the gorgeous weapon, a gasp tearing from his throat. "Is it atryxium steel?"

"Mined from our own earth."

"Bria..." His eyes meet mine, wonder staining the golden brown. "I do not know what to say other than thank you. It is the most beautiful sword I have seen."

"Well, give it a try," I say, smiling.

He stands, an eager smile curving his lips and turning his harsh features youthful. He sets the scabbard on the table before twirling the sword in a figure eight, then lunging to jab thin air. "So light. It is as if my arm and the sword are one. Fylson forged it?"

"With his metal bending power. He also had it spelled to bond with you. The more you use it, the more it will grow to know you and the way you move. Soon enough, it will become an extension of yourself and will require little to no thought to wield."

"I will carry it with pride." He reaches down for the scabbard, cinching it around his waist while carefully avoiding the sharp edge of his blade. He sheathes the sword once the scabbard is in place. "I must show Father at once," he says before hurrying for the door.

❧ ❦

"Are you finished?" I ask Wyn, my back aching from being still for so long. "I cannot sit here much longer."

"Be patient. I'm almost done."

I sigh and turn my attention back to the window, watching the line of horses and carriages as they navigate the western side of our land.

Several times today, I tried to find Father and continue our earlier conversation. He has been too busy to see me, instead informing me we will discuss it after tonight's ball. Watching the procession below, though, I am left wondering if there is any point talking with him. There is only one reason I can think of why so many fae are attending tonight: Father is going to announce my quest for a mate.

The thought has made me see red since I came to the realisation.

Much to Wyn's amusement.

"Pacing will not help you," she says, correctly assuming my need to stand is equal to my need to pace back and forth in front of the window while spewing vile words at the innocents below.

She rests a gentle hand on my shoulder. "I told you. We have a plan."

"I am not certain involving myself in the plans of you and your High Lord brother is such a good idea."

She scoffs. "Van's plan is excellent. To say otherwise only speaks of your stupidity."

"Then why do you refuse to tell me what it is?"

"I'm finished," she says, setting down the spare pins. She helps me to stand, ignoring the groan of relief that falls from my lips, and guides me to the mirror in the corner.

What I see is an illusion. It has to be. Wyn has used her magic to make me look like an entirely different fae, a fae I do not recognise but one who I relate to. My emerald eyes glow brighter with the kohl creating shadows around them, and the rosy hue to my cheeks gives me life while the lines of my full lips are more pronounced. My hair is messy, but somehow looks like it is supposed to be that way. Loose curls fall around my face and nape, giving me a wind-blown look and accentuating my pointed ears. Compared to the slick hairstyles most fae prefer, I look like a rebel.

I love it.

"What have you done to me?" I ask, my mouth hanging open.

"We call it make-up." She points to my lips. "A mixture of lard and beet juice. Let's get you into the gown."

I slide the silk robe from my shoulders, standing naked before Wyn as she arranges a mess of silk at my feet. The cool air nips at my breasts, making my nipples pucker and harden. I am not ashamed of my curvaceous body, but when something like this happens, I have an urge to wrap an arm around my chest.

Wyn orders me to step into the circle of silk. Once I am right in the middle, she drags the dark mauve material up my body, loops two thin straps over my arms, and lets the gown fall into place.

I gasp. "This is... This is surely not allowed."

The gown is simple. It wraps around my ribs, hugging me tight, before falling to the floor in soft waves. There is no flair, no hoop to keep the shape of my legs hidden. Just silk, with a slit which runs from my left ankle to just below my hip. My nipples press against the silk holding my breasts in place — I am amazed such thin straps can support anything — their shape and size on full display.

But I find I do not mind. The gown is risqué, completely against the norm, and I like that. I like that I will be the only female wearing such an item.

"This is what we wear in the Dusk Court," she says, placing a tiara of twisting vines atop my head. Three ovals of deep jade glimmer in the low light. "Tonight, we're making a statement."

I turn to face her. "What do you mean?"

Her smirk is cunning. "Vander is announcing our court to the rest of Radelea. Wearing something from Dusk sends a message."

"What message is that?" I ask, my brow knitting.

"That you have welcomed us, that you accept us, and that you disagree with the other courts claiming our land as their own." She runs a hand down the silk of my gown. "This says you're one of us and you reject the ridiculous rules the other courts play by."

My lips twist into a smirk which matches hers.

Rebellious.

Father is going to hate it.

9

SOMETIMES I DETEST TRADITION. Tonight, I relish in it.

As I descend the grand staircase, Rennyn waiting at the bottom with his hand outstretched — and his new long sword hanging from his hip — my eyes flick towards the open doors, to Father's and Fayeth's backs. As hosts of the ball, they are required to greet every guest as they arrive. It will take hours.

I will spend that time enjoying the festivities and showing off this fabulous gown before Father can order me to change. There will be nothing he can do about my show of defiance. This is an obvious message. I disagree with his plan to find me a suitable mate; hopefully the suitors realise that.

Rennyn's face is a mask of harsh lines and angles as he watches me descend the stairs. There is anger bubbling below the surface, clear in the way his rigid back straightens further, the way his hand shakes as he waits for me to take it. Contrasting to his anger and harsh features, his deep blue tailcoat is beautiful with the copper embroidery decorating the fabric.

He looks very handsome tonight, so alike our father.

I slip my hand into his, allowing him to weave my arm into the crook of his elbow. "Well met, brother."

"Well met." His hand tightens, and he hisses, "What are you wearing?"

"A gown."

He growls under his breath. "Do not give me a facetious answer. You know Father will forbid you to wear something so provocative. Every curve of your body is on full display."

"It is my body, Ren," I say as we stroll towards the ballroom. "If I wish to wear nothing but my under garments, it is my choice to do so. Besides, Father should be proud of me. I am certain my *suitors* will appreciate my attire."

"I can see the shape of your..." He waves his free hand around my chest.

"Nipples?" He cringes, and I smirk. "You are my brother, and I love you, but this is my choice. If Father cares to confront me about it at the ball, that is my fight. You have said your piece, now let it rest. Our guests are waiting."

The two guards flanking the ballroom doors avert their eyes when they catch sight of my gown, the one on the left knocking on the wooden door to alert the Master of Ceremonies of our arrival.

I hold back another smirk. Seems I will do that a lot tonight.

Rennyn leans towards me as the doors swing open. "Do not cause more trouble than you already have. This may be a ball, but it is my born day. Do not ruin it with your antics."

I blink up at him, pouring as much innocence into my eyes as possible. "Have you not noticed the endless stream of horses and carriages? Father added to the guest list after deciding on my fate. Tonight is not just about you, dear brother. Father is using your born day to announce my intention to mate."

Anger and betrayal flash in his eyes.

"Prince Rennyn Sutherland of the Autumn Court," announces the Master of Ceremonies, "and his sister, Princess Bria Sutherland."

Polite applause greets us as we enter the ballroom, faltering when our guests catch sight of my gown. Murmurs replace the claps as heads bend together and eyes track my every move.

Fayeth has gone to a lot of effort. The ballroom — an empty space with pearl-white walls and a gleaming wooden floor when we are not using it — is stunning, with beige gossamer framing the eight arched doorways on both sides of the hall, each leading to a private balcony. The golden chalices and crockery carried by servers dressed in all white is a pleasant touch, and the four chandeliers hanging from the ceiling are gleaming, the gem of our court, an enormous topaz, dangling from loops and curls of brass.

Zentha is the first to recover, pushing through the crowd to greet us, a male and female following in her wake. "Well met," she says with a curtsey.

I follow suit, dipping low. "Well met, High Lady of Day. I hope you are enjoying the ball?"

She smiles, bringing a sparkle of light to her honey-coloured eyes. "Fayeth has outdone herself. May I introduce my son, Elmon, and his betrothed, Kyra."

I curtsey once more. "Well met, Elmon, Kyra."

Rennyn takes Elmon's warm brown hand in his own before pressing a kiss to Kyra's cheek.

She is a beauty, with golden hair and amber eyes. With the way her bronze skin shimmers in the light, and the golden fabric of her gown, she looks like a statue dipped in gold. She shines brighter than most others in the large hall, with a smile to match.

"Well met," she says, dipping into the lowest curtsey I have seen.

Elmon contrasts his betrothed. He is a spitting image of Zentha, with tight black coils sitting atop his head and honey-coloured eyes that twinkle with knowledge.

Zentha leans close, whispering, "You look beautiful. Do not let anyone tell you otherwise."

We are soon bidding them farewell and moving to the next nobles. Then the next, and the next. The moon has risen by the time I have curtseyed to every High Lord and High Lady except one, and my thighs are aching from the repetition.

I am not sure who hands me a chalice filled with plum wine, but I am thankful for the liquid courage as I greet the High Lord of Summer and his son, Prince Tohminic. I sip at the fruity liquid, assessing the contrasting males. It is clear Tohminic gets his looks from his mother, a sour-faced female clinging to High Lord Iker's arm. I believe her name is Yaryn.

Tohminic's mouse-brown hair is cropped short, making the angles of his face harsher, more menacing. Perhaps it is the yellow eyes which remind me of a beast, or it could be the way his brow seems to cast shadows over his face, but Tohminic of the Summer Court makes my blood turn to ice. I have spent little time with him in the past, and I remember him to be a kind male. It is a far cry from the intimidation sparking in his eyes on this night.

He caresses his smooth chin with long, tanned fingers, waves of heat pulsing from him. "Well met, Princess Bria. It has been many moons since you last graced me with your company."

I run my eyes over his blood-red tailcoat, the shining leather boots, and the maroon frills brushing against his hands, fighting the shiver threating to race through my body. "Indeed. Though our courts share a border, it is rare we make time to entertain one another."

"Perhaps you are too preoccupied with entertaining the lesser fae of your court." My eyes snap to his, and he smirks. "My apologies. He hails from the Day Court, does he not?"

"Now is not the time to throw accusations at her, Tohm." Iker narrows his hazel eyes at his son. "Come, we have matters to discuss with High Lord Ruith. Our Winter allies are proving difficult, preferring to hide in their mountain home than prepare for battle."

My eyebrows shoot to my hairline. "Battle?"

Iker assesses me before answering. "Why, yes. The Autumn Court, Night Islands, and our own court have all laid claim to the mysterious island that appeared. If we do not begin preparations soon, we will lose our chance."

"Must we talk of war at a ball?" his mate whines, her light eyes flashing as Iker leads her to the other side of the ballroom.

"Thank the Mother Star," I murmur.

Rennyn pins me with a glare. "Play nice. I am going to introduce myself to High Lady Maude of the Night Court."

As Rennyn slips into the crowd of tailcoats and bouffant-style gowns, the High Lord of Dawn approaches, three identical males flanking him.

"High Lord Jonik," I say, dipping my chin. It is customary I curtsey, but I do not think my legs can handle another one. "Such a pleasure to see you again."

His almond-shaped eyes all but disappear with how wide he smiles. I have always liked him. His neutrality and easy-going attitude towards life give him an air of fun and laughter. Even the smallest smile brings rays of light to the darkest of days.

He grips my hands in his, my pale skin contrasting with his tan. "I have missed your cunning smile, Bria."

I laugh. "Cunning? I thought myself demure."

He runs a hand through his long, dark hair. "I think you must be dreaming. May I introduce my sons?"

I turn to the males flanking him, each of them a clone of Jonik. It is as if the four are trying to confuse me as they concurrently smile a crooked smile.

Jonik introduces the males as they each kiss the back of my hand. "Larrad, Ulakas, and Tasar."

"Oh, my. Your mother did not get a look-in, did she?" I joke. "Is there a way to tell you apart?"

The three males chuckle in unison. The one in the middle cocks his head to the side and says, "Unfortunately not. It has made for some interesting times over the past two hundred years."

"I can only imagine. To be fair to the rest of us, you could have dressed in different colours."

The left son laughs, shaking his head. "Did you know Father cannot tell us apart most days?"

Jonik scowls at his sons before offering me a wink. "If you are to be blessed with younglings, I do not recommend triplets.

Something to keep in mind for the future." He wraps an arm around my shoulders, pulling me close. "At first, my sons were not welcome at Rennyn's born day celebrations. Your Father had the unfortunate luck of being the target of one of their less than admiral pranks many moons ago. However, he invited each of them himself, claiming he has an exciting announcement to make tonight."

I side-eye the Dawn High Lord. "If you are hoping I will reveal his plans to you —"

"Of course not," he chuckles. "I would not dare, not while you are likely to incite his wrath the moment he lays eyes on you. I was only hoping for a clue."

Smirking, I twist from his embrace and curtsey to the triplets, my thighs burning. "I look forward to our garden walks tomorrow. Please be kind enough to come one at a time. Preferably dressed in red, blue, and green." I point to each son as I say each colour.

Garden walks between an unmated male and female — especially those following a grand ball — are known for one thing: courting.

"I had hoped," says Jonik, tucking a strand of his long dark hair behind his ear. "I would welcome you to my court with open arms."

"Thank you. That is very kind." In my peripheral, the guards at the entrance to the ballroom shift, gripping the handles. "If you would excuse me, I believe my father has arrived. Best I find somewhere to hide until he has said his piece."

Jonik winks while his sons chortle. "Go, fair lady. We will close the gap."

I snort and slip through the triplets, murmuring my thanks to them as they move closer together behind me, blocking me from Father's view as the doors open and the Master of Ceremonies announces the High Lord of Autumn's arrival.

Luck is not on my side, and the crowd parts just as I am sneaking towards one of the eight balconies. I freeze with my fingers wrapped around the metal handle of the glass door, looking over my shoulder at Father and Fayeth as they step into the hall, their arms open wide in welcome.

Father pins me with a glare, gesturing with his eyes for me to join him. The look only lasts a moment, unnoticed by the revellers at the ball, but in that moment, I know he is not to be trifled with. Not tonight.

"Well met," Father shouts, silencing the crowd as Rennyn steps up beside him. "I am delighted you could all attend tonight's celebration. To my son, I wish you an enjoyable eve and a healthy and prosperous one hundred years more. Happy born day, Rennyn."

A server hands Father and Fayeth a chalice each before scurrying away, the slight green tint to his skin turning a mottled purple when he blushes.

I weave through the bulging skirts and dangling swords — pouting at the Dawn triplets and Jonik as I pass, sad our plan failed — joining in the chorus of cheers and well wishes, until I am standing beside Fayeth.

"Before I encourage you to indulge in copious amounts of plum wine..." He pauses as the crowd chuckles. "I have one rule. This is one night where feuds and alliances do not exist. One night of rest for those of us in command. Do not spoil it with talk of war and battle."

A few grumbles, a single groan, and awkward chuckles fill the silence.

"One more thing before the music begins," says Father, waving a hand in my direction. His green eyes flash with anger at my gown. "Bria is at last in search of a mate. I will consider dowries in the form of alliances, trade deals, or land."

I curtsey, my entire body and soul cringing as I say, "I look forward to spending more time with the eligible males, beginning with a garden walk tomorrow and a dance tonight. Please, if you would be so kind, see Father's squire for further information."

"It is time to enjoy the festivities. Bria loves to dance, and —" Father's words are cut short by a stranger.

"Not quite." The voice is deep. Soft, but commanding and a little rough. The sound alone sends a shiver down my spine, like claws sinking into my flesh, digging and piercing until I acknowledge them. From behind me, the stranger adds, "I apologise for my tardiness."

The twang of weapons being drawn pierces the quiet.

Father's hand inches towards his sword as he spins towards the newcomer. "How did you get through the guards? Declare yourself."

I turn, stepping away from Father's glare.

The stranger does not flinch, does not so much as react to Father's anger as dense, earthy magic wafts from my father in waves that threaten to suffocate.

The male can only be Wyn's brother. They share the same light brown skin, the same dark hair — though Vander's is cropped so short he might as well be bald — and almost identical silver eyes. Dressed in all black, the doublet decorated with darker onyx embroidery, he gives off an air of power and strength. A small axe hangs from his right hip, the unsheathed blade gleaming in the fae lights. He looks rebellious.

I like him immediately.

A kiss of cool wind rushes across the hall as he turns those bright eyes to my father. "I'm High Lord Vander Theron." He pauses to let the slither of information sink in. "Of the Dusk Court."

"There is no such court!" a male shouts from the rear of the ballroom.

Many echo his words, and soon a chorus of denial fills the hall. Fae from the more reckless courts go as far as to call for Vander's head. It is ridiculous. They would not dare utter such words about any of the other high fae.

The words do not bother Vander. He rolls his shoulders, those mesmerising eyes locking on each of the High Lords and Ladies as he says, "The island you are all foolishly fighting over? It's my home. The Dusk Court has existed for three hundred years." His eyes find the High Lady of the Night Islands. "Isn't that right, Maude?"

Her ice-blue eyes blaze with anger as she grits out, "Yes."

Everyone stills. It is eerie how hundreds of fae can become so still, so... statuesque in the single beat of a heart. Not a breath huffs, not a hair flutters. This revelation is huge. Maude has kept this secret for centuries, perhaps with the sole purpose of retaining the nefarious reputation of her court.

"Explain." High Lord Iker of the Summer Court strides forward, weaving around those still frozen in shock. "This is when Night drifted from mainland Radelea?"

Vander dips his head in a show of respect. Not as low as he should, which sends a message — that he will bow to no one. "One hundred years after the Day Court fragmented, the Night Court went through a similar issue. Those of us who disagreed with Maude's ways wished to form a court of our own, just as Dawn managed. Of course, she wouldn't allow that to happen. There was a war so fierce, the land itself shuddered and reformed."

"We always wondered," mutters Zentha, the closest to Vander and one of the few fae in this hall who could have recognised the signs.

After the civil war between Day and Dawn, the land changed, just as it did with the Night Islands. The Day Court's castle was once joined to the land, but now floats on a small island near the shore. As well as the strange phenomenon of an entire castle beginning to drift to sea, the mountains to the north shifted and changed, creating a valley filled with waterfalls and creeks, all joining to form a rushing river.

The land changes after every war. I wonder if the earth on which we walk is sentient, and the disputes between courts offend the land, causing it to shift and change in warning. If another war ravages the land, will we push it too far?

My eyes find Maude in the crowd. She has her onyx hair pulled back tight, creating harsh angles on her pale face. Her blood-red lips form the beginnings of a snarl she struggles to smother as her magic writhes, sending pulses of sour rust and a throbbing ache through the air. While it is clear she would prefer her court's history to remain hidden, I cannot understand her anger.

Vander continues, ignoring the stunned faces and fury wafting from Maude. "Fourteen islands drifted from the mainland. Only five could sustain life. Maude claimed four, creating the Night Islands. The last, the Dusk Court, has been veiled since the war. Until my father, High Lord Connak, passed of old age."

"A rare feat," says Jonik. "One which deserves congratulations. How old was he when he passed?"

Vander inclines his head to the High Lord of Dawn. "Thank you. He had celebrated his eight hundredth born day mere weeks earlier."

I find it sad that his father led a lonely life. I know from Wyn that she and Vander are somewhere between one and two hundred — she would not give me an exact age, stating a female never reveals such an intimate part of herself — which gives Connak centuries of loneliness before Vander and Wyn arrived.

Their mother passed while bringing Vander into the world — a fact that haunts the High Lord of Dusk according to his sister — and had only known their father for two moon cycles before conceiving Wyn. Another feat worth celebrating; younglings are rare unless the mated pair are born from fate. It has been millennia since the Mother Star granted Radelea the wonder of true mates, leading to each generation of fae becoming smaller. Soon, we may be extinct.

"I take it his demise was the catalyst for your reveal?" High Lord Ruith of the Winter Court clasps his hands behind his back, his statement settling like a heavy blanket. "As a wielder of shadow, I am well versed in bending darkness as a veil. Tell us how your court remained hidden for such an extended length of time."

Murmurs follow Ruith's words.

"Enough of this," growls Father. "Tonight is about celebrating Rennyn and finding a mate for Bria. Talk of imaginary courts and claims of land can wait until the Mother Star graces us with her beauty. Guards, remove this male from my home."

The two guards flanking the doors march forward, each of them moving to grab Vander's arms. They stumble forward when their hands pass through his body, confusion twisting their features.

Vander chuckles deep and low, shaking his head. His eyes gleam when he says, "Dusk is a time when the light plays tricks on your senses. The land could be amber or lilac or grey as the sun and moon fight for dominance. As with the trick of the light, we from Dusk can cast illusions. While my image is here, my body is not."

The indistinct murmurs increase to a constant chatter.

Vander lifts a hand, a powerful gust of wind blowing from the tips of his fingers. "We control the air. We create wind from nothing, hardening something invisible and untouchable until we're able to hold it, to use it as we see fit." His hands splay at his sides as he gently rises from the floor, hovering a sword's length over the gleaming timber. "I don't appreciate the attempt at restraining me. You'll soon learn we are not a court to make an enemy of." He pierces Father with a glare before the illusion flickers from existence.

There is a moment of silence, of utter stillness, before chaos erupts. Shouts merge into a nonsensical stream of words, the floor rumbles as allies storm through the hall in search of one another, and guards move out hoping to find Vander's true body.

I stand in disbelief, my chest tingling with an emotion I have no name for. My head moves from side to side, the revelations of the night crashing through my thoughts like a stampeding Minotaur.

Beside me, Fayeth is shaking with what I assume to be anger. The skirts of her gown flutter from the strength of her fury, her slender hands bunching in the smooth fabric before she whips towards Father. "Do something, Kerym," she hisses. "This is Rennyn's night. And it is ruined."

Father clicks his fingers, summoning a musician and ordering her to begin tonight's entertainment. While the fae with blue-tinted skin scurries back to her corner — and the three fae accompanying her, each with a different instrument — Father calls everyone to order.

After failing to gain anyone's attention, he sends a blast of magic through the hall. The taste of earth fills our mouths, a melodic purring hums in our ears, and the soft but coarse feel of fur skates across the skin of every fae here.

Silence falls.

"We return to our celebrations," says Father, his tone leaving no room for debate. "If you wish to discuss the fraudulent court of twilight, you may do so *in your own home.* I will have no more talk of it under tonight's moon." He raises his arms above his head as he claps.

The doors behind me burst open, and twenty so-called *lesser* fae flit in, each of them carrying a large golden platter weighed down with food of every description. The music welcomes them, an upbeat piece that brings a smile to my face.

Scanning the hall, I notice several of the high fae have slipped away while the servers entered. High Lady Maude of the Night Islands. Gone. High Lord Iker of Summer. Gone, though his son, Tohminic, remains. High Lord Ruith of Winter. Gone. All having disappeared to discuss Vander's arrival, disappearance, and claims.

A rough hand jerks me to the side, and I whip my face to the left, my eyes colliding with Father's.

"Explain this abomination you call a gown," he seethes.

If I tell him Wyn is from the Dusk Court, he will have her dragged out of here before the night's end. Faster, if he knows she is Vander's sister. To save her from threat, and to keep the only friend I have in this oppressive place, I must lie. Convincingly.

I twist my arm from his grip — the bruises will come and go by the time the Mother Star rises — and say, "My new hand maiden spent some time in the Spring Court. You are aware fashions come and go, led by the nature fae there. This is an up-and-coming style."

Given that I have yet to lay eyes on the High Lady of Spring, I believe I am safe to fall back on the court I descend from. Father has always shied away from discussing my birth mother, and tonight is no different.

He recoils. "You will seek permission next time. Go dance with the unmated males. If I so much as smell any disobedience from you, I will have you confined to the castle until the next full moon. Do not test me tonight."

I bow my head. "Yes, Father."

With members of every court present, and their rulers here to witness it, Father's failure to keep the ballroom safe from outside influence will be spoken of for some time. I understand it is a heavy burden to bear, and it will force him to make some questionable decisions in the following days, but taking his anger out on me is not fair.

As a small sign of rebellion he cannot fault me for, I dance with the Dawn triplets first. At the same time.

According to — I *think* — Ulakas, the triplets and Tohminic are the only high fae to register their interest in courting me. A lesser fae from Winter, and one from Night, have agreed to garden walks tomorrow, but I have a feeling Ruith and Maude have sent them to spy, to gather information should Vander make another appearance.

While I dance with the triplets, my heart sinks. I would much prefer to join with their court over Summer, but Dawn is neutral. They have no enemies and no allies. They shy away from confrontation of any kind. The triplets will bow out of my courtship at the first sign of a threat to their peaceful lives. Leaving me with Tohminic, who makes my skin crawl.

After three musical pieces, I can no longer ignore the other males courting me. I twist away from Tohminic's ogling and search for the Night fae, finding him trailing after a server carrying a platter of fruit.

"Bim?" I place a gentle hand on his shoulder. "Would you care for a dance?"

His onyx eyes flick from the plate of fruit to the dancefloor, then he sighs and holds up a finger. "Just one."

It is the most uncomfortable and painful dance I have yet to endure. Bim steps on my toes at least four times. He does not say a single word, preferring to watch the servers as they pass, perhaps hoping one of them will offer him a refreshment or slice of ham and he will have an excuse to cut our dancing short.

I am thankful when the harpist plucks the last cord, signalling the end of the melody before moving to another, slower beat.

Bim nods before darting after a fae with bark for skin, snatching three scrolls of pastry from his plate.

Sighing, I avoid tracing my eyes over the east side of the hall, where I know Tohminic to be, and weave through the crowd of dancing fae towards Tarathiel, my prospective mate from Winter.

"I was hoping you would make time for a dance," he says, linking my arm through his and dragging me back to the dance floor.

I swear, if I am forced to dance with another male who steps on my toes, I will have metal slippers specially made. With spikes jutting from the toe and heel.

Thankfully, Tarathiel is more graceful than Bim, and my toes are safe for now. He is courteous and kind, and does not lead with a firm hand, but a gentle guide. We make small talk, discussing our home courts and preference for weather — a dull, dispassionate topic — while curling around our fellow dancers.

If given the chance, I think I could come to love Tarathiel's sweet nature. Although, I do not think I could overlook his translucent skin. I can see the blood rushing through his veins, the way his tendons lengthen and contract, and the outline of his bone and muscle. Living beneath a mountain will do that to a male.

At the end of the dance, I can no longer avoid the Summer prince. In fact, he is waiting behind me, and places a hot hand on my hip the moment the musicians strike the last cord. "At last," he says. "It is my turn."

I rearrange my features from disgusted to serene and face him. "Tohminic, I have been waiting for you to have a free moment. Would you care to dance?"

His fingers dig into my hip as he jerks me closer, pressing our bodies together. "I would very much enjoy that."

Alarm bells ring through my mind, screaming at the wrongness of his touch. His grip is a little too tight, a little too domineering. I keep the fear and concern from my face as he drags me around the dancefloor with a cruel smile curling his lips.

Halfway through our dance, he leans down, his chin brushing my cheek as he says, "You will be mine, Bria. There is nothing you can do to prevent it. And when you are mine, and our courts are united through our joining, I will take your father's land from him. Piece by piece."

I laugh as if he is telling a joke. "You have land of your own, and no need for the drying earth of Autumn."

He leans back, his yellow eyes flashing. "You are but a pawn. A means to an end. Do not think for one moment our joining will be harmonious. In fact, I have no genuine need of you other than a public alliance. You will spend your days in the Summer Court, learning from my lover how to please me. Only when you have proven your worth will I grant you freedom of any kind."

"That is not a joining I am interested in." I fight to refrain from dancing, but he is stronger than I am, and forces me into a twirl.

When I slam back into his chest, he whispers, "You are a lowly female. A bastard. You have no say in the matter."

When the music stops, I flee the ball. Having played my part for Father's sake, I am no longer required to entertain Rennyn's guests. I race to my chambers faster than I ever have, my heart pounding against my chest, only calming once my door slams closed behind me.

There is no way I am mating with Tohminic.

Not in this lifetime.

Not in any.

10

I LEAN AGAINST THE door, fighting to calm my ragged breaths. They do not pull at my throat from exertion, but from fear. The feel of Tohminic's hands lingers on my hips, making my skin crawl, and I have the sudden urge to scrub the feeling away with the coarsest brush I can find.

"Bria?" Wyn calls from the bathing chamber. She pokes her head around the arched door, her brow dipping when she sees me. "What's wrong?"

I race over to her, gripping her hands in my own. "You have to help me. Please. I cannot mate with Tohminic. He is repugnant and dangerous and everything in between. There is a vast difference between recalcitrance and pure evil. I will not survive him."

"Tell me about it while you bathe." She yanks her hands free of my iron grip and grabs my shoulders, turning me so she can work the pins from my hair. "Start with why you think you won't survive the Summer Court."

I slowly relax, my breathing returning to a somewhat normal rate while Wyn slides the pins out. "He said he will take Father's land once he is my mate, that I will have no choice but to join the

Summer Court and watch while he destroys Autumn piece by piece. He said I am nothing but a bastard female with no voice."

She snarls. "The audacity."

"He is a jerk. The way he grabbed me... He is not a nice male. He is not gentle or loving, but violent and tormenting. While I enjoy pushing boundaries, I do not enjoy leaping over them completely. Worst of all, the idea of *serving* a male makes me nauseous."

Her fingers pause. "What do you mean?"

I look at her over my shoulder. "I am to spend my days learning how to please Tohminic. Only when he is satisfied with my progress will he allow me freedom."

Her hands move from my hair to the thin straps of my gown, sliding them from my shoulders and letting the silk pool at my feet. "Did he touch you? Did he make you uncomfortable?" There is a note in her tone, one of anger and disgust she is failing to hide.

"His touch was not inappropriate. Though, he was rough." I twist my naked body until I am looking at my right hip. "He left bruises."

"You're right. You can't mate with him, not if this is what he's willing to do in a hall full of fae nobles. I can only imagine the pain he would inflict in private."

My heart sinks. She is right. If Tohminic ever gets me alone, he will do a lot more than leave five small circles on each hip.

I step over the side of the copper tub, inhaling the sweet aroma of jasmine from the whole flowers Wyn has tipped into the steaming water. The soothing aroma is a contrast to my aching heart. If only Nikolai had agreed to run away with me. I could be in the Day Court, hiding in Zentha's floating castle.

She hands me a bar of soap and a coarse sponge. "Your father's reasoning for finding you a mate is to form alliances, yes?"

I lather the soap in my hands, watching as small bubbles form between my fingers. "When the Dusk Court veil fell, and we all believed the island to be unclaimed, Father had hoped my union with another court would aid him in seizing the land. My role is to broker an alliance with a court we have no ties with, helping Father find someone who will support his claim."

She nods, a few strands of obsidian falling free of the loose plait which rests on her shoulder. "Vander wondered if that was the case. I'm not sure he'll like the news, but..." she trails off, her eyes glazing as she contemplates my predicament.

I leave her to her thoughts, my own running rampant as I scrub my skin so hard it turns red. Father is not so unreasonable that he would force me into a mating I abhor. If I could just find the time to speak with him when the Mother Star rises, catch him before he joins the war meetings I heard whispers of tonight.

"I have an idea," says Wyn, pulling me from my thoughts. "I know you don't know us well, and you owe us nothing, but hear me out."

"Go on." I set the soap and sponge aside.

"What if Vander registers his interest in being your mate?" I open my mouth to protest, but she cuts me off. "You don't have to go through with it. Once you're on our land, we can spread rumours about your joining, leaving the rest of Radelea to believe you followed through with it. I think this is the best way to get you out of this mess without making enemies. Well, more enemies."

Get me out? Tears line my eyes. Escaping the Autumn Court, fleeing my family, and hiding on an island far enough away that no one can force me to mate with Tohminic sounds like a dream. Perhaps it is.

"Will he agree?" I ask, not daring to meet her eyes lest I witness her uncertainty.

"There aren't many steadfast rules in Dusk, but one thing everyone agrees on is how to treat one another. I've already told you females are equal to males. He'll be just as disgusted to hear of Tohminic's threat as I am. An alliance would benefit us, too, Bria. We're a newly revealed court with no allies. If any of the courts wish to fight for our land, we need something to fall back on. This is a win-win situation."

I stand, water running from my body in rivulets as I snatch a towel from the small table beside the tub. I dislike the idea of asking Vander to put himself at risk for me — especially when this is not his fight — but I do not have a choice if Father believes affiliating with Summer will benefit the court.

"Let me talk to him about it tonight," says Wyn. "If he refuses, we'll find another way. I promise." The silver in her eyes grows brighter with the intensity with which she speaks.

After a moment of hesitation, I relent, agreeing to let her talk to Vander. It may be foolish to put my trust in strangers. After all, I know little to nothing of the Dusk Court. For all I know, they are far more fearsome than the Summer fae. But this is all I have right now. If trusting strangers keeps Tohminic from putting his hands on me again, then I will gladly suffer the consequences should there be any.

Breakfast is a quiet affair.

Rennyn looks like he would rather be sleeping. His head lowers to the table before he jerks upright and continues eating.

Fayeth is fuming. She is eating her fruit slices in silence while casting nasty looks my way. I guess she is still mad about my attire last night. Still mad that Rennyn's celebration was ruined.

At least he has another six days to celebrate, with a jousting tournament, village fair, and a handful of feasts to attend. Although, today, I think he would rather lounge around at the castle. Preferably with no noise, from the way he winces every time something louder than a whisper pierces his ears.

Father looks worried. I put it down to the increased security around the castle and the preparations in the war chamber. An unknown fae entering the castle while every High Lord and Lady — except the Lady of Spring — were here has caused more trouble than it is worth. Every wing of the castle was alive with action as I descended from my chambers this morning. Servants and nobles rushed from space to space, their whispers following them through the halls.

I eat my crumbling, buttery pastry in silence, wondering what the commotion could be about. If I were to hazard a guess, it has something to do with Vander's appearance at the ball. The other high fae will not let it stand. A strange male appearing from thin air, untouchable and claiming land we thought to be vacant. No. I do not believe they will leave Dusk to live in peace. Unless they can broker deals, form alliances.

Wyn informed me this morning that Vander is treading carefully, learning about the seven courts of Radelea before choosing which to approach with trade deals or other types of alliances. Everything she said went in one ear and out the other.

Father has never given me the opportunity to learn about fae politics. It is all new to me. It is all foreign. And I wonder if it is on purpose. I wonder if his beliefs align with Tohminic's, and if I have ever truly known my father.

I lose my appetite halfway through the meal, pushing my plate away as my stomach clenches with nerves. Patience is not a virtue I am known for, but today, it is essential. Especially if I am to have a private audience with Father.

As if sensing my need to speak, Fayeth slows her eating, nibbling at a slice of apple so slowly she could be pretending.

Her ridiculous behaviour is enough for me to address my High Lord and father. If she wants to act like a youngling, that is on her. She will regret her choices when her stomach is growling for food later.

"Father?" I wait until he looks at me before continuing. "I was hoping for a word in private. After the initial dances last night, I have some insight into my courtship."

"I do not have the time," he says, turning his attention back to the last of his pastry.

I clear my throat, ignoring Rennyn and Fayeth on either side. "You will want to hear this."

"Fine. Fayeth, Rennyn, leave us."

Fayeth bristles. "I should be here for this. I can offer advice."

"Mother," says Rennyn, standing and resting his hand on the sword I gifted him. "It is not your place to question the High Lord."

I flinch, even though the words are not for me. Fayeth may be cruel and cunning, but she — like every female in every court — does not deserve to be overlooked, purely because she can bring a babe into this world.

She spins on her heel and storms out, leaving most of her breakfast uneaten.

"I am needed elsewhere. Say what you need to say." Father's tone is clipped, a sign he does not forgive me for the gown.

Though I should word this with great care, I do not doubt Father will up and leave the moment he bores of the conversation, so I blurt the information out in a rush. "Prince Tohminic is not a male I wish to mate with. Just last night, he threatened to steal our land the moment the alliance is brokered. He intends to rule both Summer and Autumn, using me as a way in."

Father growls. "High Lord Iker would not allow such a thing. We have shared a border for millennia."

"I do not believe Iker will keep his position for long." I hesitate, unsure if I should bring Wyn into this.

She was adamant about this detail this morning, claiming the rumours to be truer than the fact the Mother Star rises in the morning and sets at night. For a reason I cannot explain, I trust Wyn's word. I trust *her*.

Deciding it would be impossible for me to gain this information otherwise, I skirt around her involvement and say, "I have heard whispers from the servants this morning. Tohminic plans to usurp his father. Soon, if things do not go as he hopes."

"Things?"

I make a noise in the back of my throat, somewhere between a hum and a growl. "He believes we should not allow the Dusk Court to continue, that the island belongs to Radelea. If Iker agrees to allow Dusk to join us, Tohminic will proceed with his plan."

"How do you know this?" Father asks, pushing the last of his pastry away and focusing on me. "What whispers have you heard?"

"From the servants," I say again. Knowing I cannot lie now I have his full attention, I add, "My hand maiden is new to the court and has spent a lot of time and effort trying to fit in with the others. Apparently, they talk more than we first believed."

Father snorts. "Of course they do. They are in the perfect position to gain information. Some trade it, risking their lives in the process. Is your hand maiden sure this information was not planted?"

"Why would it be?"

"Because a foreign fae entered my court last night. *Using magic.* There are lords and ladies who would wish for my demise."

I contemplate that for a moment. He is not wrong to assume the nobles will call for him to relinquish the throne. Allowing a fae to enter our court, though it is warded from such events, is a mistake that will not be overlooked.

"Then I have a proposition." I keep my emerald eyes trained on my hands. This could go either way.

"Speak."

"High Lord Vander may consider an alliance through mating. I believe it is worth considering. If I may speak freely, I would much prefer a strange new court over the Summer Court."

He is quiet, running a hand over his smooth chin. His eyes drift, as if of their own accord, as he considers my words.

Beneath the table, I cross my fingers. "I know we do not agree on much, Father, and you have done a lot for me, considering how I was brought into the world. I have agreed to mate to further your plans. Please, allow me this chance. For all we know, the Dusk Lord will refuse."

He will not. He has not. In fact, Wyn said he is determined to gain Father's approval if it means I am saved from a life of serving Tohminic of Summer.

"I will consider it," Father says at last. "However, I will need to speak with this High Lord first. I will send word before I meet with the others. He shall arrive in the royal port to avoid detection. You may leave."

I scurry away, fearing he will change his mind or I will say something that will cause my plan to backfire if I stay any longer. For the first time in my five and seventy years, Father has granted me a leniency.

11

T HE GARDENS ON THE eastern side of the court are expansive. To walk from one end — from a metal gate at our eastern wall — to the other and back again would have me returning to court when luncheon is served.

I wait beside the gate with four guards flanking me. The choice to bring guards was mine. According to tradition, a simple garden walk during a courtship does not call for protection, but with the Dusk Court's reveal, and Tohminic's threats, I do not feel comfortable venturing outside the court walls without the males and their swords. The garden entrance is within the outer bailey, the second ring of protection for the High Lord's home, and already I feel like I have ventured too far from the safety of those walls.

Fae I do not recognise wander the large space, inspecting the stalls with scrutiny. There are a lot of females here, and I wonder if Fayeth will demand I hold court for the unmated females while she entertains the mated ones. Holding court is not something I enjoy, but if I am to keep Father's good graces, I will play Fayeth's games.

The guards shift, their boots scuffing against the loose dirt.

I lift my face, swallowing down the dread of Bim's arrival. If our dance is anything to go by, I am about to endure an hour of utter boredom.

He strides towards me, still chewing on a half-eaten sausage as he says, "Well met, Bria."

"Well met, Bim. How are you this morning?" I force a smile to my face, trying my hardest not to acknowledge the grease coating his fingers. "I do hope you enjoyed the ball?"

He makes a noncommittal noise, lifting one shoulder in a shrug. "I have seen better."

"I am sorry to hear that."

He comes to a stop before me, sparing the four guards a curious glance. "I must apologise. My High Lady has demanded I return to the Night Islands and I must graciously withdraw from your courtship."

"Oh," I breathe, unsure of what else to say. "May I ask why?"

He takes another bite of his sausage, speaking with a mouth full of meat and grease. "Something about not wanting to make enemies of the Summer Court."

It is as I suspected. Although I thought it would take Tohminic longer to intimidate the other suitors, I am not surprised by the news. He wants Autumn's land for himself and will do just about anything to get it. This is just a small warning.

"Again, I am sorry," says Bim. "I hope you find what you are looking for in a male."

"I thank you for your honesty. Safe travels on your return to the Night Islands."

He does not bow or offer any kind of respect before he turns, shoves the last of the fat sausage into his mouth, and walks away.

I turn to my guards, at a complete loss for words. My mouth opens and closes, and I rub a hand across my brow as I regain my composure. Three of the guards have creases lining their brows, and the last has a strange glint to his brown eyes.

"Sounds to me like the Summer fae are issuing threats," says the brown-eyed guard.

The guard with lavender skin adjusts his scabbard. "I shall inform the High Lord. While it is likely High Lady Fayeth has brought the next male's time forward, I beg you to wait for my return before taking to the garden."

The others dip their chins in acknowledgement.

I pace the open length of the wall, refusing to allow my eyes the privilege of drifting to the gardens when I pass the gate. The brick buildings on either side seem to laugh at me with each turn, mocking my foolishness. What is the point in spending time with Tarathiel and the Dawn triplets if Tohminic will only scare them away?

The guard returns soon after, the triplets laughing as they walk beside him. They took my advice and dressed in red, green, and blue. Although I intended for each male to wear a different colour, the three are clearly fond of jesting. They each wear red boots, blue slacks, and a green tunic. They look ridiculous.

It makes me smile. "This is not what I envisioned."

"Well met, Bria," says the male in the middle. He jabs an elbow at the brother on his left. "Tasar is a genius, is he not? We look ravishing."

Tasar — I note his hair is shorter than that of the other two — throws his head back and laughs. "Ravishing is not the word

I would use, Ulakas. We have already been mistaken for the fair entertainment once."

Ulakas, whose tunic fits a little looser, smirks. "I considered stating we were on our way to perform our entertainment duties. What fun we would have had."

Larrad's almond-shaped eyes crease with mirth. They are a shade darker, almost black. "It would be a tale worth repeating over wine."

"For millennia," adds Ulakas.

I shake my head, smoothing the ivory skirts of my gown. Wyn paired it with a pink corset, and I must admit the contrast is lovely.

"Shall we begin?" I wave a hand towards the garden. "You are not about to inform me of threats to your court and your impending return home, are you?"

Their brows dip in unison.

Tasar asks, "Why would we do such a thing?"

One of my guards opens the gates, waving two of his comrades through. The triplets and I follow, stepping from loose gravel to compacted dirt. I have always loved the gardens, finding solace in the sweet aromas and bursts of colour.

I ignore the guards as I walk through the flowers with the triplets, laughing and chatting as we pass blooms the size of our faces, admire petals which change from one colour to another, and swat at the plethora of buzzing insects.

Larrad changes the conversation from Summer's interference — I informed them of Tohminic's threats so they are aware he may try the same thing with them — to their home court.

The Dawn Court sounds wonderful. Though they split from the Day Court, they somehow came out of the war with more land than Day. Dense forests, home to creatures of every description, surround their northern mountains. The triplets spend a lot of time at the lake that curls around their castle, taunting the creatures that have made the water their home.

I almost imagine my life there, spending days hiking in the mountains, lazy afternoons dipping my toes in the lake, and evenings laughing so hard my stomach hurts. As fun as it all sounds, I am not certain the life is for me.

The triplets are a package deal, apparently. If I choose to mate with one, I am choosing to mate with the three of them.

As we say our goodbyes, my cheeks hurting from how often I have smiled, I realise I have a lot to consider. If Father does not approve of Vander after meeting with him at noontime, my options will be Tohminic and his stern hand in the Summer Court, or the triplets and their three-for-one deal in Dawn.

I am not a prude or anything of the sort, but even *thinking* about how that would work makes my mind spin. Three males for one female. Would I spend every night with the three of them, or will they bless me with only one? If I were to be intimate with them all at once, I think I would be overwhelmed. Where does it all *go*?

I am so lost in my thoughts of three males to handle between the sheets, I do not register their departure. Their chuckling floats back to me on the slight breeze, and I pull myself from my thoughts in time to wave farewell.

The triplets are not even out of view when my guards straighten.

I turn to see Tarathiel walking towards me, his dark grey travelling cloak already fastened around his shoulders. I do not need his words to tell me he is bowing out. The bulging rucksack gripped in his translucent fist is sign enough.

"I regret to inform you I have been called back to the Winter Court," he says, no sign of remorse on his face or in his tone. "High Lord Ruith respects his allies and will do nothing to risk that. Especially when we have but one alliance."

"It is okay, Tarathiel. I understand. Safe travels on your return to the Bolbala Ranges." I do not watch him walk away, instead jerking my head and motioning for a guard to inform Father of yet another threat made by Summer.

In one morning, I have lost two of my suitors. Admittedly, I would not have pursued Tarathiel or Bim, but the fact remains, their departure was not of my choosing. It is just another event which validates my claim of Tohminic's controlling nature.

Again, I pace while waiting for the guard to return. I cannot help but think today is a waste. Instead of whiling away the time, pacing before the gates to the gardens, I could be enjoying the ongoing celebrations.

Rennyn's born day is one day, but we spread the festivities over seven, starting with the ball last night. There will be battles of magic, a terrifying obstacle course, and more feasts than I care to attend. Such celebrations are rare, occurring only for the notable ages — one hundred, two hundred, and so on — of the royal family.

I was excited about the village fair today. I am certain the Dawn triplets would have enjoyed it. We could have wandered through the market stalls and magic displays instead of the gardens. It is likely they would have attempted to commandeer the entertainment stage, but the laughs would be worth it.

Instead, I am pacing once more, waiting for Tohminic to arrive. My stomach is leaden, threatening to weigh me down until I am melding with the loose rocks beneath my feet. I struggle to find solace in the four guards standing rigid beside me, my mind concocting nightmares worthy of scaring younglings into behaving as they should.

When Tohminic's rough voice pierces the late morning air, I startle. "There is no need for the guards," he says, his yellow eyes flashing with anger. "You are dismissed."

I step forward from either courage or stupidity. "You have no right to send them away. They are not of your court."

His upper lip peels back in a snarl. "I am Prince Tohminic of the Summer Court. A royal male born of a mated pair. I outrank you. You would do well to remember that." He turns back to the guards. "You are dismissed."

Two of them cast furtive glances my way when Tohminic is not looking, the one with brown eyes scowling slightly. It is their duty to protect me, but they are sworn to obey those who serve above them. In this instance, they are required to follow Tohminic's order. They step into formation and march through the outer bailey towards the castle.

Though I wish they would stay, I know they will inform Father of this the moment they reach the court. And if anything angers Father, it is fae overstepping their rank. He will not be pleased with Tohminic dismissing my only form of protection, especially after last night.

"Now," says Tohminic, gripping my hand tight and linking it through his elbow, "let us enjoy the wonderful gardens."

I remain silent while we walk. We pass the carnivorous irises, their red and pink petals all but begging me to shove Tohminic into their spiked embrace. If murdering the High Lord of Summer's son would not get me into a lot of trouble, I think I would do it just to see the look of surprise and betrayal on his face. In fact, it is almost worth centuries in their dungeon. Almost, but not quite.

When we are deep enough into the gardens that Tohminic is certain no one will overhear us, he pulls me to a stop. "I do not appreciate you sprouting lies about me and mine, Bria."

I snatch my hand from his grip. "Nothing I told my father was a lie. If you believe me to have been dishonest, you can take that up with Father instead of accosting me in the gardens."

Anger twists his features as his hand whips to my throat, his fingers digging into the sensitive flesh as he shoves me against a towering fern. "You will not speak ill of me to another. Do you understand?"

My eyes bulge and I claw at his hand, fighting to draw breath.

Seeming to take pleasure in my fright, he smirks and digs his fingers in harder. "If you wish for your existence to be painless, you must learn to play by the rules. I will not tolerate disobedience."

Black spots encroach on my vision. My movements become disjointed as I attempt to thrash for freedom.

Tohminic tuts, pressing his body into mine and pinning me against the fern. "You will not fight. If you do, you will be punished."

I have no way of escape, no chance of putting distance between us. My nails cut through the skin of his hands as I continue to claw at him, my eyes begging for freedom. I cease my movements when the proof of his enjoyment presses into my lower belly.

My fear and fight arouses him. It is loathsome. Disgusting.

Just as the darkness begins to claim me, he relinquishes his hold on my neck and throws me to the ground. "This is the last time I will warn you. Dishonour me again, and I will ensure you cannot walk for seven moons."

He leaves me, panting and holding my bruised neck, with tears streaming down my face. He leaves me alone, battered with my soul cracking.

The life I would have with him flashes through my mind: abuse, torture, rules upon rules I have no hope of keeping track of. He will punish me for misdemeanours, tell me how to live, and I will pray to the Mother Star for a swift death rather than endure such a life.

When the sound of his footsteps fades at last, I leap to my feet and race through the garden in the opposite direction, not stopping until I am at the far wall and clambering over the ivy and stacked stone. I do not stop running, even as I exit the court's wards.

12

THE MOMENT THE WARD magic washes over me, I fold through the realm until I am breathing in the sweet spice-scented air of the southern redwood forest. I continue to run until the scent of the court fades, and my feet skid to a stop on the rotting leaves covering the ground, still damp from Father's tantrum-induced storm three days ago.

I sink to the ground, not caring that my gown will become filthy, and bury my head in my hands. Tears flow hot and insistent down my face. Like a phantom, Tohminic's hand squeezes at my throat.

A choked gasp pushes free, and I slap at the tender skin of my neck, a burning desire to remove the feel of his hands from my throat tearing through me. Never — and I truly mean never — has anyone treated me with such hatred, such disrespect. My life has not been easy, I will not deny that. But the sneers and taunts and belittling are nothing, *nothing* compared to what Tohminic just put me through.

I should have known. The moment he sent the guards away, I should have refused to accompany him to the gardens. I will not make the same mistake twice. Never again will I be alone with the Summer Prince.

What will the denizens think when they see the fading bruises marring my porcelain skin? What will Father think?

Father!

My head snaps up, my eyes drying at the thought of informing Father of what happened. Physically harming the High Lord's daughter is a punishable crime. Regardless of our courtship, Father will seek to exact revenge on my behalf.

I uncurl to my feet, hope filling my chest as I search for the narrow path which leads to the castle walls.

The forest is dense, with the branches overhead weaving together to form a canopy of branches and leaves. I have always marvelled at the beauty of nature, at how plants possess more strength than we will ever realise. The branches curl around one another, snaking together and fighting for survival, fighting for the small rays of sunlight in the dark forest. Although some of them are twisted and bent and look to be strangled by the others, they are thriving.

Even the miraculous sight above cannot take my mind off my throbbing neck or the ache in my heart. I do not believe Tohminic will find me here — even knowing this forest encroaches on the southern side of the castle — yet I cannot stifle the erratic beat of my heart, and I cannot loosen my tense muscles. My hands tremble as I run my palms over my exposed arms, soothing my raw nerves as I try to pinpoint my exact location.

I seldom venture into the forest, rarer still I am here alone. There are usually guards who can lead me home, correctly picking the right path through the trees to not anger the family of ogres who live here. Or Baba Yaga, the ogress who leads them.

My eyes widen, my head whipping back and forth as I search the trees for the fabled hut Baba Yaga lives in. It is supposedly magical and built from the bones of the younglings she feasts on. I hope I would *feel* if I were near such a horrible place.

The twisted trunks of the trees are too gnarled, now, too rough. Mounds of moss that were soft and welcoming, are now menacing. The gentle whisper of leaves might as well be screaming. There are warning signs everywhere I look. There is something darker about this part of the forest.

Folding through the realm is often a simple and fast way to travel, but if you are not concentrating, you may end up a little off track. When I folded from just outside the gardens, my mind was a panicked mess. I was not concentrating as I should have been.

Instead of appearing at the edge of the forest as I had intended, I have found myself in the deepest, darkest part. And though I am considered an adult, my face still holds the shine of youth. If I stumble upon Baba Yaga or any of her ogre family...

I attempt to grab hold of my meagre magic, drawing on the power of the land to fold the castle towards me. Nothing happens. My magic does not so much as flicker. A shiver trickles down my spine.

The ogres — a deformed breed of fae, created many millennia ago when the High Lord and Lady of Autumn refused to relinquish control of their animalistic magic and turned into the savage beasts we fear today — wield only one kind of magic. Warding.

I am in their territory. Whether that means I am near the castle or near the cliffs, I am unsure.

"Think, Bria. Where are you?" My words are softer than the sighing leaves as I spin in a slow circle, searching for a sign.

I quiet my breathing and freeze, listening. In the distance, far to the south, waves crash against a rocky shore. A slow smile pulls at my lips and the stiffness in my body recedes. This forest stands atop a cliff, a cliff which curls around the royal port. A port bustling with activity in preparation for the Dusk Court's High Lord to arrive.

At last, my mind catches up.

When Tohminic exited the Autumn gardens without me, those four guards would have wondered where I am. They will search for me. If they have already realised I am no longer within the castle walls, Father and Rennyn will search for me, too. They will access their animalistic powers to look through the eyes of the forest animals, searching for signs of me. No matter the direction in which I travel, they will find me.

Though I wish I could take a moment to bask in the relief, I know remaining immobile in this forest is akin to welcoming death with open arms. My scent already lingers in the air, drifting in the soft breeze and calling to whatever creatures lurk nearby.

I decide on trekking towards the ocean. It is closer than the castle, and I can exit the wards around the ogre territory faster. At least, I think so. I hope so.

Moving through the trees, I place my feet carefully. I avoid dried sticks and leaves, step over large patches of water-logged moss, and steer clear of the tiny burrows that descend below the roots of the trees. I have been lucky to go unnoticed in my short time here, lucky my sobs and gasps went unheard. That does not mean luck will continue to follow me.

In fact, I am beginning to believe I have angered the Mother Star. Why else would my life be teeming with heartache? As a babe, every night when the moon was high, my nursemaid would tell me frightening tales of the Mother Star, of how if behaved badly enough, she would blanket my word with darkness.

I always assumed the darkness Mivian spoke of would be tangible. Like shadow or night. Now I have experienced a little of life, I am wondering if the blanket of darkness is more of a metaphor, if the darkness would come from my heart and thoughts rather than the physical world.

Lost in my thoughts as I am, I almost do not notice when the forest grows silent. Between one soft step and the other, the leaves have ceased their whispers, the scurrying of insects has disappeared, and now the only sound is my pounding heart.

I chance a look over my shoulder, my blood running cold at the sight of the imposing ogre standing between the trees. His — because the creature wears no clothes, I am blessed with the knowledge it is male — skin is a sickly green-grey, rough, and riddled with scars, he carries a makeshift club which I am sure was once an established tree, and his beady eyes are locked on me. They glaze over for a heartbeat before returning to their dull black.

Whipping my head back to the front, I sprint through the forest, no longer caring if I am heard. It is too late for that. If my crashing steps alert the other ogres — or worse, the ogress — that I am trespassing on their land, it will only benefit me. The beasts will fight, each of them wanting my flesh for themselves.

Broken branches tear at my naked arms and snag in the skirt of my gown, threatening to tear it from my body as I pass through the ogres' wards. There is only one thing on my mind: putting as much distance between me and the ogre as possible.

His ferocious roar chases me through the trees, the pungent odour of carrion stinging my nose and overriding the earthy scent of moss and dying leaves. The smaller trees crumble beneath his mammoth body, the snapping of their narrow trunks ringing through the forest like the crack of a hammer against an anvil.

One moment, I am racing through the trees, and the next, I am airborne. A scream tears at my throat, my legs thrashing wildly as the ground disappears from beneath my feet. Two thick, greyish hands wrap around my torso, squeezing my ribs and organs.

The ogre turns me to face him, his stubby brown teeth peeking through the eager smile twisting his face. He brings me closer and inhales the scent at the crook of my neck. A deep rumble rattles in his chest, a sound I can only liken to glee and anticipation.

I beat my fists against his hands, screaming for him to release me at once. "I am the daughter of High Lord Kerym, ruler of the Autumn Court."

He roars in my face, spittle and chunks of something I do not wish to inspect landing on my cheeks, on my forehead, and along the curve of my bottom lip. He opens his mouth wide, revealing every crooked and broken tooth, and tilts his head towards my shoulder.

From nowhere, a blustering gust of wind tears through the forest. It brings the delicate scents of lavender and something zesty like orange. Though the scents are warm, they do not overpower the carrion of the ogre's breath as he huffs a grunt of surprise.

The ogre turns towards the distant cliffs, my back crashing through the branches as he spins without care. He takes a thunderous step forward, lowering me as he roars.

"Release her, ogre." The male's voice is deep. Soft but commanding and rough. I recognise it as belonging to Vander, the High Lord of Dusk. "Now."

The ogre roars once more — his favoured method of communication is getting on my nerves — twisting his body to the side to hide me from view.

I cannot see Vander. I cannot see if he is alone or came with an entourage of fighters. The only view I am granted is the side of the ogre's over-sized head and the greenish wax inside what is left of his ear. Which is why, when a small axe imbeds itself in the ogre's forehead, a startled scream rips from my throat.

The beast releases me in favour of groping at the weapon, and I crash to the ground, my skirt fluttering to my hips. I land hard on an arched root, my right hip taking the brunt of the impact. My eyes widen at the ogre as he tilts towards me, and I scramble out of the way a mere heartbeat before his enormous body crashes to the ground, flattening the root I landed on.

A sound somewhere between a whimper and a laugh bubbles free. I press a shaking hand to my mouth, my eyes bugging at the gruesome sight of the gaping wound in the ogre's head. His blood is such a dark red, it is almost black, stark against the moss and bronze of the forest floor.

"You alright, Princess?" Vander squats beside me. His silver eyes dart straight to the bruising around my neck.

"I..." I leap to my feet, my frantic hands rushing to straighten my gown. "Thank you for saving me."

"Of course. We heard your screams from the docks." Anger flashes across his face. "None of the Autumn fae seemed inclined to investigate, so we took it upon ourselves."

"We?" My eyes stray from Vander's at last.

Another male stands off to the side, his golden hair tied at the nape of his neck. His dark eyes crinkle at the sides, the creases forming out of habit. He bows mockingly low. "Well met, Princess Bria."

"Torin is my second," explains Vander, grunting as he pulls his axe free of the dying ogre's forehead, "and a damn pain in the arse."

"How..." I start. Finding my courage, I ask, "How did you know who I am?"

Torin throws his head back and laughs. "Well dressed, flames for hair, and piercing green eyes?"

Vander shoots him a glare before turning to me while wiping the blood from his axe. "I remember you from the ball." There is something in his tone, an emotion I cannot quite place in my frazzled state.

The reminder of the ball has reality slamming back into me, and I dip to a curtsey. "Apologies for my lack of respect, Lord Vander."

"No one bows to me," he growls. Wiping the anger from his features, he holds out a hand. "Allow us to escort you to the castle. I believe your father would like a word?"

I gulp and nod, slipping my hand into his. A cool wind wraps around me, the forest disappearing as Vander folds us both to the castle gates.

Torin appears beside us, a crooked grin lifting one side of his lips. "This is going to be so much fun, Van."

13

THE SENTRIES IN THE outpost bristle as we approach. One clambers down the ladder and dashes ahead of us, warning the guards at the gatehouse who will then send a messenger to Father, informing him of both my safety and the arrival of Vander and Torin.

The need for so many guards and sentries is ridiculous. At least, I considered it ridiculous until now. Until Father felt the need to claim an island which he has no right to. Now, the entire realm is in chaos, nobles and royals sticking their noses where they do not belong.

I walk between the males, currents of tingling power washing over me. I am unsure which male the thrilling waves pulse from, but I find I do not mind the caress of magic. It differs from the fresh feel of Vander's air powers, unlike the soft coaxing of his illusions.

My eyes flick to Torin. "May I ask what powers you wield? As a member of the Dusk Court, I assume you have control over air and illusions?"

He waggles his eyebrows. "I'm a Night fae." He pushes a little of his magic at me. The cool kiss of night licks at my arms, the soft caress of an autumn breeze chasing away the cold.

I almost forget to keep walking, and stagger a little.

His is not the magic I feel pulsing around me. No, that magic is something else entirely, something I am not sure I should look at too closely.

My surprise only makes Torin laugh. "When Dusk formed, there were Night fae who disagreed with Maude's way of doing things. We rejected her leadership and pledged allegiance to Connak. My mother remains on the Night Islands."

"I am sorry to hear that," I say, my voice low. "You wield blood and bone magic? Control over one's mind?"

He shakes his head. "Magic works in mysterious ways. I control the wind and can sift through memories of objects. I could press a hand to these stones and see who has walked by in the last four and twenty hours." When I look at him with obvious curiosity, he adds, "My mother is a Night fae, my father Dusk. You could say I'm a mystery."

"It's rare that fae with different branches of magic find a mate within a different court," says Vander. "But it's not unheard of. Clearly, your father and mother are from different courts, but —"

"She is *not* my mother," I hiss.

His brows lift and he runs a tawny hand over the scruff on his chin.

I am beginning to notice the subtle differences of the Dusk Court. The equality of females, when the rest of Radelea sees us as lesser. The scruff on Vander's chin, when smooth faces are seen as a sign of nobility. The way the Dusk fae talk by contracting their words and using a casual tone, when the rest of the realm sees it as lesser.

Though they have been cut off from us for the past three hundred years, it is hard for me to imagine why they are so different from the rest of us. It is a question for another day.

As we pass through the outer bailey, lesser fae dashing about gathering supplies for the fair in the eastern village, I apologise to Vander for my interruption and ask him to continue what he was saying.

"Sometimes, when fae from different courts mate, the babe is born wielding the strongest two powers rather than that of one court. Torin's father wields exceptional air magic and we revere his mother for her mind control. He was born with the strongest gift from each parent. However," he continues as we approach the low wall surrounding the inner bailey, "on rare occasions, the magic twists into something else entirely."

"What do you mean?" I ask, dipping my chin to the two guards on either side of the gates as we pass. "His magic is something I have not heard of?"

Torin answers, "The air magic and mind magic kind of... blended together. The wind carries memories and secrets. It whispers to me."

For once, my love of history proves beneficial. "I have read about the Whispers. I believed them to be nothing more than myth. What is the wind telling you now?"

"That your father is spitting mad," he says, smirking.

I follow his line of sight and know the wind did not whisper the news of my father's ire to Vander's second. My shoulders curl in and my steps slow as we approach Father.

He marches towards us dressed in full battle leathers, complete with a cape the colour of marigolds, his emerald eyes narrowed to slits. "Where have you been?"

I hang my head. "Please, Father, I will explain inside."

It is one thing to tell Father what occurred in the gardens, another thing altogether to speak of such events before the lesser fae. If Tohminic were to find out... A shudder tracks down my spine.

"Very well. We will convene in the sitting room." He sighs, sparing Vander and Torin a glance. "Welcome to the Autumn Court. I would very much like to hear why you disappeared from the docks."

"It's a simple explanation," says Vander as Father leads us into the castle. As we wind through the hallways, Vander explains arriving at the docks, only to hear the panicked screams of a female. How he was disgusted when none of Father's denizens bothered to investigate and folded into the forest above.

We enter the sitting room, a large space with firm sofas and too many tables, and Vander finishes with, "If this is the way you run your court, I'm not surprised your allies are refusing to aid you in your quest to claim *my* land."

Father bristles. "There is no proof of the land belonging to you."

"Only a three-hundred-year-old court," scoffs Torin.

Vander silences him with a look before turning back to Father. "You're welcome to make your inquiries. But know we won't go down without a fight. The land is ours, Kerym." He stalks into the room, giving his back to the open fireplace. "I'm sure you didn't summon me here to talk about my court."

Before we dive into the topic of my courtship, it is imperative Father understands how desperately I do not wish to mate with Tohminic.

I step forward, hiking my shoulders up in a show of confidence I do not feel. "Father, I would like to explain myself before discussing why you invited Vander here today, if you will allow it?"

Father clicks his fingers at a passing servant, ordering refreshments be brought to us immediately. Only once the lesser fae has scurried off — Vander and Torin scowling at Father when the servant's fear drenches the room — does Father all me to speak.

The guards have already informed him of Bim and Tarathiel returning to their home courts, but I recap the information, regardless. Quickly, when I sense his patience wearing thin. I go on to tell him the Dawn triplets are a package deal, adding, "I am hesitant to spend more time with them. While they are kind and humorous, I do not believe they will provide me with the emotional connection I crave. Not to mention I have no desire to belong to a harem of any kind."

Father's face screws in disgust. "I do not care to learn of your preferences in the bedchamber. I have endured enough of such speak to last a lifetime."

My cheeks heat.

Father is especially ornery today. It does not bode well for my plight.

I move the conversation along, going into great detail about Tohminic's actions and threats before explaining my encounter with the ogre in the forest and how Vander and Torin saved me from a gruesome and painful death. Because I am feeling bitter,

I add, "If the Dusk Court had not rescued me today, you would mourn my death. If they did not save me, Father, you would have lost your bargaining chip."

Father's hand twitches, as if he is restraining himself from hitting me. It would not be the first time my cheeks felt the sting of his hand. It occurs often enough that I flinch.

Vander's eyes flare brighter, the silver turning molten. I am reminded of the stars we fae love so dearly, how they shine from the night sky like tiny specks of gleaming metal. I am lost to the glow of silver, the glint of hatred and flash of disgust calling to my very soul.

He rests his hand on the handle of his axe. "From your letter, I gather you've called me here to request an alliance through mating?"

Father grunts his acknowledgment. "If you would consider courting her — and look past her antics — I believe our courts have a lot to learn from one another. An ally on the mainland would be of great benefit to you."

"I didn't need allies until *you* thought to claim my land, Kerym," growls Vander. "But if mating your daughter means she's no longer under your oppressive thumb, then I accept. I will not, however, stand by while she's treated like the dirt beneath your boots."

"You have no right to make demands of me in my home."

Torin steps forward, his mouth set in a thin line. "My High Lord has endured more hardships than you will ever know or understand. If he says Bria deserves freedom, you'll damn well give it to her. From what I can tell, your firm hand," he says, making a point of looking at the hand which twitched, the hand which is now fisted, "has done nothing but hurt your daughter. She was physically assaulted because of your greed."

"That's enough," sighs Vander. "Stand down."

Thankfully, three servers arrive, each of them carrying a tray of either food or drink, interrupting what I am sure will be a lengthy rant from Father. The food is not enough to fill us all, a sign Father does not welcome the Dusk fae. It is high noon, when luncheon is to be served, yet my father offers our guests nothing but a selection of cheese and fruit. Any other high fae would be offended.

Vander does not appear to mind, though, and helps himself to a chalice of hot cider. "Thank you," he murmurs as the servers scuttle out.

Torin pours two ciders, handing one to me before lounging in one of the wingback chairs and propping one of his ankles on a knee. He looks rather comfortable, and I wonder if it is yet another way to irk my father. Judging by the constant twitching of Torin's lips, he is enjoying himself immensely.

Ignoring the food and drink, Father stands firm before the two males and crosses his arms over his expansive chest. "You agree to take part in the courtship? I cannot promise you success."

Vander sits and leans forward, his fingers holding tight to the rim of the chalice dangling between his legs. "I have no intention of failing. Throw whatever you have my way, Kerym. By the end, your daughter will be a member of my court."

"You say it as though it is a threat," says Father, one eyebrow lifting.

"It's fact." Vander's expression does not waver. "I don't pretend to know the entire story, but from what I understand, your daughter deserves better than the life you've offered her."

My heart swells, filling with warmth. Not once in my life has another — especially a male — defended me in such a way. He is right to say he does not know the full story. He does not understand how I have been shunned, does not understand Fayeth's hatred of me. But in Dusk, such treatment would not be allowed. I cannot wait to become a part of his court.

Father scoffs. "I have given her what she deserves and then some. A bastard female with no magic to speak of... She should be thankful I gave her a semblance of life at all."

All I can do is blink and wonder if this is how Father has always felt. Has he always regretted bringing me home when my mother begged him to take me? Has he spent the last five and seventy years wishing I did not exist?

My voice is pure venom when I say, "All I am thankful for, *Father*, is the opportunity to leave this court for good. I will play by your rules during this ridiculous courtship. Vander and I will take a walk in the gardens before venturing to the eastern village to enjoy the fair, and I will hear nothing of your opinion." I step closer, making sure he understands how serious I am. "You will remove Tohminic from the prospective mates immediately."

"I am High Lord of this court," he seethes. "You would do well to remember your place. Do not push me. You will not enjoy the consequences."

"My entire life is a consequence of *your* actions. And I am done enduring the punishment." I spin on my dirty heel, leaving a smear of mud on the gleaming floor, and sweep from the room.

I have no interest in arguing with him today. Not after Tohminic. Not after the ogre. Certainly not after hearing how he truly feels about my existence. If I had any notions of bidding farewell to my home court with tears in my eyes, they are long forgotten. When I leave this place at last, there will be a smile on my face.

I will be glad to turn my back on Autumn.

14

Wyn flinches when I slam the door to my chambers closed, but I do not have the mental capacity to apologise for my rude arrival.

The conversation from the sitting room echoes in my mind, and I rub at my chest as if to rid it of pain. But the pain which should be there — the desolation I should feel after Father confirmed his true feelings for me — is non-existent. All I feel is a burning rage, the fire smothering any hint of regret which bubbles free.

I know Father well enough to know he will discipline me for my harsh words. While his favoured punishment is locking me in my trio of chambers, he cannot allow that while I am expected to be seen courting. Not knowing how he will react will be worse than the punishment itself.

"What happened?" Wyn asks from where she kneels at the hearth, stoking the fire in my bedchamber.

I lean against one of the bed posts and run a hand down my face, my teeth grinding. "Where shall I begin?"

"That bad?"

"A burning crater could open beneath the Autumn Court and I would think it a kind occurrence compared to the events of today."

She sets the steel poker — although iron is stronger against the flames, it is damaging to the fae, causing blistering wounds with a single touch — aside and stands, her eyes tracking over my ruined gown. "Let's get you into something more comfortable while you start with how your garden walks went."

I shake my head. "Vander and I are to stroll through the gardens. He will expect me soon, but I need a bath." I yank on the strings of the corset, adding, "An ogre attacked me in the forest."

She swats at my hands, taking over releasing the laces. "I'm confused. What were you doing in the forest when you were supposed to be in the gardens?"

I tell her everything, from Tohminic's threats to running away and everything that occurred after. The tub is full by the time I am finished.

Wyn adds sprigs of dried chamomile, and though her face is hidden by her long, dark hair, I know she is scowling. She gestures for me to get in. "Will your father do as you asked and send Tohminic away?"

A groan slips free as I sink into the heated water. My muscles relax, though the knot in my stomach remains. The chamomile does little to soothe my frayed nerves, and I scrub at my stained skin with more force than is necessary.

I consider her question. Father disapproves of those who overstep their rank — which Tohminic did — but he loathes insolence. I think if I had confronted him in private, he would heed my advice and refuse Tohminic's advances. But I was disrespectful towards him in the presence of Vander and Torin.

"I doubt it," I say, stepping from the tub and accepting a towel. "He will be too angry with me to consider the possibility of such a betrayal."

"Then Van will just have to win your father's favour during the courtship. You mentioned a tournament?"

I pull on my lace underclothes. "Yes. Though it changes with each courtship, there are generally three tests for the males. A fight with weapons, a magic battle, and a hunting trip. Father may decide during any of those stages a male is not worthy."

"Vander can definitely win a weapons fight. The magic battle may work in Tohminic's favour, though, since air feeds fire." She holds up two gowns — one brown and the other black — shaking them a little. "And he's good at hunting, though I doubt that's the real reason for a hunting trip."

I select the black gown. "It is more likely a test to see which male can drink the most wine before he can no longer stand."

She chuckles as she helps me into the gown.

"Wyn?" I ask as she settles the long sleeves on my shoulders and loops a thin strap around my middle finger. "Why me?" It is a question I have asked before, but her answer has never felt right.

"What do you mean?"

"Why didn't Vander send someone to spy on Rennyn or Fayeth or anyone else in the Autumn Court? Why did he send you to be my hand maiden?" It has been bothering me for some time, but I have been too afraid to ask again until now.

She is quiet for a moment, searching for the right words as she works on fastening the black pearl buttons that snake down my back.

The gown is beautiful, if not a little strange. The high neck covers the yellowing bruises on my neck, the long sleeves hide the few scrapes and cuts along my arms, but the skirt falls to knee-length. Something I have never seen in Radelea. Ever. She has dressed me in another scandal.

"It's not so much about you as it's about the other servants here. They talk, probably more than they should. We've gained a lot of information from their murmurs." She hesitates, her eyes glazing as she is lost in her thoughts.

"There's something about you," she says after a long pause. "That day when you fell from the ship, Vander, Torin, Nyree, and I were watching from the shore, and Vander was so... enraptured by you. He couldn't explain what he was feeling, but he knew we needed to know more. We're still not sure what magic you cast on us to make us so interested in you."

So many questions run through my mind. I cannot begin to understand the rest of her words, so I choose the one question I can easily find an answer to. "Who is Nyree?"

"The leader of the Ill-fated. They're a group of Night fae who were unfortunate enough to be on our island when the land broke apart. When Maude learned of their fate, she refused to allow them to return home. They banded together to protect one another."

"That's horrible," I say.

I am stunned for a moment at my slip of speech. Wyn is wearing off on me, causing me to contract words which should be spoken on their own. Lazy words make for lazy lives, according to Father. Mashing words together — such as 'that is' — is frowned upon.

Although I should correct myself, I do not. In fact, I kind of enjoy talking with a more casual tone like Vander and Wyn. It is such a small thing, so inconsequential in the scheme of things, yet I feel like I have taken a step towards choosing my own path in life. I feel as though I am pushing back against Father's rule.

"They've long since made peace with it," says Wyn. "They don't follow a lot of our rules, instead choosing to live by the old ways, the life we lived before the war."

"Why do they stay? Why not seek refuge in any other court?"

"Both Maude and my father wouldn't allow it." She pushes me into the wooden seat by the window and smooths my hair, pulling the occasional leaf free. "If the Ill-fated entered any court and explained their predicament, the rest of Radelea would have discovered our weakness. At the time, both Night and Dusk were weak, and couldn't afford another war."

"But it has been three hundred years. Maude has still not forgiven them for being in the wrong place at the wrong time?"

"Oh, she has. A century ago, she sent a messenger with the news. Some returned home, but Nyree and the other Ill-fated didn't want to leave their homes. Some of them have families, many of them have lovers and friends. After two hundred years, they had built lives for themselves. Leaving didn't feel right."

I can understand that. Until today, I could not imagine leaving the Autumn Court because I believed it to be my home. Now, I have realised my family is a lie. I am related by blood, it is true, but I am not related by heart, by soul.

"I am thankful to you for telling me all of that," I say as Wyn moves to my front and slides black leather boots onto my feet. "Though my original question remains unanswered."

"To that, I have no answer. Vander knew he could send someone to spy on Rennyn, but he chose you instead. Though if he knew how unappreciated you are here, I doubt he would have."

I hang my head. She knows a lot of my history — I have grown close to her over the last few moons — including the hardships I have faced through the years. The one thing I have not confided in her is how I was brought into the world.

"I will explain to Vander today. He has a right to know he chose wrong. If he chooses to free you from your obligations here, then so be it."

She looks me right in the eye. "I'm not going anywhere, Bria. We're friends. We've only known one another a few days, but it's enough for me to know we're *meant* to know each other. You're my soul sister."

Tears build in my eyes, but I push them back. "Thank you," I whisper. "I have never had a friend."

15

BY THE TIME MY guards escort me to the garden gates, the Mother Star is drawing close to the horizon. Only a few hours of daylight remain.

I dismiss the four guards when Vander arrives, ignoring their protests to follow us into the gardens. I am not afraid of Vander, and though he may seem intimidating and dangerous to some, I know he will not harm me.

We walk in silence for a few moments, enjoying the low buzz of insects and sweet aromas until we take a left turn deeper into the maze of flowers and shrubs.

"I would like to apologise," I say, pausing to admire a patch of brightly coloured sneezeweed, "for how I behaved with Father. I should have waited until I could speak to him in private."

He barks a laugh. "If you didn't say something, Torin would have. Then I'd be the one apologising."

I straighten, turning to face him. "Regardless, I am sorry for how I acted. I spoke out of turn and said things I should have kept to myself. I feel I should explain, if you will hear it?"

He gestures for me to continue through the garden. "Please."

"You will have gained a lot from my conversation with my father, learned that Fayeth is not my mother?" I pull my cloak tighter around me, warding off the slight chill in the air. "My true mother is a Spring fae."

He slides his hands into the pockets of his leather jacket. It is a style I have not seen before. "While I appreciate your honesty, I'm not sure why it's important to know who your mother is."

"I do not know who she is. Father has always kept that from me. The point is, I am a bastard. I do not have the privilege of overhearing sensitive information. Wyn will not gain much by spying on me. You are better off sending someone to watch Rennyn."

His eyes flash. "Bastard is a disgusting word used by cowards who can't shoulder the responsibility of their actions. You're not a bastard."

The afternoon air crackles with power. It licks at my hands and face, sending tingles of warmth through my body.

He sighs. "I have no need for inside information from Autumn. You're the closest court, and we can easily keep an eye on your land from Dusk. What I need is a fae inside those war meetings your father holds. I need to know how to protect my court. I sent Wyn to you hoping to gain something, *anything*, that could help."

"And have you gained any such information?"

"I have." I turn to him, surprised. He says, "Don't worry, Wyn hasn't let slip any of your secrets. She's the reason I revealed myself at your brother's born day ball."

I nod, understanding. "You wished to prevent war by revealing yourself. You had hoped the other high fae would see sense and would not attack an island already ruled by another."

"Time will tell if it worked. At the moment, peace is tentative at best. One wrong move by anyone, and Radelea will suffer."

I can't help but think my refusing Tohminic's hand could be that one wrong move. It may be enough to tip the Summer Court over the edge. And if the Mother Star has broken our land after two wars, I shudder to imagine the destruction she will cause if there is another war.

"For the sake of your court, I hope the others see sense." I place a gentle hand on his arm, the warmth of his body seeping through the dark leather. "Thank you for doing this, for agreeing to participate in this deplorable courtship. I do not know what I would have done if my only choices were Tohminic or the Dawn triplets. It is not something required of you, especially when you are in mourning. I am very grateful."

"Don't thank me yet, Princess."

"Whatever do you mean?" I ask, snatching my hand back.

The silver in his eyes darkens to slate grey. "I'm not your knight in shining armour, on a mission to rescue your jaded soul and capture your heart. I'm doing this because I hate how females are treated, passed around as if they're mere objects to possess. When I win your father's permission, we won't be running off into the sunset, happy and in love."

"Wyn told me it is nothing but a ruse," I admit. "She said we do not have to mate once we are in the Dusk Court. I understand this."

"Then you understand love isn't something I'm interested in. Any ideas you have of falling for me... you can forget them right now. With my father's death, my home under scrutiny, and the possibility of war on the horizon, I don't have time for anything other than protecting my court."

I know all of that, but his words still sting. It stings that wherever I go, I will be unwanted. At least if Vander gains Father's approval, I will have Wyn as a friend. In a world where I have nothing, the prospect of friendship is all that keeps me going. Without that, I might as well cease to exist.

Having done our duty by walking through the gardens, Vander and I meet with Torin and Wyn at the eastern wall of the court.

Wyn looks stunning with golden-brown hair, black leather pants, and a ruby blouse. She has used her illusion magic to make her eyes more blue than silver, too. No one will recognise her as my hand maiden, and she will be free to enjoy the village fair without scrutiny from the Autumn nobles.

Torin wears the same clothes from earlier today: full leather, as if ready to run into battle. He even has twin short swords crossed over his back, their hilts poking over his shoulders. He greets us with a crooked smile. "How was your stroll among the flowers?"

Vander snorts. "It was good. We talked things over, and we both agree on the terms of this arrangement."

Wyn punches him on the shoulder. "You're such a dick, Van."

My eyes grow wide. No one treats a High Lord like that, sister or no. Strangely, Torin and Vander do not seem bothered by Wyn's show of disrespect. In fact, Torin howls with laughter.

Vander groans, rubbing a hand over his shoulder. "Ouch. What did I do to deserve that?"

"Sometimes I wonder if you were born without tact or sense. Don't you think Bria has endured enough without you acting like a fucking twit?"

"F-fucking?" I ask, my brows pinching.

Torin slings an arm around my shoulders. "Fucking is a worthy pastime, and a crude word that should never pass a female's lips."

I am more confused than ever, but let the subject drop. Somehow, I do not see Torin's explanation becoming any clearer if I ask for clarification. Perhaps I can determine the meaning from its use if Wyn or the males use it again.

Vander's eyes narrow at where Torin's hand rests against my shoulder. He tears his gaze away with a growled, "Let's go then."

One moment I am standing just beyond the castle's wards, the next, Torin folds us to the eastern village, and I am inundated with the sounds of the fair.

Cheers, claps, shouts, and laughter mingle with ringing bells, clashing swords, and ethereal music, the sounds drifting towards us on a salty ocean breeze. Tents of every colour line both sides of the wide road, the stores behind them brightly lit as high and lesser fae alike gather with their friends and loved ones. Babes dash between the legs of whoever steps in their path, giggling as they twist from the reach of their parents.

A smile curves my lips. I have always loved fairs.

"Where to first?" asks Torin, pulling me closer to his side. "Food, drink, or trade?"

Wyn's stomach growls. "For the love of the Mother Star, find me some food."

The eastern village is twice the size of the western village and docks put together. Weaving through the throng of fae towards the far end of the fair, where there are many food tents and stalls, takes far longer than it should.

We are stopped several times by fae wishing to greet their High Lord's daughter, and with each instance, Wyn grows more unpleasant. The ninth time a member of Father's court holds us up, she leans towards Vander and whispers in his ear.

He pins me under his starlight stare, running a hand over his chin before nodding. He jerks his head towards a gap between stalls and steps into the shadows.

I raise my brow in question at Wyn, but she only waggles hers in return.

Torin is just as elusive with the plan. He slides his arm from my shoulders — how he has kept it there this entire time is beyond me — and slaps my buttocks. Hard. "Off you trot."

I shoot him a scowl before following Vander into the darkness. Hidden by the stalls on either side, with a solid brick wall behind us, we are essentially alone in a village crawling with fae. It is a strange feeling to be among them, but not.

"Do you enjoy the attention?" he asks. "Do you enjoy everyone knowing who you are?"

"Of course not," I say, clasping my hands.

"I figured as much. How do you feel about a few hours of freedom? I can cast an illusion over your face to make you look like someone else. What do you say? Are you up for a night of fun?"

I look back over my shoulder, watching the fae pass our hidden alcove. If Vander can make me look like someone else, I will not be forced to endure polite conversation with Father's acquaintances. I can do whatever I wish without fear of consequence. Perhaps I can sit in a tavern and cradle a mug of ale, dance without restraint, or I can tell Lord Gorred — Father's second, a male I have detested my entire life — to keep his wandering hands to himself for once.

A wide grin pulls at my cheeks as I turn back to Vander. "Do it. Please, make me look different."

He waves a hand over my face. "Enjoy yourself. Freedom doesn't come around often."

A youthful giggle slips past my lips and my insides vibrate with anticipation of what the night will bring. For the first time in my life, I am nobody. Just Bria.

"What do I look like?" I ask as we rejoin Wyn and Torin.

Torin winks. "I approve."

Wyn shoves him playfully. "You have brown hair and grey eyes, your nose is a little longer, and your brow a little flatter. I would have given your chin a sharper point than Vander has, though. You could belong to Autumn or Dusk. Good thinking, Van."

My fingers trace over my face, finding nothing unusual.

"It's just an illusion," says Vander. "You're still you."

Our quest for food is easier now. With no one stopping for pleasantries, we find the stalls within moments. Wyn drags us towards the largest tent, where the mouth-watering aroma of buttery pastry wafts from the depths of the canvas.

Inside is stifling hot with all the bodies pressed in together. Three long tables cut through the space, the bench seats all taken, groaning under the weight of so many fae. Crumbs and plates and empty mugs litter whatever space remains on the wooden tables.

A lesser fae with bark-like skin scurries about, working extra hard to ensure the stall runs smoothly. She passes us without a glance. "There is no space, I am afraid. Try the stall next door. They offer roasted meat."

"I don't want meat." Wyn crosses her arms over her chest. "And I'm sure my brother, the High Lord of Dusk, doesn't want meat, either."

Torin whispers in my ear, "Never get between Wyn and food."

I nod, seeing that for myself. In fact, I am surprised she is not stomping her foot.

The female visibly shrinks before dropping the used plates on the nearest table and dipping to a curtsey. "My apologies, Lord."

"We do not need seats," I say, saving her from Wyn's wrath. "We can eat while observing the fair. If you do not mind bringing us plates, we can make do."

She hardly spares me a glance, keeping her evergreen eyes on Vander. "Of course, miss. I will be back in a moment with your food."

"Thank you," says Vander. The moment the server disappears through a side door, he turns on his sister. "Don't throw my title around to get what you want. Unless you're willing to take your rightful place as High Lady?"

Her eyes narrow as she caresses the hilt of her dagger. "Threaten me again, brother, and see what happens."

"Now, now," says Torin, stepping between them with a smirk. "All will seem better once you've eaten. You don't act like yourself when you're hungry, Wyn. And Van, you know better than to rile her up on an empty stomach."

The siblings look as if they are ready to smack Torin up the side of the head. If he were to speak to me like that, I do not think I would restrain myself. Though, I am beginning to realise this is just how Torin acts. He is the lovable jester of the Dusk Court, here for the sole purpose of making everyone laugh.

Thankfully, our food arrives, and we each take a plate, Wyn shovelling food into her mouth before we have even stepped foot outside the tent.

She groans. "This is so good."

I take a bite of a flaky pastry with sliced almonds on top. The buttery goodness melts on my tongue, and a groan of my own slips free.

We eat while we weave through the crowd towards the entertainment side of the fair, where displays of magic captivate the crowd, the court jesters steal laughs from younglings, and fae use their magic to operate thrilling rides.

Torin orders us to a comedic act, the four fae on stage dressed as the High Family of Autumn as they hyperbolise the odious life I live.

The female portraying Fayeth screams and throws her hands in the air. "How am I to enjoy my luncheon when *she* is here, Kerym, darling?"

It is unnerving to see my father's scowl on another male. The actor draws a wooden sword, pointing it at the female portraying me. "Be gone, bastard daughter, so my beloved may dine in peace."

"Why do you refuse to love me, Father? Am I so despicable?"

The crowd cheers when my actor brother slides onto the stage and shouts, "You magicless wench! Impurity be gone!" before piercing my back with his sword.

The cheers continue as I slowly die, on stage and in my true heart. A life of being mocked, a life of being hated by the denizens should have prepared me for this moment. It has not.

I turn away from the stage, fighting the tears in my eyes as I whisper, "I think that is quite enough."

The trio of Dusk fae surround me as we leave the travelling actors without leaving a coin for their efforts. Their anger and surprise radiates from them in waves and threatens to bring me to my knees. The pity should not bother me, but somehow, because it comes from three fae I do not know well, the feeling is suffocating.

"Let's try the rides," says Wyn, attempting to lighten the mood. "Maybe the one with the giant teacups."

"It looks so boring," says Torin.

I drag my eyes from the ground and search for the ride in question, finding it straight ahead. The bright and colourful teacups are stationary while excited fae clamber into the false cocoon of safety. As soon as they are seated, a male shouts for them to hold on, warns them once more he is not liable for injury, then waves his arms through the air.

The cups shoot for the sky, all but disappearing with the colourful sunset as a backdrop, before spinning faster than my eyes can track. The fae within the cups squeal with both delight and fear when they plummet towards the ground.

"Guess I was mistaken," says Torin.

"You know what, Wyn?" I loop my arm through hers. "We came here to have fun. Let's do it."

Her grin is borderline maniacal. "I knew I liked you."

We join the long line curling around the roped area surrounding the teacup ride. My foot jitters with nerves — I have never done something as outrageous as this — with every slow step we take closer to the ride's entrance.

The sun has set completely when it is our turn to climb into the cups. We choose a dark purple one with a chip in the side, sitting on the narrow seats and tying the meagre rope around our waists.

I am not certain it will hold me for long.

"Hold on tight," the male operating the ride shouts. "Do remember, we are not liable for injury of any description. Failure to prevent your fall is by fault of yourself. Enjoy the ride." He shoves his hands into the air.

My stomach quits on me. It remains on the ground as I am thrown into the sky, nothing holding me but a frayed rope and stone teacup. The scream that tears at my throat is one of exhilaration and fear, and it is the ugliest sound I have ever made. My knuckles are white from strain as I grip the sides of the cup, my grip slipping a little with every rotation through the air.

We dip and weave and spin, we plummet and slam to a halt. We laugh and squeal — Wyn and I laugh and squeal, the males grunt now and then — as our eyes water from being frozen wide. It is the most fun I have ever had.

Vander is not fond of carnival rides, apparently, and refuses to endure another, so we spend hours tasting ale and wine while

Wyn drags us from stall to stall, purchasing wares she cannot find in Dusk.

By the end of the night, she is carrying a bag laden with goods — spelled candles, jewellery, wrapped sweets, a bottle of spiced mead, and a bolt of glittery fabric — and talking about the absurd dance moves she witnessed from Torin on the dancefloor.

I am exhausted when I collapse into bed well after the moon begins to sink. Exhausted, with aching cheeks from smiling so often. It is the first time I recall being genuinely happy and I cannot help but wonder if life in Dusk is always this carefree, this... warm and welcoming.

Wyn, Vander, and Torin share a tight bond of friendship and respect, something I yearn for and something I vow to obtain. Regardless of Vander's refusal to allow love into his heart, it is clear the three of them care deeply for one another.

I am both envious and awed.

I could be friends with these three. It would be easy for me to fit into their lives, just as I did this evening. Easy to be happy. It is the first time in many moons I fall asleep with a smile on my face, and my heart filled to the brim with warmth.

16

I HAVE TO MARVEL at Wyn's brilliance. She knows when to dress me appropriately and when to put me in something a little more risqué. This morning, she has selected a traditional fae gown in garnet red.

A lot of fae believe red to be the colour of love, and many will assume that is the reason behind today's gown. But love is not red. It is not pink or white or any other colour one might deem as happy.

It is grey.

Love is calm and strength, it is timelessness, wisdom, stability. Love is not good or evil, it is not right or wrong, and it does not conform to any singular definition. It is all-consuming and knows no rule or tradition or expectation. Love is not black and white. It is the grey between, where there is no reason. Only a desperate need to hold on to that feeling of warmth, security, and home.

The corset is built into the bodice, giving my already curvy body more shape. The sleeves flare at the hands like trumpets, covering them completely and creating loose folds that swish with every movement. And the skirt itself offers a strip of gold down the centre, as if there was not enough satin for the red to join at the front, instead giving that material to a widening train.

But the back — the best part of the gown — reveals the tight corset, laced with gold ribbon. It matches the gold lacing that has been sewn onto every hem and the golden tiara resting atop my head, the rubies glittering in the light.

This morning, I am every bit the princess. It is such a shame I am dressed to impress a hall filled with nobles and high fae.

I enter the dining hall, where breakfast is to be served any moment, to find I am the last to arrive, and Father is about to begin his speech of welcome. My face remains neutral as I sweep through the hall towards the empty seat adjacent to Fayeth, but inside, I am quivering.

Father has that look in his eye. It is a look I have seen only thrice in my life, one of unfettered rage and the promise of retribution. He has not forgiven me for my outburst yesterday. I did not expect him to, but I had hoped.

"Well met, Father," I say, offering him a curtsey before taking my seat. "Fayeth, Rennyn."

They murmur their greetings, hardly sparing the time to pull themselves from the conversation the three of them share.

To distract myself from Father and his wrath, I run my eyes over everyone here.

Across from me, Rennyn is handsome in emerald. The colour brings out the brightness in his eyes, making him seem softer than is usual. There are shadows beneath his eyes, a sure sign he remained at the fair until the early hours of the morning. I did not see him there, but we threw the celebrations in his honour and I know Father would ensure he remained until the event wound down.

Beside him, the triplets and Jonik laugh and joke with Torin — with Torin beside me, I doubt this breakfast feast will be nothing short of eventful — and Vander who sit opposite. Jonik's mate, Leilani, sits silently with an amused smile playing on her plump lips.

Vander seems tense with Iker's mate, Yaryn, beside him, and Iker to her other side. Tenser still that he is in the same space as Tohminic, who sits at the end of the table seething beside his father. At least Father had half a mind to seat me well away from the Prince of Summer.

Standing rigid on the outskirts, too many lesser fae and guards watch over us all. They line the walls like statues, always watching, always listening. It is unnerving.

Father stands and clears his throat. "Well met, my friends. While feasts are common during a courtship, it is rare they occur so early. There is a reason I have called you here this morn. I am sure you are delighted to hear I have hastened the events of this dalliance."

Murmurs run the length of the table.

My spine straightens, my fingers curling in my lap.

"These things often take many moons," Father continues. "With the threat of war looming over us, I do not wish to linger on such trivial matters. Today, combat with both weapons and magic. In mere days, we venture into the forest to hunt. Then Bria will visit your homes."

Anger fights to be free as I shake my head. "No, I am afraid not."

"I saw it," says Vander. "I found it lacking."

He has dressed in his usual leather jacket today, which only intensifies his air of masculinity and strength. He is a High Lord, and his title demands the respect of those beneath him.

Fayeth does not offer him such grace. She sniffs, her nose lifting. "Your taste is unique in the Dusk Court. Tell me, Vander, what is quality entertainment where you are from?"

"I can't speak for my denizens, but *I* think insulting a member of your family is nothing short of disgusting. It's a petty attack that speaks volumes of your character."

"Watch your tongue," snarls Father. "I have allowed you entry to my home and lands. I will revoke that permission as easily as I gave it."

Vander turns back to his plate, seemingly uninterested in anything my father has to say.

It only serves to anger Father further. He jerks to his feet, his fist slamming against the wooden table. Just as he opens his mouth to speak, however, a chalice clatters to the table and a choking sound fills the silence.

All heads whip to the far end of the table, where Iker has two trembling hands clasped to his throat. Foam trickles from his gaping mouth, gathering in the corners before dribbling down his smooth chin. His body jerks and his eyes grow so wide, I catch a glimpse of dilated pupils.

His mate screams from beside him, her hands pulling at his arms. "Iker! What is it?"

Iker turns his face towards Yaryn, those wide eyes almost entirely black. He stands, pressing a hand into the table to keep his balance as his legs shake.

"Someone call for the healer!" shouts Tohminic, his chair skittering back as he stands. He wraps an arm around his father's shoulders. "Now!"

"There is no need," says Jonik, racing around the table. "Lie him down."

My hand flutters to my chest as Jonik kneels beside a convulsing Iker. The High Lord of Dawn is a tier two healer — he can heal physical injuries or ailments, but not completely if the fae is too far gone — and should have no issues healing Iker.

But when Jonik's hands hover over Iker's now still body, his brow creases in concern. He grits his teeth, smoky white light emanating from his fingers and seeping into Iker's pores, probing and searching for the cause of his illness.

Tasar skids to his knees beside his father — Larrad and Ulakas can heal only physical wounds — his white light joining his father's as they attempt to bring life back to Iker's body.

Everyone freezes. Not a word is uttered as we all watch and wait for Iker to recover.

My throat grows tight and I realise I am standing. I do not recall getting to my feet, and I do not recall Father moving from his own seat, as intent on Iker's recovery as I am.

He stands behind Rennyn, fists clenched at his sides and breathing hard. He narrows his emerald eyes to slits as reality sinks in, the realisation he may soon share a border with a court ruled by Tohminic.

While Summer has not been our ally under Iker's rule, the northern court has not been our enemy either. If he is to die today, they will crown Tohminic High Lord, and everything will change for the worse.

I send a silent prayer to the Mother Star, begging her to have mercy on Iker. If she has any compassion towards this land at all, any hope of saving Radelea, I am sure she will see the sense in Iker's soul remaining in his body.

"Heal him!" screams Yaryn, her hands flying into her hair. Her eyes are wide and panicked, crazed as they dance around the hall. "What are you waiting for, Dawn? Heal my mate!"

My heart breaks for her. Losing a mate is one of the most difficult things a fae can endure. Though not as devastating as losing a true mate, the loss of a chosen is still debilitating in its own regard.

I have read stories of mates losing their minds to the despair. I have read of their will to live fading. That is just the chosen mates, like Iker and Yaryn, like Father and Fayeth. True mates losing one another is utter destruction, plain and simple. If one dies, the other soon follows, lost without the other half of their soul.

"I.." Jonik starts, his hands shaking. "I cannot. He is too far gone."

"What are you saying?" Yaryn cries. "You are saying he is dead?"

Jonik stands and places both hands on Yaryn's shoulders. "He is not dead. At least, not yet. We have halted the spread of the poison. It could be mere moments before his heart fails him, or it could be days. You have time to say your goodbyes. I am very sorry."

"Sorry?" Tohminic's voice is a deadly whisper. "Your apology means *nothing*. Heal him, Dawn. You do not wish to make an enemy of the Summer Court."

Jonik raises his hands in surrender. "I have done all I can."

"You and you," says Father, pointing to two of the guards. "Move Lord Iker to the infirmary. Give Lady Yaryn anything she needs."

They dip their chins in acknowledgement and march from their places by the wall.

Yaryn screams at them to leave Iker be, clawing at their hands and arms as the males lift him and carry him away. It is a hard scene to observe, one which I hope to never experience for myself.

Tohminic and Yaryn rush after the guards, Tohminic spitting insults and threats as he leaves. Someone has poisoned his father on our land, brought him to the brink of death in our dining hall. He will not allow this to slide without further investigation. He will not rest until he finds justice.

"You," Father commands once more. "Collect Lord Iker's plate and chalice. Do not touch them with your bare hands. Deliver them to my study and stay with them until I arrive. Rennyn, you will support Tohminic in this difficult time. Fayeth, be a dear and console poor Yaryn."

Fayeth presses a light kiss to Father's cheek as she passes him. "Find whoever did this, Kerym."

Father growls, "If it is the last thing I do."

"What am I to do, Father?" I ask. "I would be glad to help in any way I can."

He does not face me as he says, "You are to hold court with the unmated females. I will send word if the tournament is to go ahead today."

Though I try to withhold the groan, I fail miserably. Holding court is the last thing I should do today. The threat of death is within our walls, and Father expects me to entertain the females? Am I so worthless I cannot so much as support a lady in mourning?

I call for Wyn as I enter my chambers. If I am to hold court with the unmated females, I would very much prefer my hair tied back, lest a fight erupt and my hair get pulled. The females are known to bicker, those venomous words flowing from their mouths to their palms if the argument carries on long enough. Especially if they are quarrelling over a male. And history believes the males are the ruthless, violent, antagonists.

"Yes, Bria?" She enters from my bedchamber, where she was likely making the bed or airing the chamber. "I thought you were at breakfast."

I sit in the seat by the window. "Can you please tie my hair back? Father has ordered me to hold court with the other unmated females. I am to distract them."

"From?" she asks, gathering my hair in her hands.

"High Lord Iker took ill at breakfast. Poison."

Her hands lower. "No. Are you serious?" When I dip my chin in acknowledgement, she breathes, "Fuck."

I turn in my seat and raise my eyebrows.

She forces me back around. "It's like 'blessed Mother Star', I suppose. An exclamation."

"Where did you learn such language?"

"I can't say. When you're safe in the Dusk Court, we'll tell you everything. Until then, you'll just have to accept our strange way of talking and get used to it." She twists some of my copper locks to the back of my head. "All up or half?"

"All, please. I cannot believe what happened to Iker. Who do you think did it?"

She contemplates my question for a moment before saying, "You know the servants whisper among themselves. There have been rumours over the past two days of Iker softening towards the idea of helping your father take rule of the Dusk Court. I think someone doesn't like the thought of two of the largest courts forming an alliance. That, or it was Tohminic."

I stiffen. "He would not dare."

"After everything he's done to you, the threats he's spewed, do you honestly believe he wouldn't stoop as low as murdering his own flesh and blood? You know I'm always honest. I'll always say what's on my mind. So forgive me when I say you're being daft if you refuse to believe he'd do something so unforgivable."

A few moments later, she has finished pinning my hair away from my face. She is not a true hand maiden, yet she has extraordinary skill.

"Wyn," I begin as I open the door, "Father has moved the timeline of my courtship forward. The males will fight today. I thought you would wish to know."

"Vander will be fine." Though her words are confident, her eyes flash with concern.

⁂

"And so, if you would believe it," I say to Princess Xaria, "an axe flew from nowhere and stuck into the beast's head."

She gasps, her hand flying to her mouth. "What did you do?"

"The disgusting creature dropped me. I scrambled away before he collapsed, right where I had landed. I will never forget High Lord Vander's words. *You alright, Princess?* They comfort me in my dreams." I'm exaggerating, of course, but holding court requires me to keep the females entertained.

"He certainly has a strange way of speaking," says Xaria. As High Lord Jonik's niece, she resembles the royal family of Dawn a little too much. Her almond-shaped eyes are dark and gentle, her glossy ebony hair straight as a pin.

I smile. "I have yet to spend much time with him, but from what I have noticed, he *contracts* his words." My eyes flick around as if I hope none of the other females heard. "He will say things like don't instead of do not. It is... confusing."

She sips at her wine, a pale pink liquid that matches her gown. "I have always enjoyed the tales you weave. You bring a certain brightness to these events."

"Thank you, Xaria. That means a lot to me."

I run my eyes over the small drawing room — I have always detested this space, with its blood-red walls, gilded frames, and vaulted ceiling — ensuring the rest of the females are not dying of boredom. Why the males force us to endure the company of fae we would rather not associate with is beyond me.

Though, given the males refuse to allow us any real responsibility, I do suppose they believe this is a kindness.

My eyes snag on a female with chestnut hair I have not yet met, and I make my excuses to Xaria before flitting through the room towards the newcomer.

"Well met," I say, smiling. "I am Princess Bria Sutherland."

"Chlora." Her eyes are a blue so bright, I am reminded of the glittering ocean at noontime. But where the ocean is calm and sparkling with life, Chlora's eyes are roaring waves of chaos which threaten to smother. "My father is Lord Iker's Commander General."

A male of discipline. Commander General is the highest rank any fae army offers. Chlora's father is the male responsible for training, commanding, and deploying Summer's armed forces. Foot soldiers in the infantry, the armada, and the horseback cavalry all answer to him. If we ever go to war, he will be the one to order the troops to invade our lands, to murder our denizens and ravage our villages.

"An admirable way to spend one's life." The words are ash on my tongue. "How are you enjoying the Autumn Court?"

"It is rather enjoyable. Though not nearly as pleasant as home."

Ah, a compliment preceding an insult. It speaks volumes of her character.

"Do tell, Chlora, how we could improve. I would very much like for you to enjoy your time here."

"There is little *you* can do," she says, waves of fury crashing in her eyes. "Other than beg the Mother Star for mercy if you choose Tohminic as your mate, of course."

I force my eyes to remain still and not roll towards the heavens. Tohminic mentioned a lover. If Chlora believes I willingly choose him, she is as deluded as the male she loves. A powerful urge to fling stinging words at her overwhelms me.

"Such nasty business with Lord Iker," I say, my words cutting. "I do hope Father catches whoever is responsible and brings them to justice. He believes he is close to discovering the culprit." It is a lie. I have not spoken to Father since breakfast.

Her face twitches, her eyes darting around as she leans closer. "Back off, bastard. You know nothing."

I am saved a scathing response by the arrival of Father's messenger. He stands by the door, a scroll of parchment clenched in his hand.

"This has been illuminating, Chlora." I turn my back on the Summer fae before she can respond, knowing it to be considered offensive. The knowledge makes me smile.

Father's messenger brings news of the tournament going ahead, regardless of Iker's declining health. According to the note, Tohminic has stated a distraction is both welcome and needed. Or perhaps he wishes Father's attention lie elsewhere.

17

THE LIST FIELD IS buzzing with activity when I arrive with the other females. The roped-off area reserved for magical jousting has been transformed to an arena, with tiered seats lining the perimeter. Five males stand before a short tower lined with orange and gold, Father, Fayeth, and Rennyn looking down on them from above.

I peel away from the other females and ascend the rickety steps behind the royal stand, two ribbons gripped in my fist. I am required to gift them to two of the males under the promise he will return the ribbon upon victory.

"Well met, Father," I say, taking my seat on his right. It is the only time he will grant me the privilege. "It surprised me to hear the tournament is going ahead."

"Tohminic was quite determined," he says, jutting his chin towards the males. "Have you made your selection?"

I dip my chin in acquiescence. "Vander and Larrad." It does not matter which of the triplets I choose, because they come as a package deal. Wishing one of them well is wishing them all success.

"Very well." He stands, his voice magically booming over the list field as he welcomes the spectators and competitors.

"Bria has chosen two males to gift with her well wishes. Prince Tohminic of the Summer Court and High Lord Vander of the Dusk Court, step forward."

I bristle with anger. How dare he choose on my behalf.

The two males step closer to the base of the stand. They will catch the lengths of silk; if they do not, it is to be considered a sign the Mother Star does not bless the union.

I rise with one length of gold in each hand. Holding my fists over the edge, I release the shining strips, watching them flutter to the ground. The gold catches the light, and the fabric seems to blaze as the twin ribbons catch a slight breeze and entwine together, both of them landing in Vander's waiting palm.

I huff a laugh, clapping with the rest of the crowd.

Tohminic is not impressed. His face screws in anger, and he accuses Vander of using his air magic to cheat. There is little he can do without proof. How can you prove Vander influenced the wind when the Dusk Lord did not so much as twitch?

Vander shrugs, claims that if he *did* use his powers, there is no rule stating he cannot do such a thing. He dismisses Tohminic and saunters to the wooden bench to the side, where he will wait until Father calls him to combat.

Father, with his cheeks reddened from rage, shouts, "For Bria's honour, these males will fight to prove their courage and strength. Once a winner has been determined, they will fight with magic to prove their ability to protect. In five moons' time, they will hunt and show their ability to provide. Winner draws first blood. Begin!"

The crowd erupts with cheers and applause as four guards blow a long note on their bugles, urging Tasar and Tohminic to walk to the centre of the list field. The area is nothing but loose dirt and rock with a crude red line bisecting the space.

Tohminic draws a long sword that makes Tasar's bow seem almost laughable. The moment Tohminic grows near, the fight will be over.

My assumption is proven correct not five heartbeats later, when Tohminic slices the bow into two uneven pieces, the blade following through until it collides with Tasar's arm.

I cannot say I enjoy the males fighting with weapons. The clang of metal against metal rings in my ears — I am sure I will hear echoes of the sound for days to come — the potent scents of sweat and blood permeate the air, and the gasps and cheers of the crowd grow irksome. Though when it comes to the last pairing, I sit straighter in my seat.

Father will crown the winner of this duel as the victor.

Tohminic circles Vander, his sword gripped tight in his hand, a smear of blood gleaming from the silver blade.

Vander, with my two ribbons tied to his black gambeson, readjusts his grip on his axe, his knuckles turning white with strain. His silver eyes are intent on Tohminic's face as he carefully moves sideways, countering the Summer lord's movements.

Tohminic lunges, bringing his sword slicing forward on an angle towards Vander's hip. The grunt he releases upon the collision of his weapon against Vander's axe is guttural.

There is no space in my mind for thoughts, no space for anything other than concentrating on the two males circling one another once more. I suck my bottom lip into my mouth, biting down and drawing blood. The anticipation and anxiety are unbearable.

Vander's feet move with smooth agility as he dances from Tohminic's reach, a mocking smile curving his full lips. He twirls his axe in his hand, blocking Tohminic's every attempt at slicing into his skin.

While Tohminic wields his long sword with brute force, Vander's axe is an extension of his arm. He is graceful as he swings the blade down and around, as if his purpose in life is to bring grace to the axe, a weapon often seen as belonging to those of lesser status.

Tohminic slices his sword through the air in a figure eight before jutting it forward, using an enormous step as momentum. A small cloud of dust kicks up around his leather boots, hiding them from view.

Vander avoids the sharp blade by curling his back over, as if he intends to plant his hands on the ground and walk on all fours like an animal. The sight of his back arched in such a way makes my stomach churn, and I slap my hands over my face, peeking through a gap in my fingers. My heart pounds, the poor thing struggling to handle so much excitement and nervous anticipation.

The males continue to dance around one another, the clang of their weapons and their ragged pants the only sound in the list field. It goes on for too long — they are so perfectly matched — and the crowd grows restless.

Looking closer, I note Tohminic's increasing anger. I flick my eyes to Vander as he twists away from yet another jab, huffing a laugh when I realise he is still taunting his opponent. He glances my way while Tohminic regains his footing, and I give him a look that says *hurry it along, Lord.*

He cocks an eyebrow, bowing in mocking acceptance of my expression.

This time, when Tohminic lunges, the Dusk lord does not evade the attack.

He lifts his axe until it reaches shoulder height while putting his weight on his left leg, then he steps forward and a little to the side with his right and brings the axe swinging down towards Tohminic's shoulder, imbedding it in the flesh of his arm before ripping it free.

Tohminic roars — the sound pained and filled with fury — as his hand slams over the wound, crimson seeping through his fingers.

"We have a victor!" It is difficult to hear Father's shout over the cacophony of noise from the spectators. "Vander of Dusk has proven his courage and strength. Congratulations to you, High Lord."

Vander swings the hand still gripping the axe across his body, bowing over his arm towards the crowd on his left, then his right, before finally bowing for Father.

Behind him, Tohminic throws his sword aside and stalks from the field, his hand still gripping the wound on his arm.

I nod to the two guards on either side of the infirmary tent, and they each pull one side of the loose canvas away, revealing the mayhem inside.

Five cots, each of them occupied by one of my prospective mates, take up the far length of the tent. To my right, five guards — if Torin could be called that — watching their charges intently, their eagle eyes flicking over the space every so often. To the left, three harried Dawn Court healers.

The five males are arguing with a fierceness I wish I could hide from. From what I gather of their concerns, Tohminic has accused Vander of being a cheat. I am not surprised by his reaction to losing, not at all.

"You all look a little worse for wear," I say, smiling and dragging their attention to me. If I could avoid this part of my duties, I would. "You all fought with exceptional bravery."

Ulakas snorts. "It is not brave to duel for a female's heart. Foolish, yes. Brave? No. We would all rather court you with flowers and sweet words."

"Speak for yourself, brother," says Tasar. "I did not believe you to be a sore loser."

Ulakas reaches across to his brother's cot and shoves him to the floor. "Says you, who fell beneath my blade. May the Mother Star curse you with blisters on your cock."

Larrad roars with laughter, his dark eyes sparking with mischief.

I step forward, cutting their antics short. If I allow them to, their jesting will carry on well into the night. "Father has decided two of you will be removed from the courtship after tonight's magic duels. I am very sorry for the haste in which we conduct this. The stars know I wish we had more time to get to know one another."

Vander shakes his head. "Kerym's need to hurry this along is understandable."

Tohminic says, "I am surprised you see that, Dusk, considering he wishes this to be over to allow more time to plan the downfall of your court."

Before another argument can ensue, I curtsey and say, "I wish you luck in the coming duels. Fight with honour." I spin and dash from the infirmary tent before any of them realise what is happening.

My own tent, a small space of ivory canvas, is a mere twelve paces away. Close enough that I will hear any shouted arguments. I can only hope the males retire to their individual tents before that can happen.

"There you are," says Wyn as I enter. "How's Vander?"

"You were right to say he would do well. I have not seen a male move with such grace, especially with an axe as a weapon. He is the only male who did not require healing. He is fine."

Her relief is clear as she adjusts the fur draped over the wooden seat in the corner. "I think I'll watch the magic duels. I can't stand not knowing."

"Use an illusion. If Fayeth realises you are Vander's sister, or worse, catches a hand maiden avoiding her duties, you will be out of this court before you can blink. I believe neither of us wants that."

She pours iced water into a chalice, adds a slice of lemon, and hands it to me. "Fayeth's hand maid helped me set up your tent. Iker's getting worse, and apparently, Tohminic refuses to be near him."

I collapse into the fur-lined chair. "I met his lover, Chlora. She's a..." I lower my voice to a whisper. "She's a real jerk."

We spend the next few moments discussing Chlora. Wyn calls her a bitch, whatever that means. I do not ask, deciding the way they talk in Dusk is not my concern until I am there. If I learn to talk as they do, if I allow that hope to blossom, it will only hurt more if Father forces me to mate with Tohminic or one of the triplets.

It is not long before Father sends a messenger requesting my presence for a family meal before the magic duels commence. I would much rather eat in my tent, but angering my father today — after Iker and my reluctance to grace Tohminic with a ribbon — would not be smart.

So, I swallow my protest, slip on my cloak, and join my so-called family on the royal stand, where two maids are already serving dinner. With the dying light of day, a bitter chill is creeping over the court, and I am thankful for the warmth the lamb stew will offer.

The moment I take my seat beside Father, a long table is placed over our knees, the maids quickly setting the stew, steaming rice, and buttered rolls down before filling our chalices with wine and disappearing.

I do hope they find a moment to fill their stomachs and wet their mouths.

"Tohminic should do well tonight," says Rennyn, spooning lamb and gravy onto his bread roll before biting into it.

Father makes a sound of acknowledgement and sips at his wine. "I believe he will emerge victorious. The light and healing magic of the Dawn Court will do little against his fire and necromancy. I am not so sure of the illusions and wind of Dusk."

"The air might feed the fire," I say, spearing a carrot. "Unless Lord Vander can use his illusions, I agree Tohminic will end the night victorious."

"After everything he has said and done over the past moons, I am hesitant to support him," says Father.

My lips part, and a jolt of surprise tingles through my body, trapping a breath in my lungs. If I agree with Father's words, it is likely he will rescind them out of spite — or Fayeth will fight for the opposite — so I remain calm and still, but continue to eat while straining my ears to listen.

"You may be right, Father. He has proven his lack of consideration and has a blatant disregard for our rule," says Rennyn. "Though, I wonder if we would benefit from allying with Summer."

"If we join forces, we will be the most powerful courts in Radelea," says Fayeth. Though I am not looking her way, I feel her cunning eyes on me as she says, "Not to mention, if that dastardly ogre had mauled Bria, Tohminic is likely the only male who would not mind the scars."

I swear Ren snorts under his breath, though from so far away, I cannot be sure. The mention of the ogre makes me wonder if Fayeth had anything to do with the attack. She has, in the past, had her guards follow me. If she had known I was in the redwood forest, she could have ordered a servant to use their animalistic magic to control the ghastly creature. I shove the thoughts away. She would not do such a thing, and I am foolish to believe so.

As they continue to discuss the merits of each male — as if my opinion does not matter — I am acutely aware of every word, every movement. I note Father softening towards their words, Rennyn's determination to voice Tohminic's positive attributes, and the hint of cruel intention in Fayeth's voice. The more they talk, the less hope blooms in my chest. By the time the maids have cleared our plates, not a single shred of hope remains.

Father agrees with them.

I cannot help but feel a sting of betrayal. Rennyn and I have never argued, and we have never so much as whipped cutting words at one another. In fact, I have always felt as though he is the only fae in this court who would defend me. Now, I am not so sure. Perhaps celebrating his one hundredth born day altered the way he thinks, altered the core of his being. Or has he always been this way?

I am unaware as our guards throw invisible barriers around the royal stand, leaving the denizens in the stands below to fend for themselves against the magic that will blast through the list field within moments. Father's shout of welcome and the brief explanation of rules he offers both fall on deaf ears as my mind spirals.

Rennyn was supposed to be the one fae I could count on here. He is my brother, and he is supposed to love and support me no matter what. He said as much the day I told him about Nikolai.

So why do I feel as though our relationship is nothing but a lie? Why is it, when I need him most, his loyalty lies with Father and Fayeth?

Father clears his throat and nudges me with his foot.

I pull myself from all thoughts of my brother and stand, facing the five males below. "After tonight's duels, two of you will prove unworthy of my love." My mind cringes at the words Father is forcing me to speak. "It is the way of life, survival of the fittest. I wish you luck and delight in witnessing your power. Begin!"

First up, Father has two of the triplets on the field. I cannot tell who is who from here, but according to Father, Tasar and Larrad will be an even match.

After several long moments of beams of light being thrown back and forth, one tense moment when the crowd is thrown into blazing brightness, and a clever net of golden rays, I am enraptured. The males react as if reading the thoughts of the other, volleying attacks back and forth while chuckling.

Their easy going nature brings a smile to my face that only grows larger with every shout of encouragement and dissuasion from Ulakas. It seems as if he favours Tasar to win, but perhaps he knows he can beat that brother.

The Mother Star is sinking beyond the horizon, painting the sky with streaks of teal and indigo and an orange so bright it's blinding, when Father grows tired of the repetition and calls it an even match.

The crowd cheers in approval as Tohminic and Ulakas stalk onto the field. Fae lights shine from above, casting a bluish glow over the scene that only adds to the excitement.

Tohminic appears unaffected by the crowd, the imminent battle, and the scrutiny of my father as he adjusts his leather tunic and massages the palm of his hand in preparation. His eyes are golden, reflecting the sunset, and he has never looked more dangerous than he does at this moment.

Father calls for action, and in the same heartbeat, Tohminic throws four orbs of crackling fire at Ulakas.

The duel is over before it begins.

Larrad and Tasar meet the same fate, the former receiving burns from a fiery spear, the latter succumbing to Tohminic's blast of intense heat.

The crowd goes silent when Vander saunters onto the list field, a kind of darkness swirling around him with the twilight sky as his backdrop. He looks as if he was born for the moment. His silver eyes glitter like the stars we love so much as he faces Tohminic. The idea of meeting the same fate as the triplets does not trouble Vander, he does not fear Tohminic's wrath.

At Father's call for them to begin, neither male moves. They stare at one another, assessing and contemplating as the world around them goes still.

My breath freezes in my chest and my heart pounds in anticipation. My eyes are so wide they might just roll from their sockets.

Then, as if called forward by the Mother Star herself, they move as one.

Tohminic sends a wall of blistering fire straight for Vander, the heat palpable even through the guards' shield surrounding the royal stand. It roars as it tracks across the field, crimson and amber and the brightest of whites.

Vander sweeps his hands through the air before him, crossing them over with his fingers splayed as he creates a churning tornado. The tornado, fierce in its power, rips through the wall of fire with ease.

Screams from the crowd cause me to peel my eyes from the males to observe the scattering denizens. Wind rips at loose strands of their hair and embers catch on their woollen clothes. Some linger far enough back that the magic will not injure them further, though most of them tear across the spongy grass for the castle walls, too frightened to linger and await Father's announcement of the victor.

I would join those fleeing if I could. The males are so stubborn, so filled with hatred for one another, that I fear this might end in tragedy for both Summer and Dusk.

Tohminic wields fireballs, tornados of glowing embers, and swords of flame. Each coming too close to Vander for comfort.

My stomach drops impossibly further as my eyes track a high-pressure jet of air. Vander seems to almost fly as his wind power throws dust and pebbles across the field.

On and on it goes until the scene disappears, replaced by a buzzing wetland. Fat trees that seem to be made of nothing but reaching roots as far as the eye can see, thick mud that reeks of decay, and mossy rocks that are slick and dangerous.

I am not the only fae to witness the illusion.

Everyone gasps. Everyone.

The power Vander wields... It is frightening.

When Tohminic uses his necromancy magic to drag a decaying body from the depths of the earth, commanding it to call for its kin and attack, Father decides we have seen enough. He stands and shouts for a ceasefire, claiming the duel is too close to determine a winner.

He decides Ulakas and Larrad have not shown him proof of their strength and valour, and orders them back to the Dawn

Father notices my approach and peels away from the group, meeting me out of earshot.

"What is it, Father?" I ask, pulling my cloak tighter around me. The clouds swirl overhead, a sure sign Father's emotions are warring within him. "Has something happened?"

"I have cancelled the hunting trip. High Lord Iker has succumbed to the poison. He died as the Mother Star rose." Father's tone does not reveal a shred of sympathy or sadness. "Prince Tohminic has returned home to oversee his father's farewell and claim the crown. In light of this, I offered him the chance to bow out of the courtship, to which he refused. In fact, he was adamant you shall still visit his court."

Any hope I have of using Iker's death to avoid mating with Tohminic dies before it blooms.

Tohminic is the High Lord of Summer.

My chance at finding happiness elsewhere is little more than a speck of light in a world of impenetrable darkness.

"You leave for Dawn at first light," says Father, his tone leaving no room for argument.

"Is it necessary for me to leave so soon?" If I can remain in Autumn while Tohminic handles his father's death, my chances of convincing Father of Dusk's merits increases tenfold. "Perhaps it would be better for me to remain here, to help with any fallout that may arise. A High Lord dying on our lands is sure to create dissent among the courts."

"You will leave at first light," he growls. Already on edge, Father is in no mood to deal with my pouting.

His eyes track a stable hand leading his horse, Tycho, back to the stables. Using it as the perfect opportunity to cut our conversation short, he hurries away, shouting for the poor horse handler. "You! Have you removed the sacks and bed roll?"

Alone on the outskirts of the other males, I am unsure what my next move is. Do I comfort those remaining, or do I retire to my chambers and help Wyn pack for my trip to Dawn?

The look on Vander's face makes my decision for me — the crease between his brows is severe as he frowns at the eastern horizon — and I bunch my skirts, hurrying over to where he stands a little away from Torin, Tasar, and the handful of guards still discussing Iker's death.

"What bothers you, Lord Vander?"

He tears his gaze from the lapis lazuli sky. "Wyn said the servants were whispering among themselves. One of your maids found hemlock in Tohminic's chambers. It's a little too convenient, don't you think?"

"We have already surmised Tohminic is responsible for Iker's death. Was it hemlock poisoning then?" They drum the poisonous plants of Radelea into us from a young age to ensure no fae ingests the pretty white hemlock flowers by accident. An easy feat, given they look astonishingly similar to parsley flowers.

"It would seem so," he says, his lips flattening to a hard line.

"But you do not believe it was Tohminic?"

His eyes lock with mine, silver clashing with emerald. "Finding the plant in his chambers is too obvious. If he did poison his father, he'd get rid of the evidence. He'd be foolish not to."

"Then we have a murderer within our walls who walks free. I wonder who would stoop so low."

"We may never know."

I leave him to his thoughts, walking back through the outer bailey and heading towards the stables. If I am to travel to Dawn tomorrow at first light, I need to be sure Solana is ready. Though it is possible to fold there from Autumn, the courts are quite the distance apart. With such a large travelling party — the triplets and their hands, myself, Wyn, and the guards — it is more likely we will travel by horse and wagon. It will be two or three moons before we reach Jonik's castle, and it has been a while since Solana made such a long trip.

The comforting scent of old leather, manure, hay, and that mellow scent of horses tickles my nose, and I breathe deeply to enjoy the moment before wandering through the stables to Solana's stall.

"Hello, beautiful," I say, holding my palm out for her to sniff.

She snorts in response, scraping her hoof against the hay-strewn floor.

"I know. It has been too long. Tomorrow, we are travelling with the Dawn males to their home. It will be a long walk, likely two or three days." I run my hand down her neck. "We will enjoy the freedom of the forests and plains, possibly cross a creek or two."

She whinnies. It makes me smile so wide my cheeks hurt.

"Excuse me, miss, but you can't be in here." The stable hand's voice is firm. "I must ask you to leave at once. These horses belong to the High Lord and his family."

"I do not believe it will be a problem," I say, turning towards him.

His greenish skin pales. "My apologies, Princess Bria."

"That is quite alright." My smile is genuine. "You are just doing your job. I expect nothing less. I am taking a trip tomorrow. Has Father informed you?"

He bows his head, some colour returning to his cheeks. "Indeed. Solana will be groomed and ready at the rising of the sun."

"You have my thanks." I turn to leave, adding, "Please pack extra apples for her."

I am slow to wander back through the inner bailey towards the castle doors, hearing nothing but talk of Iker's death among the lesser fae who serve the court. Forgers and horse handlers and seamstresses all rush to inform one another of the news, whispering their thoughts on who is responsible and what will happen now.

I wonder right alongside them.

The death of a High Lord is no small thing. The death of a High Lord in the castle of another is reason enough to incite war. With the tension surrounding Dusk's reveal and the hope of many courts to claim that land for themselves — regardless of the fae living there — things in Radelea are already beginning to crumble. This could shatter the realm entirely.

Inside is no better, with the maids and guards muttering amongst themselves. It takes only five steps through the grand foyer to grow tired of the whisperings.

In my hope to find a moment of peace from the constant murmurs, I find myself standing outside the lecture hall, listening while another fae reads a tome on the history of the Winter Court to my students — they are discussing Lord Ruith's mate, Uma, and how she refuses to leave the castle. My heart aches for the lost responsibility — if I could take the younglings with me when Father chooses my mate, I would.

I steel my spine and knock on the door before letting myself in. "My darlings," I say, a warm smile pulling at my cheeks. I do not feel the joy I portray, yet I am expected to be nothing other than ecstatic about my hand in life.

"Bria!" Mykaela calls. "We have missed you."

"And I have missed you. Unfortunately, I do not think I will return to you. Father is sending me to the Dawn Court tomorrow, and from there, I will venture to Dusk and Summer."

Dey does not appear impressed. They have a distinct frown and creased brow. "You do not wish to continue teaching us?"

"It is not that." My frown matches Dey's. "While I would very much like to continue educating you on the history of Radelea, my duties as the High Lord's daughter are considered more important right now, especially with the threat of war hanging over our heads."

"Then why are you here?" asks Dillon.

"I wished to say goodbye and wish you well. Know I will think of you often, and I will write to Father asking of your progress. Do not think I will forget you. It is impossible."

They all smile at that, Hamon the largest, and I leave with my heart a little lighter. Knowing my younglings understand the love I have for them will get me through the toughest of times while I visit the other courts, more so than the thought of my father, Fayeth, and Rennyn.

I have not seen my brother since the duels, and I wonder if he is avoiding me. He shoulders more responsibility now he is one hundred, though I do not believe he has no time to sit with me for a cup of peppermint tea. The distance between us is greater than I thought. Rennyn does not yearn to strengthen our relationship, as I do.

As I make my way to my chambers in the western wing, I vow to find time to sit with him upon my return. I will not leave the Autumn Court without Rennyn at least promising to write once a full moon.

When I enter my chambers at last, Wyn is dragging my travel cases into my bedchamber. She pauses mid heave, those silver eyes rolling. "Why are these things so damn heavy?"

"Because they are made of wood and metal, I suppose. You could call for a guard to move it."

She huffs, "I'm nearly done. There's no point waiting for a guard." She grunts and yanks on the case once more, pulling it a hand's length closer to my bedchamber. "This will do, won't it? It's not in the way?"

It is most definitely in the way, resting a mere sword's length from the door. I shake my head and say, "It will be fine where it is. Do you have a case of your own?"

"I have a sack. It'll do." She kicks open the lid of the chest. "What's the weather like in Dawn?"

"Mild with gusty winds. It is known for their morning dew and misty nights. I will need several cloaks and sleeves on my gowns." I open the armoire. "And a hat and shawl."

She plops a leather sack on the bed. "And for travelling?"

"The thickest cloak I own and three comfortable gowns."

"You don't ride in pants?"

I freeze. "You *do*?"

We turn towards one another, each of us just as baffled as the other. I have never heard of such a thing as a female wearing pants, even while riding. It is unbecoming.

Wyn shakes her head. "There's no reason a female should always wear a gown. It's ridiculous. We wear whatever we want in Dusk."

"I have never tried pants before. Perhaps I could borrow some when I visit Dusk. For the sake of curiosity, of course." I worry at my bottom lip. "Though I am not certain they would be comfortable. All that fabric so close to my legs..."

"How's it different from being in bed, with the blankets twisted around you? I've spent many mornings waking you, and let me assure you, I've never seen someone become so tangled in their sleep."

"I'm sure you have." The laugh which bubbles free is both surprising and welcome.

She pushes me aside, so she has access to the armoire. "So, plain gowns and cloaks? What about a ball gown?"

"This is much too difficult," I groan. "How am I to know what I need in Dawn? There could be a heat wave or torrential rain."

"Leave it to me," she says, taking an emerald gown and folding it neatly. "There's tea in the sitting room."

"Are you sure? I don't mind helping."

She waves me off. "This is my job. As much as it's a lie, if I don't do all this, your father will replace me. Just like he did your previous hand maiden."

The reminder of Lymsia makes my heart clench with sadness. I must remember to send her a fruit basket or something of the like to show my appreciation for her years of dealing with me. Between the ages of forty and sixty were not my best years. Lymsia spent many an evening calming my adolescent fury and placing sacks of warmed lavender beneath my pillows to help me sleep.

I pour the steaming tea into a glass chalice — a new design I adore — the scents of lemon and ginger chasing away the ache of Lymsia's departure. A satchel of lavender would be wonderful for the trip to Dawn.

Often times, I find it difficult to give in to slumber in the depths of the forest, and the ride will most certainly take us through the forest which borders Day and Summer.

"Wyn?" I call, setting the warm glass down. "When you are finished with the travel cases, I would very much like to visit the herb master in the eastern village. Would you care to accompany me?"

She pokes her head through the door. "What do you need?"

"Lavender," I say, smiling, "to help me sleep." I don't add that the scent alone will calm my jaded soul, bringing memories of home and safety in a world of unknowns and strange fae.

❧ ❧

"It is just around this bend," I tell Wyn, clutching my cloak tighter. The winds are ferocious this evening, reflecting Father's frustration and unease.

He has been in meetings with the nobles all day, trying to avoid confrontation with Summer over the death of their High Lord. Word from the servants is High Lord Tohminic — he has already assigned himself the title — sent a messenger declaring us enemies of his court.

It is the last thing Father needs.

What I do not understand is the stipulation Tohminic placed at the end of his scroll. *Our courts shall remain enemies until my mating with Princess Bria, when I will meet with High Lord Kerym to discuss the possibility of alliance.*

In other words, he and his court will be enemies of Autumn, and likely declare war on us, if Father does not agree to offer his daughter to the Summer High Lord. With a sizable dowry, too.

Wyn holds open the door to the herb master's store for me. It is a weathered timber door which has seen better days. The herbaceous scent that wafts from inside is overpowering.

"May I help you?" The aged male stops trimming a sprig of cedar as I enter the warmth of the store. "Princess Bria. How lovely to see you."

"Well met." I take in the store, noting the array of green. I cannot determine the difference between most of the herbs, but I recognise the basil, sage, and chamomile. Turning back to the bronze-skinned male, I ask, "Have you any lavender?"

"Of course. May I ask what you intend to use it for?"

"I am to travel to the Dawn Court come morning. Sleeping in the forest is difficult for me. I merely wish to ease myself into slumber."

His smile is warm. "Shall I wrap it in hessian for you? It will be easier to transport and should keep the bees away. Nothing worse than a sting on the cheek while you are trying to sleep."

"That would be lovely, thank you."

He hums while he gathers a bundle of the purple flowers, wraps them in beige fabric, and ties it with a white ribbon. "I must say, two members of the High Lord's family in as many moons is a rare occurrence."

"Whatever do you mean?"

Wyn stiffens beside me, her brows pinching as she listens for the herb master's answer.

He hands me the bundle, accepting a silver coin as payment. "High Lady Fayeth was here two mornings ago. She had need of parsley flowers."

I thank him for his time and effort, and slip into the twilight outside, wondering why Fayeth would need parsley flowers. Unless she planted them in Tohminic's chambers — the servants would not know the difference between the parsley and hemlock — hoping to create the rumour he killed his father, there's no reason for it.

This whole thing is getting stranger by the day.

19

THE WAGON IS READY to go by the time I exit the court and approach the outer bailey. It is quite amazing how a wooden board with a large wheel on either side can hold so much weight. My two travel cases are but a small portion of the cargo, with the triplets' cases, the maids' and guards' cases, and several crates filled with food, all neatly tucked beneath a canvas cover.

"Everything is ready to go, Princess Bria," says one of the stable hands, a muscular male with warm brown skin. "We will connect the horse harnesses to the wagon shafts, and then you are set to leave."

"Thank you." The smile I offer the hand is tight. I would much rather remain in Autumn than spend days riding with the Dawn triplets then endure their jesting for seven moons at their castle.

Father has not yet arrived to bid me farewell. It would be disrespectful to mount my horse before he is here, so I settle for running a hand down Solana's golden brown fur. Someone has braided her flaxen mane, and my smile turns genuine that she and I match — Wyn tied my hair back with two braids this morning, hoping to keep the copper strands from my face.

"Are you ready for a trip?" I ask her, twisting so I am standing in front of her and laughing when she grunts. "Perhaps we will find a nice open plain to run through. It has been a while since you stretched your legs."

"Talking to your horse again, I see."

I turn to Rennyn, my smile slipping. "What are you doing here?"

He holds a hand to his chest. "You wound me, sister. I have come to bid you farewell and wish you success on your journey."

Turning back to Solana, I continue running my hand over the curve of her shoulder. "You should wish me luck, not success. Father is aware of my preference for Dusk, yet he is determined to see this ridiculous courtship out."

"You have a duty to the court," says Father, approaching from behind. "You would do well to remember your responsibilities."

"Responsibilities I did not ask for. If you hate me so, why not send me to my birth mother and let her deal with me?"

I do not miss Rennyn's hiss of breath. He, like everyone, knows the topic of my mother is a sore spot for Father. I am pushing too far by asking. I know that. Yet, I cannot help it. My life would be better in the Spring Court, regardless of Mother's social standing.

"May the Mother Star bless your travels," Father grits out.

By the time I have turned around, he is halfway back to the castle doors, his cloak swishing behind him.

A ragged sigh slips past my lips. "He will never tell me who she is, will he?" I ask to no one in particular.

Rennyn takes it upon himself to answer. "Best just forget about her."

"It is difficult to not wonder about the female who brought me into this world, Ren. I am always wondering if she caressed her swollen stomach while envisioning my life, or if she smiled when I kicked from inside her for the first time. Does she think of me now, regretting her decision to leave me with *him,* or is she glad I am not a burden?"

"All questions you will never know the answer to. Push them from your mind. Wondering only leads to heartache." There's a hint of something in his hazel eyes, an emotion I cannot quite place. "You have my well wishes for your journey, sister." With that, he turns and follows in Father's footsteps.

I sigh and gesture for the stable hand to place the step beside Solana, fighting to keep my thoughts from the emotion I saw glinting in Rennyn's eyes. We have never discussed my mother, too scared of Father's rection to so much as utter *Spring Court* in case the walls listen in. Although, I wonder if it has only been me who is too scared to talk about it, and whether Rennyn does not wish to speak of it because he knows more than he lets on.

The thought follows me as I pull myself onto Solana's back, settling into the leather saddle and hooking my feet into the stirrups. I wrap the reins around my hands, a habit the horse master could never break when I was learning to ride. There's something about the security of the leather around my hand that centres me.

Three midnight black horses pull to a stop beside me, each stallion carrying a Dawn triplet. Dark eyes assess Solana, the horse closest to her dismissing my beautiful mare with a snort.

"It seems we have some competition," I say, giving Solana a quick pat.

"Pay him no mind," says the triplet closest, Tasar, I think. "He is always a touch temperamental in the mornings."

His horse nickers.

"Shall we begin the long and odious journey?" Tasar asks, a smirk playing on his lips. "We hope to reach the border between Summer and Day by nightfall."

"It is a futile hope. If we are to avoid the hills of Summer — which we should, if we do not wish to tire the horses — our only option is to take the coastal track."

Tasar's face contorts in anger. It is the first time I have seen such an emotion on any of the triplets' faces. "We do not have permission to linger. High Lord Tohminic granted us passage through his lands and nothing more."

I throw a quick look to Wyn, where she sits upon a chestnut mare, and roll my eyes before turning back to Tasar. "The hills it is, then. You are right, it is best we leave." I glance at the rising sun. "We are already cutting it fine."

He nods to a pair of guards, who jerk on the reins of their horses and set out at a trot. Wyn and the triplets' private hands follow, all riding identical horses of chestnut with ebony manes. I ride beside Tasar, with Ulakas and Larrad — who have remained in the Autumn Court to support their brother — laughing with one another behind. The wagon, pulled by two horses who are being led by two stable hands, creaks as it rolls forward, leading two more guards who take the rear of our large party.

Fourteen horses, fourteen fae. Four royals, four hands, four guards, two stable hands, and one wagon. The size of the entourage makes me nervous. If we run into any trouble on the road, it is not likely we will find luck in hiding. And we are to travel through the Summer Court today, likely not crossing the border with Day until nightfall.

Our trip through the forest between Day and Summer will take most of tomorrow, given we have no choice but to ride from east to west because of the wagon. If we could cut from the south and exit at the northernmost point, we would be within Dawn's lands by late tomorrow. Unfortunately, the forest adds another day to our trip.

Three entire moons of riding.

I am not sure my legs and buttocks can endure such a journey.

After exiting the castle walls and crossing the grassed viaduct I often use to sneak to the western village, we turn north, circling to the north before crossing into Summer's lands mid-morning.

Solana does not seem to mind the warmth. I believe she is the only one.

The guards ahead shift uncomfortably on their horses. Their heavy tunics would be dreadful in the scorching heat. Not to mention the weapons strapped to their backs and hips, the knee-high leather boots, the vambraces on their arms, and the rabbit fur hats that are part of their uniform.

Wyn hides her discomfort the best, but even from such a distance, I can see the beads of sweat coating the back of her neck and wetting the thick fabric of her grey grown.

The Mother Star shines so brightly in Summer, I fear she will set the realm ablaze with undying fire. She is larger here than at home, and her brightness is blinding if I look at her for too long. Already, she has blinded me twice for daring to meet her gaze.

Trickles of sweat track down my spine, causing me to squirm in the saddle. The move does not ease my discomfort but frees space for the sweat between my breasts to track down my stomach, dipping into my belly button. This is the most uncomfortable I have ever been.

It is so hot in these lands, even the triplets have ceased their banter and laughter in favour of sipping from their water skins and scowling at the sky. Not a single cloud dots the aquamarine above to provide brief moments of shade.

The land is little more than an open, browning plain, with a scorching desert to the east and a forest somewhere in the north. What trees are brave enough to grow in the heat are mere twigs compared to the sizable ferns of the Autumn gardens.

I fan my face, which is surely the colour of glittering rubies, while attempting to mop up some of the breast sweat with my gown. An entire day drenched in sweat, panting, and wishing for the cool caress of a wind which will never come. I do not think I can handle it.

The sun has reached her peak by the time we exit the last of the rolling Summer hills, and the guards decide it is as good a time as any to stop for luncheon.

Though we cannot hide from the Mother Star when she is at her highest and brightest, the rest is welcome. Especially for the horses, who have it harder than the fae riding atop their backs. The stable hands feed and wet the mares, stallions, and geldings before seeing to their own needs. It makes me both happy and uncomfortable.

I sink into the long, soft grass, glaring at the yellow wild flowers dotting the sloping field. I have never liked the colour, thinking it the symbol of cowardice and deceit. It is fitting these flowers should thrive here.

"Water?" Wyn asks, handing me a chalice. "It is warm but will wet your mouth."

"Thank you." I take the offering with a smile and gesture for her to sit.

It is not unheard of for hand maidens to be granted permission to sit with their charges, but a friendship such as the one I share with Wyn is rare. Hand maidens are to be treated as lesser, kept at arm's length.

I do not care about those traditions. Rebellious. Father has said it many a time.

"I am hoping for a spot of shade soon," I say before sipping at the — too warm, it is much too warm — water.

"I doubt we'll find any until we hit the forest." She grimaces as she crosses her legs in front of her.

It makes me smile. "You are not accustomed to riding for so long?"

"We just fold wherever we need to go in Dusk. We have horses, but they're recreational."

"You ride for fun?"

She winks. "We do a lot of things for fun, just like you and your angler friend from the Day Court." When I am quiet, she adds, "Why did you do it? I've always wanted to know."

"I guess I was looking for a kind of reprieve," I say, ripping some of the yellow flowers from the ground and beginning to pluck the petals. "That, and freeing my body of a little stress helped me to endure life at the castle."

"Why didn't you just handle yourself?"

I turn to her with wide eyes. "What do you mean?"

"You've never given yourself an orgasm?"

My face heats as I run my eyes over those gathered around us, praying to the Mother Star none of them overheard. When I am certain our conversation remains private, I pin her with a glare. "I would never. It is unbecoming of my title."

She snorts as she stands and wipes dry grass from her gown. "Try it one day. You might just enjoy yourself."

Luncheon is a brief affair. The sandwiches and fruit are warm, and we all rush to get them down before storing everything back on the wagon and setting off once more. The heat is unbearable and the quicker we exit the Summer Court, the better off we will be.

Waves crash against the western cliffs far in the distance, begging me to turn and urge Solana into a gallop, if only to feel the cool, salty tang of the ocean breeze on our faces. The desire is only made more difficult to resist by the arid desert to our east, and the knowledge the Summer Court's castle lies beyond the burnt sands and the peaks of the dunes.

The sun is cresting towards the horizon when the forest appears in the distance, at long last. There is a kind of cheer to the travelling party, chatter starting anew for the first time since crossing the border between Autumn and Summer.

The triplets are growing more and more lively the closer we ride to the long-awaited shade, and I wonder if they have ever heard the stories. Tales of a fearful creature who wanders through the trees at night, listening to the whispered conversations of those who dare draw close to its den.

The Dullahan.

A headless being who rides a skeletal horse and wields a whip of spine. It is said that meeting the stare of the head he carries blinds you, your eyes gouged out by the sharp tip of his whip. A shudder runs through me, leaving gooseflesh in its wake.

I have long since feared the Dullahan. Legend states the headless rider will claim your life if he whispers your name, which is why I have ordered every fae riding with me to not say my name out loud for as long as we are within the confines of the forest. I have no intention of allowing the Dullahan to feast on my soul. None at all.

The sun disappears, igniting the sky with yellow and gold and burnt orange, and my sweat turns sticky. I pray for a creek crossing the moment we enter the forest, so I may wash away the day of riding.

Instead of a bubbling creek, four royal guards meet us the moment we step into the shade of the trees and onto the Day Court's land. Four guards, all in Dawn uniforms, surround a lone messenger with a golden gleam to his skin.

Tasar slides from his horse's back. "State your message."

"Well met, My Princes," the messenger says, refusing to meet their gazes. "It is with regret High Lord Jonik commands you home. You are no longer considered an option in Princess Bria Sutherland's courtship."

The messenger hands a tight scroll to Tasar, who unfurls it with a frown while the rest of us slide from our horses.

He reads the letter out loud. "Dearest sons, while I am certain you are enjoying your ride to Dawn, and entertaining Bria with your wit, I regret to inform you I have decided an alliance with Autumn is not in the interest of the court. Not when your joining with the princess creates an enemy of Summer. Make haste on your return home and do not linger, especially if you remain by Bria's side. Sincerely, High Lord Jonik."

"Sounds to me that Summer threatened us," growls Ulakas, snatching the note from Tasar's hand. "That fire wielding bastard."

"You heard him," says Larrad. "Let us divide our belongings and return home."

"Do you mean to leave me here alone?" Anger crashes through me and taints my words. Tohminic has gone too far in threatening the Dawn Court. They are a neutral court with no enemies and no allies. They provide the entire realm with healers.

Tasar has the audacity to look surprised by my outburst. "We are in no position to question our father. I am sorry. We have no choice."

"You have two guards, Bria," offers Larrad. "And your hand maiden."

I wish they would all stop speaking my name. My eyes flick left and right, seeking signs of the Dullahan and his spine whip.

When I am certain he is not near, I growl, "If you believe Tohminic would act on his threat against your home, you are foolish males indeed. There is not a single fae in Radelea who would be so reckless as to incite the anger of your father and risk him calling his healers home."

"It is what it is." Ulakas scowls. "Arguing the point does not change the fact our High Lord has ordered us home. We bid you farewell, Bria of Autumn."

How easily their jesting masks have slipped now they are not required to fight for my affection.

A growl slips free as I throw my hands in the air. I stalk to a guard and order him to fold home and inform Father of this ridiculous turn of events. He is to return before the triplets leave.

"What do we do now?" Wyn asks, watching the princes' hands move their cases from our wagon and onto one from the Dawn Court that the guards have summoned. "I don't think riding home at night is smart."

"I agree. We will make camp here for tonight and return home come morning. I am sure Father will send word agreeing." I lean against a large tree and sink to the ground, resting my elbows on my bent knees and burying my head in my hands. "He will not stop, will he? He will continue to threaten and fight every male until I am locked in his seaside castle."

"It's just Vander now. I doubt he'll succumb to Tohminic's threats."

By the time the triplets have finished unloading and reloading their cases and half of the food, night has smothered the land in its blanket of darkness. The forest is still as they urge their horses into a gallop and disappear beyond the dense trees, leaving me with Wyn, two guards — the guard I sent to inform Father returned with a note ordering me home in the morning — a stable hand, the wagon, and my withering hope.

The two guards lead us farther into the forest, searching for a clearing large enough to set up camp. They find one soon after setting out. The eerily perfect circle of towering pines will be the perfect place to rest and hide from the Dullahan.

As Wyn prepares a light meal, cooking fat sausages over the flickering flames of the fire, I head off in search of a stream to bathe in. I do not have to go far and follow the trickling of water for mere moments before coming across the pebbled creek.

It would be so easy, I decide as I splash water onto my face. So easy to slip through the trees and disappear. No one will realise I am gone for a while, leaving me free to escape my father's clutches, to escape Tohminic.

I could be anywhere in Radelea. I could be in Winter or Dusk or Dawn. Even if I folded out of this creepy forest and find a village to call home, my life will be much more enjoyable that what it is now.

Leaving Wyn will be difficult. I would think of her often as I make a life for myself as a hand maiden or seamstress or something of the like. I could build a hut within this very forest and live off the land. Although, I would spend my every night fearing the Dullahan will find me.

If I fold to the Spring Court, I can blend in as one of them, my copper hair serving as a kind of disguise. I may be so lucky as to find my birth mother and beg for help. She could show me the ways of the Spring fae, help me fit into their world seamlessly.

By the time I have washed the day's sweat from my body, I have all but decided to enact on my plan to hide in the Court of Blooms.

That is until Wyn comes searching for me. It would be no matter — she can come with me or take me to Dusk — if it were not for the guard accompanying her.

"Bria? Are you about done?" she asks. The way she avoids looking in the guard's direction speaks volumes. She wished to come alone, perhaps guessing where my thoughts have taken me.

I stand, drying my hands on my gown. "Yes. I am done." Done with this courtship, done with my father and his court. Just... done. I am done.

Dinner is sombre. The guards refuse to join us for a meal, instead patrolling the clearing and keeping an eye out for the feared headless rider. Wyn does not speak much, and I guess she is wondering if Tohminic's latest threat is enough to send me over the edge of madness.

I find myself wondering the same thing as I mindlessly chew on the burnt sausages. Just one day of riding through the Summer Court's lands was enough for me to know I will not enjoy spending every day of my life in the scorching heat. That's not to mention the hell my life would be if Father were to order my mating with Tohminic.

All of a sudden, the greasy meat is dry in my mouth, and I struggle to swallow. With little else to do, and unable to eat through the bout of nausea, I retire for the night.

Wyn follows me into the tent, helping me from the gown. "You're quiet tonight. What's going on?"

"Tohminic." I lower my voice to a whisper. "While I washed at the creek, I considered folding to the Spring Court."

She begins on the buttons down my back, leaning close so the guards and stable hand do not overhear. "I figured as much. You know, we can do it. Pretend to go to bed, but stay in this gown. When the others are asleep, we can leave in the dead of night, head for the Dusk Court. Once you're on our land, no one can touch you."

I look over my shoulder, gauging her reaction. "You would do that for me? You would risk my father's wrath?"

"Of course I would." Her face is set in stone, not a flicker of uncertainty or dishonesty to be seen.

"Then we do it." I allow her to button my gown back up. "Tonight, we flee. Tonight, I am a free female, no longer ruled by the Autumn Court or cowed by Summer."

"You're going to love the Dusk Court," she says, patting the neck of my gown.

20

A LL IS QUIET. SOFT snores sound from the tent beside mine, one guard and the stable hand having fallen asleep somewhere around midnight. The second guard is supposed to be patrolling the clearing, and I am pleasantly surprised to find him asleep on the job, his chin digging into his chest as he rests against a tree.

"We are good to go," I whisper to Wyn, letting the opening of the tent fall closed.

She reaches for my hands, so we can fold together, but a booming shout rings through the forest.

My first thought is the Dullahan has found me at last, here to whip my eyes from my skull with his spinal column weapon. My next thought is of Father, here to ensure my return to the Autumn Court. Then my mind catches up to the words.

"By order of High Lord Tohminic of Summer, you are hereby detained on the grounds of trespassing."

My wide eyes find Wyn's. "Are we not in Day territory?"

"I thought we were," she says, her brow creasing. "I'm almost positive this land belongs to the Day Court. This must be part of Tohminic's plan: get you alone, then take you in the middle of the night when the guards are too groggy from sleep to fight back."

I gather my magic, folding the western village — the closest point to the Dusk Court — towards me. Before I can so much as step through the void of time and space, someone slices my tent open from the outside, two burly guards sneering at us from a crude gash in the canvas.

"Found her," says the guard on the left, a selkie fae with greyish skin. It would be a terrible idea to get on his bad side. He turns back to us, noting our travel clothes and leather bags with a sneer. "Going somewhere?"

I step in front of Wyn. "We are yet to retire. What is the meaning of this?"

The second guard says, "Would you be kind enough to exit the tent, or shall my friend and I drag you out?"

"You will do no such thing." I cross my arms over my chest for good measure.

"I do like it when they refuse," says the selkie.

There is no question where they are from. If their words did not give them away, the selkie does. Born of the Summer waters, selkies do not leave their home court often. Tohminic likely paid this guard, and handsomely, to retrieve me.

Wyn whispers from behind, "Best we go with them for now. They'll follow if we fold."

"We will come without a fight," I tell the guards before turning towards the tent's exit, only to find a third guard waiting.

I frantically try to think of a way out of this. Nothing is off the table, from folding away to fighting for freedom. Though when I step from the tent to see my guards and the stable hand bound and gagged, I realise escape is unlikely. Impossible.

"Release them at once!" I shout, gesturing to the males. One of them has blood trickling from a wound on his temple.

I count five guards, though a faint shimmer in the air to my left indicates a sixth has just folded away. To the Summer Court to inform Tohminic of our capture, I suppose.

This just keeps getting better and better.

"That will not happen." It is clear by the selkie's tone he is not one to bargain, it is also obvious he's in charge of these males. He nudges the leg of one of my guards, huffing a laugh. "They did not put up much of a fight. In fact, this one was asleep when he was supposed to be watching for attacks like this one. A waste of life, if you ask me."

"No one did," I snap. "Now, if you would kindly leave so we may rest in peace, we would very much appreciate it." I move to turn back to my tent, but a guard grips my elbow.

"I do not think so. His Lordship will be here soon."

"You have no reason to detain us. This land belongs to the Day Court."

The selkie laughs. "Darling, the first thing Lord Tohminic did upon being crowned High Lord is seize this entire forest. The Day Court did not so much as blink at the loss of their land."

I do not believe Lady Zentha would allow such a thing without a fight. The selkie is bluffing, I am certain.

"Regardless," I say, attempting to free myself of the guard's hold, "we have done no wrong. You have no cause to treat us with such disgrace."

"I disagree," says a voice which sends shivers down my spine. He steps closer, his yellow eyes alight with glee. "Someone from your court *murdered* my father. I will take my revenge in any way I see fit."

Wyn snarls from beside me, where she is being restrained by one of Tohminic's guards.

My upper lip curls. "I am not a bargaining chip. Nor am I a prize to be won or a female to be used as an example."

He moves closer, so close the scent of his breath invades my nose. The bitter notes of ale, something greasy, and a hint of lemon. "You are all of the above."

I spit at his feet. "You are a disgusting male, Tohminic. Leave us be."

The back of his hand cracks across my face, the sting raw and burning. "You will treat me with respect." He leans closer. Too close. "We are at war, Princess Bria. Best become accustomed to such brutal treatment."

"We are not at war!" I scream.

"While you were traversing across *my* lands, blissfully unaware, I have declared war on a number of courts, including your father's. War is not kind, Bria. You will learn just how cruel it can be soon enough." Tohminic's smile is cunning and mocking. His hand whips out and wraps around my wrist in a vice-like grip as he pulls me closer. "I will rule over Radelea with Chlora by my side. You, the bastard daughter of Autumn and Spring, will be nothing more than a façade. You will be by my side at all times, silent and waiting for any command I shall give. Do you understand?"

My entire being burns with anger, and I am sure my eyes would spit fire if I were born of Summer. "I will do no such thing."

"I have spent many moons pondering how best to gain your cooperation." He drags me away from the camp, farther into the forest. "You would not care for the lives of your family if I were to bargain with them, nor that of your court. The younglings you teach, though..."

"You would not dare to touch them," I hiss.

He is right to assume I would not do as he asks if he threatened Father, Rennyn, or Fayeth. I am aware they would not do the same for me, and I am not so foolish that I would risk my life to save theirs. Especially after recent times. But my students, I would die for.

I must admit, his desire to rule runs deeper than I thought. For him to go to such lengths to trap me, and use me as he sees fit... Well, it does not bode well for me, that is for certain.

Tohminic's gaze meets that of the selkie guard, and he nods once, his eyes flashing with triumph.

I whip my face in that direction, ice filling my veins as the selkie brings an orb of churning water to one palm, and fire to the other. He sends one orb hurtling towards each of my guards, encasing them in glittering blue and blazing red.

Their screams will haunt me until the end of time.

Before I can bargain for Wyn's life, the realm's magic encases Tohminic and me. He drags me through the fold, stepping into the balmy midnight air just outside his keep. He does not bother with any of my belongings, leaving them in the forest for the Day fae to find.

The castle, made purely of sandstone and rather small, sits at the very edge of the eastern cliffs, protected on three sides by sheer drops and raging waters far below. It is a keep built for defence; the battlements are sturdy and able to withstand the harshest of attacks. Inside such a well-built keep... It is nothing more than a trap. A cage.

Tohminic yanks my wrist and pulls me forward.

My heart sinks as I move closer and realise I was mistaken in my first assessment of the keep. We are standing on a low land bridge that forms part of a long, narrow walk past the entrance of a gatehouse. It cuts through the sea, curving away from the land and dipping lower. Steep steps descend to the true keep, which rests on jagged rocks below, the waves lapping at the outer walls.

The keep itself is a simple square, with each corner marked by a cylindrical tower, and likely a protected courtyard in the centre. The battlements that join each corner appear narrow from where I stand, the crenelations taller than I have ever seen. It's enormous, at least twice the height of home and four times as wide.

"Welcome to your new life," says Tohminic, the humour lacing his tone unmistakable.

I yank on my wrist in a useless attempt to be free. "This is not my life. It never will be."

"So naïve." His magic whorls around him, pulsing with suffocating heat as he pushes it towards the sandstone steps leading to the keep. Water sizzles and turns to steam, leaving the once slippery steps dry.

If I slip and tumble down these steps — which are ancient, perhaps as old as time itself — I would not survive, so I allow Tohminic to drag me lower and lower. My stomach tightens further with every step towards the sandstone keep. Tohminic tells me it is named Ad'Starrag, which means harsh stone in the ancient first language of the fae. How fitting, given the ruler of these lands.

The keep's obsidian backdrop, dotted with pricks of glimmering gold and silver, does little to calm my ravaged nerves. The stars I love so much are gorgeous at this hour, shining their brightest before dawn approaches. It is a trick. It is a cruel joke. Nothing could be so beautiful in a land so vicious.

Behind me, Wyn is being dragged down the steps by the selkie guard. She is protesting every step of the way, giving the selkie a hard time. It is pointless. She can fold home whenever she wishes. Born to be High Lady of Dusk, her power is far greater than any guard Tohminic controls. She endures this for me. To protect me, to keep me company, keep me sane.

I face forward once more, just in time to appreciate the delicate work involved in creating the arched entrance to Ad'Starrag. The interior is just as stunning, with open arches on either side of the wide hallway allowing the moon to cast streams of light over the floor and walls.

Tohminic leads me through the keep to a secluded wing on the eastern side. It is clear he chose this chamber for me because the glassless windows show nothing but a churning ocean and sharp rocks. I would likely drown if I attempted to escape.

"You have five hours to rest and change," he says. "Then you are required to attend breakfast with the court. Attempt to flee if you wish. I am curious to see how far you make it before the selkies retrieve you."

The selkie guard shoves Wyn inside after me, growling for her to behave.

She seethes in silence as he slams the door closed and slides a bolt across the outside, locking us in. Her head cocks to the side as she listens to their receding footsteps. Only when she is certain they are gone does she turn to me with concern in her eyes. "Are you okay?"

"I... Yes, I am." I graze my teeth along my lower lip as I move to the open window and gaze out at the churning ocean. When I try to fold the Autumn Court towards me, nothing happens. "I am not sure there is a way out of this. I cannot fold. They have us trapped."

"There's always a way out. We just have to find it."

To distract my mind from negative thoughts, which will rule me if I allow them to, I take in the chamber Tohminic has chosen.

The sandstone walls are drab — beige and brown and pale orange are not colours I would choose for myself — but the space is airy, bright, with the four arches open to the elements. Gauzy fabric, in a blue so pale it is almost white, frames each window. The curtains flutter in a slight balmy breeze, their rustling a mere whisper compared to my racing heart.

Time has turned the copper frame of the bed a delightful teal, and the gossamer hanging from the corner of the four posts is the same colour as the curtains, both matching the slightly darker silk sheets.

A chaise lounge and table, both teal copper, rest in the corner. In the opposite corner, beside a window, an oak timber armoire and a lace screen to change behind.

Just beyond the screen, a tiny area with a small bed. For Wyn.

It's a beautiful cage. Nothing more.

I drag my weary eyes back to Wyn. "There is no reason for you to suffer alongside me. Flee, while you can."

She huffs a laugh. "How? We're trapped."

I shrug. "Encase yourself in a bubble of air and swim for freedom?"

"Actually, that could work." She chews the inside of her cheek. "But I can't just leave you here."

And I do not wish for that. I do not much like the idea of being here alone, but this is not Wyn's fight. It is mine. Besides, no one knows I'm here, and if Wyn informs Father of what has happened, he will fight for my freedom.

"Vander used an illusion of himself to appear at Rennyn's born day ball. Are you that powerful? Could you send an illusion whenever I need you here? That way, Tohminic and his guards will not know you have fled."

The courts of Radelea did not expect a court able to illusion their way through their wards. Until they figure out how to prevent such a thing, Wyn is free to use her magic to come and go as she pleases.

She opens the armoire, curiosity getting the better of her. Pulling a sheer skirt free, she grimaces. "I'm all for loving your own body, but this is too much. Everything will be on display." After shoving it back inside and closing the door, she turns to me. "I can do that. I can help you when you need it while

Vander figures out how to get you out. Promise me you won't do anything stupid whenever I'm not here, though."

"I promise."

❧❧❧ ❧❧❧

Wyn was right. The clothes are ridiculous. The gossamer skirt does little to hide the shape of my legs. Only the cotton panties stitched into the skirt give me any semblance of privacy. The bust of the gown is nothing but a sheer corset, the fabric ruffled over my breasts. One wrong twist of my body and the folds hiding my nipples will shift, and I will be on full display.

I am not a prude by any means, but this is too much. I look like one of the village harlots.

The selkie guard — I have learned Xaler is second in command — leads me through the keep to the dining hall.

Summer fae crowd the long, open space. They are all balancing on low stools that line the longest table I have ever seen.

"Welcome." Tohminic sneers from the head of the table. He gestures to the stool beside him. "Sit."

The eyes of every fae in the hall linger on me as I pass them, my silk slippers silent on the sandstone floor as I keep my eyes forward. I feel them assessing me, sneering at my bastard status, and wondering if I am worthy of their High Lord. It is easy to ignore their scrutiny.

As I take my seat on Tohminic's left, I take solace in knowing Wyn is escaping. The moment she is free of the court wards, she will fold to Autumn with a message for Father declaring Vander the victor of my courtship.

I will not accept Tohminic as my mate. If Father so much as threatens to force me, I will reject the bond the moment it is created, cursing both of us to a future of madness. Losing my mind is something I will gladly accept if it means I am free of the monster beside me.

It is unfortunate that breakfast is delicious. I did not need more reasons to find the Summer Court alluring, but the creamy cheese and sliced tomato are just as enjoyable as the stewed beans and flat bread.

While everyone is eating, Tohminic speaks of war. He claims Autumn will be the first to fall, with the eastern village already in his sights. He will work from east to west, claiming our land for himself. Once he has control of the court, and Father is either dead or kneels before Tohminic, the Summer Court will reassess and determine which court to target next.

Likely the Day Court.

The raucous laughter that follows his words only serves to amuse him. He stands, clapping his hands once. "To celebrate our guest's arrival, we convene in the rotunda for wine and pleasure."

His words are met with cheers from the nobles of his court, but a chill dances down my spine. I do not like the sound of that at all.

21

T HE ROTUNDA IS A courtyard in the centre of the keep with a bubbling water fountain marking the middle. Lining the perimeter, ten alcoves are open to the elements, framed by gossamer curtains, with beige over-sized cushions in each of them. The plants are all green or purple, none with flowers or leaves to bring bursts of colour to the place. Succulents are the only flora brave enough to grow in Summer.

Though it is still early in the morning, the heat is already unbearable. It is no wonder the members of the court are removing their clothes. Thankfully, the Mother Star has yet to rise to her peak, and long shadows fall over the rotunda, beckoning me into their cool embrace.

"You will stand beside the fountain and you will watch," says Tohminic. "You will learn, and at the next full moon, when we convene here once again, you will participate. There is no debate."

Take part in what? I wonder as he disappears amongst the naked bodies filling the circular area.

Wine flows freely from golden carafes, filling chalices and glass cups before they are anywhere near empty. Some of the Summer fae pour the deep red wine straight into their mouths or over the bodies of those closest. It is strange to witness. Made more so when the moans begin.

I whip my head around, peering beyond the fountain at the group of three staggering towards an alcove. The female, a gorgeous fae with shimmering lilac hair, wraps her legs around her male friend, while a second female drags them forward. They are all naked.

I thought this was a kind of garden party to celebrate my capture. I was so very wrong. Everywhere I look there are naked bodies, lips parted in ecstasy, and bursts of fire magic. The cacophony is loud, overwhelming.

My eyes, which are wide with shock, find Tohminic in an alcove, gripping the back of Chlora's neck with so much force, his fingers turn white from the strain. His other hand cracks across her exposed buttocks before he thrusts inside her in a single, rough move. The reddened mark his hand left is stark against her porcelain skin.

Chlora's scream of delight is so loud, I hear it over the two groaning males beside me.

If I am being honest with myself, I am curious. I am not oblivious to Chlora's pleasure. It is clear on her face and in her delighted moans, but I cannot envision taking her place. The thought of Tohminic touching me in such a way dries up any arousal before it can so much as dampen my panties.

A splash from beside me has me whipping my face towards the two males as a female joins them. She lowers to her knees, right in the tepid water, looking up at them both through dark lashes before dragging one of them closer and wrapping plump lips around his thick erection. The other male moves behind her and sinks into her from behind with an animalistic groan.

Behind them, a third male watches with lust burning in his eyes, his tanned hand stroking his engorged cock, his pace increasing with every moan from the trio beside me.

Turning my face away, I am stunned to find Tohminic and Chlora right in front of me. Chlora is on her knees, her eyes watering as Tohminic holds her head to his pelvis. I cannot see a single slither of his cock — Chlora is surely choking.

He jerks his hips but does not allow Chlora the gift of air. His eyes meet mine as he groans. "Does this remind you of your lover from the Day Court? Does it bring back memories?" His neck pulls taut, and he clenches his teeth. "I will take great pleasure in severing his cock from his body, so he may never enjoy the feel of you again. I may be lenient and leave his hands."

Chlora moans, her fingers digging into his hips and her eyes watering.

I cannot stand the sight of it and turn away with Tohminic's words crashing through my mind. If he intends to torture Nikolai purely for *my* choice to sneak from the castle every full moon, I must warn him. I cannot allow someone to be harmed because of my actions.

My focus sharpens, and I realise I am staring at a group of four females. One of them looks at me through hooded eyes, beckoning with a curl of a finger before sliding it inside of one of her companions.

My eyes widen and I turn away yet again, but there is nowhere to look without seeing bare breasts, throbbing erections, or contorted bodies.

When a servant offers me a chalice filled with wine, I greedily accept. The only thing that will get me through this is the courage the wine brings. Again, Tohminic's words filter through my thoughts. *When we convene here once again, you will participate. There is no debate.*

My mouth runs dry, the bitter wine turning to mud on my parched tongue. There is no world in which I am interested in participating in this... What do I call this? There is no word I know to describe such an event.

I wonder if every court behaves in this regard. Is the Autumn Court unlike the rest? Perhaps I have lived a sheltered life, not understanding the ways of the world. This could be normal. I make a mental note to ask Wyn, knowing she will not shy away from the truth.

The reminder of my princess-turned-hand maiden makes my chest tighten with anxiety. My insides quiver as if to flee my raging emotions and I send a prayer to the Mother Star — who is reaching her zenith, casting a stifling heat over the rotunda — for Wyn's safe escape. If the guards catch her, or if she comes to any harm, it will be my fault. I should not have urged her to flee so soon.

Several pairings disappear into the shaded keep, giggling and panting as they race through the open hallways towards their chambers. Some linger in the alcoves, lost in their pleasure, and do not look to be leaving soon. Especially the two males opposite. From their delicate touches and loving looks, I assume they are mates.

Strange they would be here, given how over protective mates are, especially in the early stages. Though, the bond between chosen mates is less potent than that of the true mates I have read recounts of.

I cast my tired mind back to last night, trying to remember how full the moon was. Tohminic stated I must take part in this chaos when it is full. By my guess, I have nine, maybe ten, moons until then. I vow to be gone before it happens.

Back in my chamber, I rush through writing two letters. One for Rennyn, begging him to make Father see sense and free me from this nightmare, and another to Nikolai, demanding he run, hide if he must, and warning him of Tohminic's intentions.

I seal them with crimson wax and hand them to one of the two guards stationed outside my door, instructing them to find a messenger and send the letters off as soon as possible, though I am uncertain they will follow my command. Honestly, it surprises me that Tohminic allowed me parchment and a quill.

A maid brings a meal not long after, a meagre soup and bread that is far less tasty and extravagant than this morning's breakfast.

I spend the afternoon pacing, not knowing what else to do with my time other than worry about Wyn. She has not sent an illusion of herself into my chamber to tell me she made it out okay. She promised she would as soon as she was free, yet I have not heard from her. My mind creates all number of horrible scenarios she may have found herself in, and I have to force myself to think positive thoughts.

The Mother Star has sunk beyond the horizon by the time I am collected for the dinner feast. Unlike in the Autumn Court, everyone in the keep shares breakfast and dinner, welcoming and farewelling the Mother Star as one. It is the only good thing about this dreadful place.

Again, I am the focus of all scrutiny as I walk the length of the long table, all eyes narrowing at my copper hair, pale skin, and the curves of my body. It is clear they do not appreciate me watching their morning... celebrations instead of joining in.

Forever an outcast, no matter the court in which I live.

Dinner consists of buttery fish with a tangy lemon sauce, crisp green vegetables, rice with a mixture of brown and white grains, and more of the flat, round bread from this morning. I hardly taste the food.

Again, the conversation revolves around Tohminic's plans for the war. He has proclaimed himself an enemy of Autumn, Dusk, and Spring. It is not difficult to determine his reasons for such declarations. Autumn, the court I call home. Dusk, the court of the male I have chosen as my mate. Spring, the court of my birth mother. They are all foolish reasons to declare war.

I have long since acknowledged Tohminic's depravity. But when the selkie guard drags a beaten male into the dining hall, I am stunned into silence. Not even my nightmares could have imagined this.

Cuts and bruises cover Nikolai's face, though they do not prevent him from scowling at the High Lord of Summer. He thrashes against Xaler's hold, spitting venomous words at his captor.

Xaler laughs and hauls him through the hall before throwing him at Tohminic's feet. "Nikolai of the Day Court, as requested, My Lord."

"Excellent," says Tohminic as he stands.

The Summer fae bristle with anticipation.

Nikolai leaps to his feet, sinking into a defensive position that makes everyone laugh. The Mother Star knows he has no hope of fighting his way out of here, not with his weak water magic, and certainly not against over one hundred Summer fae.

His eyes find me in the hall, his fight evaporating in an instant. "Ria?"

I beg him with my eyes to understand why I must not step in and prevent the pain he is to endure. I coat my emerald irises with guilt, regret, and pain, hoping he will see my heartache and forgive me. Not that I deserve a shred of his forgiveness.

Though it is cruel to think it, I cannot prevent the thought from flashing across my mind. If only Nikolai had agreed to run with me when we had the chance, we could both have avoided such pain.

"You know," says Tohminic, "I would have spared his life had you not attempted to warn him of my intentions. His blood is on your hands, Bria."

He holds out a tanned hand, and his long sword appears in his palm. The sound of the blade being freed from its scabbard is deafening in the quiet, too loud for my sensitive ears. "Have you any last words?" he asks Nikolai.

Nik only glares.

"I'm sorry," I whisper. Tears line my eyes, revealing my weakness to all. "I'm so sorry, Nik."

Tohminic arcs his sword through the air, severing Nik's head from his body in one precise move. The thud that follows reverberates through my skull, echoing until it is all I can hear. Blood sprays towards me, coating the fine gossamer of my gown in bright crimson, but it is not the cause of my roiling stomach.

Tohminic fists his hand in Nikolai's flaxen hair, blood dripping from the severed head as he lifts it and places it before me. All I can see is Nik's bright eyes, now dull and lifeless, and the steady drip of blood on the sandstone floor, stark against the pale stone, as if to mock me.

My breaths turn ragged and all I can do it stare at the disembodied head on my plate, the oozing crimson staining what remains of the rice and fish. There's a buzzing in my ears, a kind of incessant screech that grows louder and louder the harder I pant.

I slap a hand over my mouth, fighting to prevent the bile that burns the back of my throat from joining the mess before me. After a mere heartbeat, I know I will fail, and jerk to my feet. I ignore the clattering of the stool as it crashes to the ground, ignore the jeers and laughter from the Summer fae — none laughing harder than Tohminic or Chlora — and ignore the urge to lose my dinner in front of so many.

My legs move fast, carrying me through the keep until I am in the safety of my chamber, where my dinner wins the battle. My body heaves as I lean out of the arched window, the bitter aftertaste of lemon and cream disgusting as it resurfaces. Cold sweat dots my forehead, and I blink rapidly, trying to rid my mind of the image of Nikolai's frozen shock.

My fault. It is all my fault.

I pursued Nik. Me. *I* snuck from the court to meet with him every full moon, knowing what danger I was putting him in. *Me.* Bria Sutherland, magicless bastard. I am responsible for Nikolai's death.

Tohminic was right. Nik's blood is not only coating my gown and skin, but it stains my hands. They were crimson the first moment I placed a hand on his shoulder and asked if he was unmated. My hands were red with his blood when I first leaned towards him, whispering my wishes into his ear. They were red when I asked him if he had a cabin on the Day ship where we could go.

My hands are red. *Red, red, red.*

He was right to refuse me when I begged him to flee the court with me. He was right. His concern was of my father's punishment, as was mine. Both Nikolai and I were unaware of the danger lurking in the shadows.

My head pounds, matching the racing of my heart as I pace the length of my chamber. Back and forth I walk, fighting with everything I have to clear that same image from my mind. Lifeless eyes, dripping blood, stained rice... My throat clogs, the emotion brewing with every twist back in the other direction.

Red, red, red. Nikolai's blood coats my hands like gloves.

A choked sob tears at my throat and I can take it no longer. I dart to the window and clamber onto the sandstone ledge, gripping the side with one hand as I assess the water and rocks below.

The Mother Star has blessed me with a low tide tonight, as if knowing I would need to escape. After a quick glance over my shoulder, blurred from the tears, I leap from the window and land harshly on the uneven rock outside before racing towards the water. If Wyn can get out, then I can, too.

My slippers skate across the slick rocks, seeming to find every patch of silky kelp left from the high tide. Tiny crabs scatter at my approach, disappearing into miniscule crevices between the harsh angles of the rock, making me envy their size. I splash through the shallow water, my heart in my throat and hands fisted at my sides.

A cruel laugh echoes through the night. "Going somewhere, *Ria?*" Xaler uses the name I gave Nik as an added torment before he lunges for me. The seal fur he wears in the ocean, a gift from the Mother Star, ripples as he sails through the air, changing from shimmering brindle to fae skin as he crashes into me.

"Let me go!" I shout, smacking my fists into his arms.

He only laughs and collects me as if I am nothing more than a sack of grain, hurling me over his shoulder and jogging back towards the keep.

I cannot hold back the frustrated scream as he throws me mercilessly through the window and back into my chamber. "Please," I beg. "Please let me leave. I do not belong here."

My attempt at finding a shred of pity within the ruthless selkie is a waste of breath and effort.

He laughs harder, his body shaking from it. "You are amusing, I will give you that. You are not going anywhere. This is your home now, whether you accept it or not."

I fall to my knees, my hands clasped before me. "Do not tell him. Please, do not speak of this again."

He arches a brow, his laughter dying. "Why would I keep this to myself?" His eyes ravage my body. "Unless you will offer a trade?"

The bile returns. "I would rather die."

"I so look forward to your punishment." They are his last words before he races across the jagged rocks and dives back into the depths of the ocean.

22

"Bria." Something fresh and cool brushes across my shoulder. "Bria, wake up."

A groan ripples free, garbled by a jaw-cracking yawn. "What's it?"

A snort. "Wake up."

I squint my eyes open, blink the remnants of sleep away, and stretch my arms over my head. The pull of my gown surprises me enough that I jerk upright, the memories of last night flooding my mind as a gasp tears at my dry throat. I drag my weary eyes to Wyn.

"Care to tell me why you're covered in blood?" she whispers, throwing a glance at the closed door. "And would you care to tell me why you now have a guard stationed at your windows and two at your door?"

I run a hand down my face, holding back the fresh bout of tears that are stinging my eyes. "It was horrible. So horrible. After breakfast yesterday, the Summer fae celebrated with some kind of sex party. I have never seen so many naked bodies in my life."

She chuckles, opening her mouth to speak, but I hold up a hand and silence her before continuing.

"He made me watch the whole thing. He told me I will be required to participate at the next full moon. But that is not the worst of what occurred after you left."

She sits beside me — it's eerie how the bed does not dip with her weight because her illusion cannot affect anything here — her hands curling into fists. "We won't let that happen, Bria. Why are you covered in blood? They're not into blood play or anything?"

"I do not know what blood play is and do not care to find out." My throat clogs, but I force the words out. "The blood is Nikolai's. Tohminic beheaded him in front of me. Placed his head on top of my dinner."

She is silent for a moment. It's as if she is too stunned for words, too shocked by the news to so much as attempt to embrace me. After a long moment of silence, she breathes, "Fuck."

I stare at my hands, hands which are still stained with blood. While the worst of the pain has faded, the heartache, guilt, and regret still linger, smothering me like a blanket of flames. I despise the emotions, yet I deserve to suffer through them.

"We have to get you out of here as soon as possible."

"There's something else," I say, standing and beginning to pace. If I have to stare at the red on my hands any longer, I am not sure I will survive. "After Tohminic killed Nikolai, I attempted to flee. I climbed from my window and raced for the ocean. It was low tide, and I believed I could make it to the wards and fold to the Dusk Court from there. Xaler found me."

"I understand why you did it, but it was incredibly stupid." She nods to the door. "Let's get you cleaned up, and we can talk more once you're not grimacing every time you look at your hands."

"You noticed?"

Her smile is warm and genuine. "I notice a lot."

I have never been more thankful for Wyn than I am right now. Though it is the early hours of morning, and Tohminic expects us both to be sleeping, Wyn threatens the guards with bodily harm — which she cannot act on because she is an illusion — if they do not allow us access to the bathing chamber.

They relent soon after, and escort us down the open hallway towards the bathing chamber, a large space with four tubs built into the ground. The guards stand by the door with their backs to us. It is pointless, given the six arches leading to the ocean on the opposite side of the chamber. Anyone could pass by and look in.

I am not brave enough to attempt escape twice in one night, though I make a note of the way here. Just in case.

"I can't help you," says Wyn, "but I'll guide you, okay? Start by loosening the ribbons of the corset."

Her instructions are easy to follow. Twisting my body so I can reach the laces, not so much. It takes twice as long as it should to loosen the corset bust of the gown, and by the time the gossamer is in a pile at my feet, I am panting.

"There are two pins in the back of your hair. You'll feel them. Pull them free, then you're ready to step into the bath."

She guides me through where everything is, and I collect soap, oil, and a sea sponge to scrub my skin with.

I keep my eyes on the sandstone wall while I scrub the blood from my skin in the heated water and say, "I am so thankful you escaped without issue. Will you tell me about it?"

The distraction is welcome. If I allow my mind to focus on what I am washing from my skin, I will succumb to the suffocating emotions bubbling inside.

"I left as soon as you went to breakfast. There were no guards in the ocean or on the surrounding rocks. Actually, the wards are close to the keep. I didn't have to use my air magic to breathe underwater, and folded to the Autumn Court the moment my lungs began to burn."

"You met with Father?" I ask, moving the sponge from my arms to my legs. "What did he say?"

"I'm really sorry, Bria. He said whatever trouble you've found yourself in isn't his concern. He has enough on his plate with Summer's threat of war."

I scoff. "It is not a threat. Tohminic took me as an act of war. Father is not concerned in the slightest? I always knew he would rather me gone, but this is beyond what I expected of him."

"Fayeth was there, if it makes a difference."

"It doesn't. I am beginning to wonder if she has always been honest, while Father and Rennyn are nothing but lying jerks. At least I have always known where I stand with her."

"I didn't linger," she says, continuing her story. "As soon as I realised Kerym had no intention of attempting to rescue his daughter, I headed straight for home. I've been with Vander, Nyree, and Torin ever since, trying to figure out the best way to get you out. So far, we have nothing."

My stomach sinks. "But he is trying? He will fight on my behalf?"

She meets my eye. "He was furious when he found out. He claims Tohminic's lying and cheating are the foundation of his anger, but I think there's more to it. Maybe you can get it out of him once you're free."

"He does not appreciate the mistreatment of females. He told me as much on one of our walks."

I can tell she does not believe that is all there is to it, but I let the subject drop, moving on to ask how I can escape this hell. "Low tide would be the perfect time to escape, but after last night, Xaler will send guards to watch the ocean."

"Which rules that out. Is there anywhere within the keep that leads to the western side of the court? Anywhere with tunnels or even a tall tower you can jump from?"

"I am not jumping from a tower."

She tilts her head, her lips curling into a smile. "We would catch you. We can slow the fall with our magic by making the air denser."

Her smile falters, and she seems to disappear for a moment. Her entire body freezes. Her chest does not rise and fall, there is no throbbing pulse at her neck for several heartbeats before she blinks. "I have to go. I'll be back soon." She disappears entirely.

The bathing chamber is too quiet without her. My thoughts become louder, screaming in my mind as I fight to shove them back. *Red, red, red.*

My hands are red with Nikolai's blood.

I lather the bar of soap between my hands, the scent of carnations and lavender wafting from the white bubbles. Raking my fingernails over my palms, over the backs of my hands, and between my fingers makes my skin turn pink. The pink darkens. *Red, red, red.*

My fear and guilt come to life. My hands are stained a pink so dark it appears red in the ebbing light of the moon. It only makes me scrub harder, my breaths becoming more ragged the harder I scrub.

The image of Nik's head on my plate flashes in my mind, the stained rice and blood mixing with lemon sauce bringing bile to my tongue as sweat beads on my forehead.

I sink lower in the bath, lower and lower until I am submerged, my breaths no longer ragged, but catching in my chest. The tainted water blurs the domed ceiling, the image rippling with the movements of the water. The sandstone turns hazy like a mirage. If only my life were a mirage. If only the past days were a dream.

I do not surface from the depths of the bath until my lungs are burning and my eyes are stinging. Even then, the image of Nikolai still torments my mind. Nothing will rid me of the haunting picture. Nothing will make me forget, even for a moment. The Mother Star will force me to acknowledge my failures. Even if it kills me.

I break the surface and gulp down precious air, my hands sliding into my tangled hair and tugging. The sob crawling up my throat is so intense I almost choke on it.

"Bria? Shit, you okay?"

I manage a brisk nod and nothing more.

Wyn's return calms me, it anchors me to the here and now, and I push down the scorching emotions and turn to her. "Where did you go?"

"Van wanted a word. I filled him in on everything that's happened here, too."

I nod again. It seems I can do nothing other than nod.

She says, "We have a plan. Obviously, I'll have to go back and help with the finer details and such, but there *is* a plan. We're getting you out."

"How?"

Her silver eyes are as intense as the sharpest blade. "We're going to declare war against the Summer Court."

"Tohminic has already declared war against Dusk. I do not see how declaring war against him in return helps matters."

"War is fickle. If we do not acknowledge Tohminic's threat, the other courts will side with us if he ever attacks. Declaring ourselves as his enemy puts us in a difficult position with the rest of Radelea, but we're prepared to do that for you."

This time, I shake my head. "I cannot allow it. War is not a game to be played, choosing pawns and pieces as you see fit. It is cruel. It is brutal. You are putting your court at risk unnecessarily." I stand, water running from my body in rivulets, leaving clean skin behind. "You cannot declare war because of me. I would rather die."

She steps closer. "You're one of us now, and we take care of our own. No matter the consequences. You chose Dusk in that fucked up dating circle your father forced you into. You *chose* us, Bria, and we choose you right back. Dusk is your home. Fight for it."

"You have only known me a matter of days."

"It's enough."

My voice rises. "It is not enough to put your denizens at risk. I will not allow it."

"This isn't your call. Vander has to make a big move, regardless of your circumstances. He has to make a stand against the other courts who are fighting for their claim to *our* land. This is how. This benefits us as much as it benefits you. Now, as heir to the throne of Dusk, I refuse to hear more on the matter." She gestures to the towels, her expression daring me to continue arguing.

I snatch a bundle of rough fabric from a low cupboard. "This is a mistake. I'm not worth it."

She says nothing more while I dry myself and slide a sheer robe over my body. She says nothing while the two guards escort us back to my chamber. And she remains silent while I struggle to dress myself in a two-piece gown.

A single strip of lavender silk covers my breasts. The lace sleeves, which are separate from the bodice, are rough against my raw skin, made worse by the flames stitched into the netting. The skirt is also lace, with the same fiery pattern, and nothing but a narrow strip of silk at both the front and back that slides between my legs as I walk. I might as well be naked.

The piece is complete with a silk belt low on my hips, a heavy gold necklace, and several bangles clinking together at my wrists.

I have no mirror to determine if I look as ridiculous as I feel, and nothing to help me with my hair, so I braid it over one shoulder to keep it from my face. There is not a shred of care inside me wishing for the approval from anyone in the Summer

Court, though I am afraid if I do not dress appropriately, my punishment will be severe.

A low screech outside my door has me ripping it open to see what the commotion is about, only to stagger back at the sight that greets me. "What is this?"

My eyes widen at the twin wheels, at the metal bars forming the grid of a tall structure, and at the two guards gripping the long wooden handles in front. It's a cage. And Tohminic's gloating face looms from behind.

"This is how you move through the keep," Tohminic sneers. "I once told you freedom has to be earned. Your pathetic attempt at escape has proven you are not to be trusted. Get in."

23

A QUICK LOOK OVER my shoulder, and I am pleased Wyn had the sense to duck into her miniscule, hidden space when I opened the door. The less the Summer fae see her, the less they will expect to see her. She will be able to illusion in and out as she sees fit and not raise their suspicions.

I step closer to the cage, unwilling to anger Tohminic today. The scent of metal tickles my nose. "But it is iron," I say, my feet stilling. "It will burn me, kill me if I am touching it long enough."

Though it smells no different from any other metal, I am one hundred percent certain they made the cage of the dangerous iron. If I so much as graze my skin against the bars... If Tohminic forces me into it, I will endure untold pain.

"You should have considered that before you tried to escape," snarls Tohminic. "I will not ask again. Get in the cage like the disgusting animal you are."

I make myself believe the pain of touching the iron will be nothing, *nothing* compared to the pain of being responsible for the murder of an innocent fae, but even with the words repeating in my mind, a cry escapes as I wrap my hands around the bars of the cage.

My palms sear with such intensity, I fear scorch marks will forever mark my flesh. The scream that tears at my throat as I haul my body into the confined space is piercing and brutal. It lingers as I settle in the middle of the cage, then fades to a whimper.

The bars are woven so close together, I have no chance of finding a reprieve from the scalding metal. Each miniscule movement causes stabs of intense pain, the crossing bars branding my skin even through the fine fabric of my skirt.

The cage rocks as Tohminic slams the door closed. "I do hope you are hungry," he says, his smile cruel and cunning.

I lurch forward when the cage rolls, and catch myself on the side wall. Again, the iron torments my hands. My tear-filled eyes meet Wyn's as the guards wheel me away, and I am begging her with every fibre of my being to save me from this torture.

Her chin dips ever so slightly and she mouths, "Soon."

The relief that fills me at the single word is short-lived.

The cage tilts as we take a tight left turn, and I am thrown to the side, my upper arm pressing against the horrid metal. This time, I hold the whimpers in. I will not allow Tohminic to witness another shred of pain or fear.

I straighten, adjusting the silk strap at my rear so I am sitting on it. It eases some of the pain, though my hands are throbbing and uncomfortable. They will heal before breakfast ends. I just have to remain still.

But breakfast is unbearable.

The moment I am wheeled into the dining hall, I realise why Tohminic hoped I was hungry. I am only granted the privilege of eating if the Summer fae wish it. A handful of them throw crumbs and half-eaten food at my cage, and if it does not fly through the gaps, then it is too bad for me. They leave it on the floor, where it mocks my growling stomach.

I am taunted and laughed at. I am ridiculed. It is the lowest point of my life.

The little food I eat does nothing to soothe the cramps. It may be one grain of rice, one slither of flat bread, or rabbit meat which has already been chewed. Whatever it may be, I eat it.

This is the first time in my life I have not known where my next meal is coming from, and I am reluctant to take any chances. If Tohminic decides I have not earned the right to eat… I do not want to think about the consequences.

After breakfast, the rest of the court disappears to do whatever it is they do here. Likely torture innocent souls or skin fae from other courts alive or something just as nauseating.

Alone in the dining hall with Tohminic, Chlora, and Xaler is not something I would wish for ever again. Especially when the Summer lord wields his necromancy magic to call forward an additional guard.

The headless male saunters towards me, his hands cradling a bloodied head. The gaping wound at his neck causes bile to coat my tongue. Nikolai is unmistakable, even in death.

Knowing it is a reaction Tohminic is seeking, I do not offer him one. I keep my lips pressed in a firm line and meet his gaze head on.

"Do you have nothing to say of your guard?" he taunts.

I glare harder.

"Very well." He turns to Xaler. "Take her on a tour of the castle and our lands. Have her back by sundown."

"Am I to abide by any restrictions?"

Tohminic smirks. "She is to remain in the cage. Otherwise, there are no rules to speak of."

Xaler rubs his hands together in glee before heaving on my cage and wheeling me out of the dining hall.

He takes me to the throne room, where nobles gather to throw rocks at me. They clang against the iron, reverberating and shuddering the bars. Then to the kitchens, where even the servants sneer. I would say I am grateful for the fresh air of the courtyard if it were not for the younglings poking sharpened sticks through the gaps in the cage. The Summer Court is a cruel, cruel place.

We visit the outskirts of a scorching desert close to Ad'Star-rag, where the bars of my cage grow so hot I cannot bear to touch them. The burning sand blows against my skin, causing pin pricks of blood to rise to the surface. I am soon covered in miniscule blisters which have no right to hurt so badly.

The eastern village rests on a rocky shore, and the denizens are happy to oblige Xaler's request for luncheon while they taunt me with wine and ale. One kind female — an aged fae with pink skin and a stained apron — sneaks a slice of mouldy bread into my cage, demanding I thank her for her efforts. I do, and I force myself to eat it.

After Xaler enjoys a meal of roasted turkey and buttery pota-toes, he takes me along the border with Autumn, where my father's guards are patrolling the demarcation of the courts. They turn their faces away. It hurts more than the rest of it, the knowledge my home court will not bother to rescue me. It hurts so much not even the sight of Nikolai's broken body bothers me in that moment.

The rolling hills in Summer's west are rife with wildlife, and even the small creatures seem to shun the broken female in the cage.

Throughout the entire day, I endure the pain of the iron. My skin is red, raw, blistered, throbbing with intense pain. Every bump in the road sends me crashing into the cage walls, every tight corner has my face smacking against the metal, and every damn gust of wind ravages my tender wounds. None of it is more intense than the burning gaze of the Mother Star, who threatens to engulf me in flames with her strength alone. Sometimes I wish she would.

By the time Xaler wheels me back into the keep, I am thankful for the setting sun and the safety of the sandstone walls. Twilight blazes across the sky, painting the horizon in indigo and deep pink, seen through the open arches of a hallway I have yet to see.

The guards who took over from Xaler refuse to tell me where they are taking me. They are too intent on their task of dragging my torture cage through the keep to so much as utter an explanation.

They wheel me through a set of large oak doors and push me into a grand chamber before retreating with smirks on their evil faces.

My body goes rigid when I realise where I am. The extravagant furniture, all gleaming under the shimmering fae lights. The gauzy curtains around the bed and many open windows, all fluttering in the evening breeze. This chamber is fit for a High Lord, and only a High Lord.

Voices travel along the open hallway behind me, laughter piercing the quiet. "The way she cringed when Xaler poked his trident into the cage was worth the annoyance of her presence at dinner."

"I am glad you approve, Chlora," says Tohminic as the two enter the chamber.

"Does she have to be in here?" Chlora whines, freezing in the doorway. "Seeing her at dinner is one thing. Having her in your bedchamber is another."

I scoff. "I would much rather be anywhere else. It is not like I *chose* this."

Tohminic pushes against the cage with his foot. I topple sideways from the force of it, my face colliding with the side. "You will not speak unless I grant you permission to do so." Turning back to Chlora, he fists his hand in the back of her hair, angling her head so she is forced to look into his yellow eyes. "Ignore her. You are here because I allow it, Chlora. Do not test me. Not tonight."

She traces a finger down his chest, dragging it across the ridges of his abdominals and to the waistband of his pants. "You know I do not mind observers to our intimacy, Tohm. It is just... She is so *plain*. She detracts from the moment."

"Then I will call for Ayda. Unless you would prefer she join us, rather than replace you?"

Chlora pouts. "I would rather have you all to myself, but if you wish for Ayda to join, I will not refuse."

"Good, because she is already here." Tohminic sweeps an arm out, beckoning a naked female from the adjoining bathing chamber.

Ayda is stunning. So stunning, I find it impossible she is from the Summer Court. How can a place so disgusting and violent produce such a beauty? Her deep brown skin reflects the fae lights hovering overhead, as if she is covered in golden glitter. Perhaps she is. Her eyes, twin pits of molten amber, drip with desire, matching the dampness gathering between her legs.

Tohminic pulls her to him, his mouth closing over a pert nipple. The bulge in his pants grows instantly.

I look away. I do not need to witness this.

Before I can close my eyes, a gleaming blade is sliding through the bars of my cage, sticking into the delicate skin of my throat.

"You will watch," Tohminic growls. "Or I will gouge your eyes out and set them on the table, and force you to observe every night for the rest of your miserable life."

"Why?" I spit. "Why must I watch you?"

"Because you tried to run and I refuse to let you out of my sight. That, and it pleases me to know you have no choice. It pleases me that you will be reminded of Nikolai from Day every night in this bedchamber. You will watch because I demand it." He rests the long sword against the exterior of the cage before returning to the females and demanding one of them sit atop the table in the centre of the main chamber.

I watch in seething silence while Ayda sits on the gleaming tabletop and spreads her legs wide. I am just as enraged as Chlora pushes her back as far as she can go before slipping her tongue inside Ayda. Bile burns my throat when Tohminic slams his cock inside Chlora without warning, eliciting a delighted moan from the female.

Tohminic thrusts hard and fast. The force of his pounding is bruising.

Chlora moans and screams while grazing her teeth over Ayda's clitoris.

Ayda grasps Chlora's head in a tight grip and holds her face still. She grinds her hips against Chlora's face, her eyes never leaving Tohminic's.

Tohminic's movements become so rough, I am concerned for Chlora's wellbeing. He grunts with every brutal thrust, the veins on his neck pulsing.

Chlora fights for freedom desperately, but neither Ayda nor Tohminic are prepared to let her go. When her movements grow slow and jerky, and her body sags, Tohminic roars his release at the same time Ayda screams through an orgasm.

When they release Chlora, she does not move. She remains still for several heartbeats until she bolts upright, her hands groping her neck as she gasps for breath, those intense blue eyes wide with... Not fear, but desire.

"Ayda," growls Tohminic, stroking his still engorged cock, "give Chlora what she is dripping for."

Ayda complies.

It goes on much the same for the rest of the night. I lose count of how often both females lose consciousness from lack of air, lose count of the orgasms, and I lose track of the time.

Our fae bodies can endure a lot, though I am not certain repeated asphyxiation is good for anyone, no matter the strength of the body and mind.

The hell I am living through only gets worse from there.

Over the following four days, I am shamed, I am threatened, I endure torture, and I am forced to witness Tohminic's pleasure. Each night it is different. Sometimes it is just Tohminic and Chlora. Sometimes a different male or female joins them. Always different, never the same.

I stop seeing it after the second night. Though I direct my eyes towards the bed or table or wall or floor, wherever Tohminic performs, I do not pay attention to what occurs. I see naked bodies and hear bliss-filled moans, but my mind is numb.

All my skin matches. Scars in the shape of the lace flames cover my arms and legs, as if to remind me I will never be free of the Summer Court. Even if I find freedom from these sandstone walls, the flames on my skin will forever remind me of this torture.

24

I CANNOT SEE PAST the pain today.

All I know is the torture of metal blistering my skin.

Wyn tells me the Dusk Court has gathered at the border of Autumn and Summer, ignoring Father's threat to attack if they remain in his territory. They know he will not do so when they are marching to save me, Princess Bria Sutherland, of no court, no magic, no family.

No freedom from the red.

I cannot focus through the pain. Is it worry or anger or something else on Wyn's face? I cannot think why Dusk would do such a thing. Why march on Ad'Starrag? Why ally with Day and Dawn? Dusk and Dawn and Day. D, d, d. *Red, red, red.*

She leaves after mere heartbeats, too afraid of being discovered in Tohminic's chambers. Again, I am left alone with the torturous metal and my equally tormenting thoughts.

The Mother Star comes and goes. Seven days of blazing heat.

Seven moons of being guarded by Nikolai's gruesome body.

Red, red, red.

I lose my mind to the pain.

Wyn sneaks into Tohminic's chambers to tell me Zentha's forces have joined the marching army of Dusk. But what does it mean? An armada in the west. An infantry of foot soldiers to the north.

The note of pride in her voice when she speaks of Vander's accomplishments means nothing to me. The surprise when she tells me of Dawn sailing south to trap Summer from the east means nothing.

I gasp through the pain and beg her to leave me be. Leave me to die from the pain. It is too much. I cannot think past the hatred I have for myself every time I look at my undead guard, at Nikolai, his skin grey and buzzing with flies.

⁂

The Dusk Court has infiltrated Summer's eastern village.

Tohminic is unaware, too wrapped up in my torture and his pleasure. He urges younglings to poke me with sticks while spilling his seed in Chlora's mouth. He encourages the prodding of swords while he abuses another female's body. The dead body of my former lover still obeys Tohminic's every command, haunting my days and nights both.

There is a voice whispering in my ear, telling me to bend and meld and control. I do not know the voice and I do not know where it comes from. I do not know if it is real, or if it even uses words. There is a voice, but I cannot hear it because my skin *burns*.

I cannot see. My vision is black around the edges, blurred in the centre.

Pain is my life now. Pain and sorrow and red. *Red, red, red.*

In the brief moment I see Wyn, she tells me Jonik's armada has anchored to the east — Dawn and Dusk are allies in this war. Zentha and her court will not march with them, but she is holding the western and northern borders — indeed, it was a lie that Tohminic seized the forest bordering Summer and Day, just as we thought — which is more than enough given Zentha and Father are so close.

Tohminic finally takes notice. He spends the day, the ninth since I entered the cage, raging throughout the keep, threatening fae and spitting venomous words at whoever will listen. Most of it is aimed at me, yet I do not notice.

I cannot think of anything through the continued pain or the whispering voices telling me to bend and meld and control. To contort. All I know is Tohminic is too late to realise, too late to act. Too late, too late. *Red, red, red.*

25

EVERY DAY I HAVE been in this cage, I have tied a torn strip of lace to the cage bars. It is the only way I can determine how long I have been enduring the constant pain. I stare at the nine crude ribbons, though there seems to be eighteen, and blink back the ever present tears.

It is seldom I am lucid enough to notice such things — the pain keeps my mind distracted, my eyes blurred and black at the edges, and I can smell nothing other than the blistering flesh covering my body — but today I am aware of the lace ties, I am aware of what they mean.

Tonight is the full moon.

I feel as though more time has passed than a single full moon. So much has happened since the last time I snuck from the Autumn Court to meet Nikolai at the docks of the western village.

Father wished for me to find a mate to secure an alliance for our court and rushed through the courtship to be rid of me sooner. I endured the males I was to impress, I suffered through feasts and walks, and an ogre attacked me. I learned of Father's true feelings towards me. For the past five and seventy years, I have been nothing but a burden on the Autumn Court, nothing but unwanted and unloved. It is a harsh reality to come to terms with.

Then there is Tohminic.

Not wishing to recall every twisted thought relating to the High Lord of Summer, I drag my eyes from the lace tied on the cage bars.

I am in the rotunda today. Xaler wheeled me into the centre of the enclosed space, directly in the path of the Mother Star's scorching rays, so I may watch the preparations for tonight. So far, I have almost fainted from the onslaught of pain and heat three times, and each time, Xaler has thrown a bucket of iced water over my cage.

There will be no rest for me today. Not even the false slumber of unconsciousness I have succumbed to often over the last nine moons.

The fountain bubbles innocently beside me, the rare droplet of cool water splashing against my ravaged skin.

The lace and silk two-piece gown clings to my fading body, ruined from days of wear. Where I have torn strips of lace from the skirt, the frayed edges are becoming unravelled. Soon, there will be nothing of the narrow length of silk between my legs to hide behind. Stains cover the lavender lace from the scraps of food thrown into the cage, from the blood seeping from my many wounds, and from the spittle the Summer fae love to disrespect me with.

The wounds themselves are red and angry. The repetition of touching the iron and my fae body healing the wounds has left an array of scars over my arms and legs. Some of them take the same shape as the flames stitched into the lace, some are mirrors of the crosses of the cage, others are lines made by the occasional sword or stick poking into me.

I will not be the same if I am ever freed of this torturous life. Every scar is a reminder of what I have endured. Though sometimes, I believe it is my fate to suffer after what I did to Nikolai.

Red, red, red. The simple word has lost all meaning. My hands are the usual ivory. I know it to be true, yet I can only see crimson whenever I look at them. I can only see it when I look at the undead guard who is always by my side.

Nikolai's abused body is its own form of unbearable pain. I can cope with the physical abuse... just. But seeing my dead lover's body day in and day out is a special kind of torture. My mind is in anguish with every glance at the decaying body, and I take great measures to avoid looking in his direction.

He is beside my cage now, so still it is unnerving as he awaits his next command.

I had hoped Tohminic would grow tired of the mental and emotional abuse, or at least his magic would become drained from the constant use, yet every time he lays eyes on Nikolai's severed head, there is a triumphant gleam shining from the yellow, a kind of sick pleasure in the knowledge I am suffering, that he is the cause of such pain.

Maids and other lesser fae scurry about the rotunda, placing decorations on the sandstone walls surrounding the circular space. They add silk sheets the colour of a blazing flame to the beds in the alcoves, pulling them taut and smoothing the surface. Some weave large carnations onto twine, others scrub the stone pavers on the ground until they are impossibly gleaming, and two work together to cleanse the water in the fountain.

In the time it takes for the sun to meet her zenith, the rotunda is sparkling and decorated in shades of amber, deep orange, and ruby red. So much effort for a sex party. Too much effort for a court so deplorable.

There is a hazy memory flickering in the back of my mind, a demanding pulse urging me to pay closer attention. There is a reason I am being forced to remain conscious today, when Tohminic often takes great pleasure in my fading strength. The memory is slippery, though, as if made of water or the finest of sand, and I cannot focus on it.

It is a word on the tip of my tongue, my mind unable to connect the dots and find the right way to form the letters. It is the end of a rainbow, forever teasing that it is near, only for me to crest the last hill to find another mountain hiding the pot of gold. A sigh flutters through my lips, and I leave the memory be. It is not as if I could focus through the stabbing pain, even if I wanted to.

A servant carrying a tray of pastry rushes past. From here, it looks to be buttery and flaky and stuffed with some kind of creamy concoction dotted with raisins. My stomach growls and cramps, the pain miniscule compared to that of my throbbing thighs, reminding me I have not eaten a full meal for nine days.

"Please," I croak. "Please, if you would be so kind."

The servant does not deign to acknowledge me.

Xaler, who has been monitoring me from the shade of an alcove, laughs. "Are the crumbs you receive not enough? Are you ungrateful?" His voice is distant in my ears, the buzz of anger too loud. He pushes away from the sandstone wall, his predatory gait meant to intimidate. "Do you know what we do to those who are not grateful for their hand in life?"

"No." My dry tongue flicks out to wet my cracked lips, doing little to ease the discomfort. "Though I am sure you will tell me."

His trident appears in his hand, gleaming in the noonday sun as he balances it in his open palm. His fingers curl around the bright metal — brass, I believe — and hold it tight, the three prongs aimed at my face. "We give them something to be grateful for. Life."

"While I would pay good money to watch you taunt the bastard," says a cruel voice I know all too well, "I have need of her."

"My Lord," says Xaler, his chin dipping.

Tohminic's eyes don't stray from my cage. "It seems Dusk has us surrounded. The Dawn Court has anchored their armada off our eastern shore. The Day Court has sent an infantry to the northern border and an armada to the west. Your friends march on my keep as we speak. What should I do about that?"

The memory that was nagging for my attention blazes in my mind, an image of Wyn desperately begging me to hold on for one more day until Vander and his army reach the Summer Court's keep. By nightfall, Ad'Starrag will be surrounded by enemies.

"I do not know. Surrender?" My voice comes out weak and rough.

"I spent the entire day yesterday in a fit of rage," Tohminic admits. "Did you know I blamed myself for allowing this to happen? But it is not my fault. In fact, I am the last fae who shall shoulder blame."

My face remains neutral, but in my mind… In my mind, I am screaming. He is so very wrong. If he did not threaten each of those courts by declaring war against them — and the Spring and Autumn Courts, though they are unlikely to come to my aid — this would never have happened. There is no one else to blame but Tohminic.

He continues, "No. The blame rests on the shoulders of your hand maiden, does it not?"

My spine stiffens. It is not possible. Wyn has been so careful.

"My Lord?" asks Xaler, gripping his trident tighter.

Tohminic's lip curls into a snarl. "She is Wynetta Theron, sister of the High Lord of Dusk. I was pleasantly surprised by the revelation when I received Vander's message to free her at once. I would have released her if he had not revealed her identity."

She was supposed to find me this morning. When she did not show, I thought nothing of it, believing her to be busy with preparations for the siege.

Tohminic turns to Xaler. "Take her to her chamber. When you have done that, I need you in the war chamber. We are under siege."

Xaler's trident disappears with a swish of his hand, and he moves to grip the long wooden handles of my wagon cage.

"Wait." A cough tears at my parched throat. "You cannot harm her."

Tohminic laughs. "Why not? I can do whatever I wish within the walls of my home. A bastard daughter with no magic to speak of will not give me orders. I worked hard for my position. I earned the respect my title demands, earned the right to make decisions here."

"He will kill you." There is not an ounce of uncertainty in my tone.

He and Xaler laugh, clearly believing my words to be nothing more than a joke.

Xaler shakes his head and wheels my cage through the keep towards my chamber.

I am certain I speak true. Vander will not rest until he exacts revenge on his sister's behalf. Though I do not know him well, I know this to be certain with every fibre of my being, as if my soul is looking into his and seeing the truth. I have witnessed the bond the Dusk siblings share. The Mother Star knows I have suffered the envy upon seeing them laugh together, wishing I could share such a connection with Rennyn.

The moment Xaler pushes my cage into my chamber, which I have not entered in days, and I see Wyn trapped just as I am, I lunge for the iron bars and grip them with all my strength. "Forget Vander," I spit at Tohminic. "*I* will be the one to end you, Lord of Summer." My incredulous stare lingers on the closed door, a rush of adrenaline coursing through my body and making my entire being tingle.

They left us here. I am alone for the first time in nine moons.

The pain makes itself known, and my thoughts catch up to me. I snatch my hands from the iron bars and twist to face Wyn. "Are you okay?" The disbelief in my tone is clear as a summer sky.

She shifts against the bars, her maid's gown serving as a blanket of protection against the iron. "I'm not worried about me. My skin won't touch the iron, not with this hideous gown on. Blessed Mother Star, the only time I don't send an illusion, and I'm captured."

"I am so sorry."

"It's not your fault," she says, her face screwing in confusion and disbelief. The emotions settle, and her eyes soften. "How are you?"

"I do not know how to answer that." The iron scorches my skin as I settle back in the cage. "Not well. I am not well at all."

"At least you're lucid today. The past few days you've been... You haven't been yourself. I don't think you even noticed when I was here."

"Not that I am ungrateful you are here, but why are you in my chamber? Why risk coming back?"

She sighs. "Vander ordered it. He wants you out. He was hoping the Dusk Court's arrival would distract Tohminic, and I'd be able to slip in and break you out of that damn cage."

A laugh — a foreign concept to me these days — bubbles up my throat. "And how did you plan on doing that?"

"With an Atryxium blade. They can cut through anything, even diamond."

"But they are rare." I cast my eyes over the chamber to find the blade. When I do not find it, I ask, "Where is it?"

"Confiscated by the guards who found me sneaking into your bedchamber."

For the first time since they threw me into this torture chamber, tears line my eyes. "What are we going to do? He will not let us go, even with the siege."

"Vander is prepared to wait it out, but I think you're right. Tohminic will kill us and attack our army before letting himself or his fae starve. They haven't received a delivery of food since we moved on the village. I've already sent an illusion of myself to Vander and told him about all of this. He's discussing our options with Torin. He's our army commander."

"Will he come here to tell us what is to happen?"

She speaks too quickly. "No. No, I have forbid it."

"Why?" She looks away, training her eyes on the hundreds of Dawn ships dotting the ocean. I growl, "Wyn."

"There's something you should know," she says, still not looking at me. "I haven't mentioned it to Vander yet, but I believe you —" She snaps her mouth closed when the door squeals open.

We both turn to Tohminic, surprised to see him back so soon. Unless... He must have been listening at the door.

I throw my mind back, trying to pick apart our conversation and discover if we let anything important slip. Other than Vander's willingness to see the siege through, I do not believe there was anything damaging. Thank the Mother Star for small mercies.

Four guards trail in behind Tohminic, acting on silent orders and heaving our cages into the hallway. We roll through Ad'Starrag in a strange line, two cages pulled by two guards each, with the High Lord leading the way.

While they drag us to wherever Tohminic has commanded, the High Lord tells us of his plans. I try my hardest to ignore his words, but when he mentions death, I strain to listen carefully.

"Our plan is simple. Upon seeing his sister and her friend so destroyed, Vander of the Dusk Court will act out of rage instead of careful planning. My denizens will wait for the right moment to attack, and when Vander is distracted and enraged by your state, he will be too slow to react. We will allow him glimpses of you both from the battlements, and his rage will slowly grow until it gets the better of him. He will snap when we kill the Dusk female."

When Tohminic is looking towards the ocean, I whip my head to Wyn, my eyebrows raised in question. *Will it work? Will he succumb to the anger?*

She rolls her eyes and shakes her head. *No, he's not that stupid.*

The guards struggle to drag us up a curved incline towards the battlement's crenelations, heaving and panting as they pull with all their strength.

Tohminic ignores their struggle and continues gloating. "The Dawn Court should have remained neutral, as they have for the past four hundred years. Their light and healing magic is inconsequential compared to the might of my selkie army."

I watch Wyn as her face slackens, her eyes flutter closed, and her body tilts to the side. Her cheek presses against the iron bars on the side of her cage, but she does not react.

Mere moments later, she jerks upright with a gasp, her hand clasping her blistered face. She glances at me, smirking through the pain causing her face to contort.

Though it is nearing dinner time, the Mother Star's light is blazing when we exit onto the battlement, and I squint my eyes against her brightness.

Having never been granted access to the battlements in my time at Ad'Starrag, I have yet to witness the magnificence of such a view. The crenels in the sandstone bricks reveal the glittering eastern ocean beyond. The Dawn ships with their golden sails bob in the rippling waves that steadily grow larger until they crash against the rocky shore the keep rests atop.

To my right, the battlement is open and looks over the rotunda, where the Summer fae are already beginning to gather, unaware of the mayhem outside the keep walls.

Tohminic leads us towards the southern battlement, where soldiers and guards stand at every embrasure, some hiding behind the higher merlons. Though he does not linger, and continues on to the western side of the keep.

Halfway along the western battlement, the guards pulling my cage lower the handles, setting the iron trap in full view of the army far below.

They stand to attention on the low, narrow bridge arcing away from the mainland, preventing access to and from Ad'Starrag. They stand in long lines beyond the lapping waves, weapons of every description at the ready. The Dusk Court is large, intimidatingly so, and does not look to be leaving anytime soon. Thousands. There are thousands of them.

More difficult to see is row upon row of indigo tents stretching as far as the eye can see, across the plains and into the rolling hills far in the distance. Thin curls of smoke trail to the ever-darkening sky, the amber of small fires casting an eerie glow over the war camp.

Standing on the land bridge with his axe at his hip, Vander is the image of vengeance. His silver eyes are noticeable even from my substantial height atop the keep. The flutter that ignites in my chest is one of hope and relief; it is a moment of gratitude to the Mother Star for blessing me with meeting the Dusk High Lord, gratitude for his strength and determination, for his morals. The flutter grows in intensity until it is all I can think about.

26

Tohminic steps between the two iron cages. "Can you see his anger? It is brewing. From his station on *my* land bridge, he can only see your outlines and the cages that hold you. But even from there, he can hear." A long sword appears in each of his hands, and he stabs them through the bars of both cages.

A scream tears at my throat, the attack so fast and surprising, I cannot react fast enough. The blade slices across the top of my thigh, cutting through the lace of my dress as if it is made of air. Blood dribbles from the wound, and I clamp my hands over my leg to stem the flow.

Wyn, with her healthy body and rested mind, reacts faster. She jerks out of harm's way in time to avoid being sliced open, though her palms grip the iron bars and are soon covered in fresh blisters. She does not make a sound.

It enrages Tohminic. He pokes both blades through Wyn's cage time and time again until he pierces the soft flesh of her stomach.

Pulling the sword free with a satisfied chuckle, Tohminic turns to the Dusk army below and shouts, "The females you fight for will not survive past the setting of the sun." He pokes a blade into my cage, causing a scream to tear from my throat, even knowing I am untouched. "You see? Why risk your court for two worthless females?"

Vander does not deign to respond.

Instead, a whisper runs along the army. The soldiers part, their thunderous steps a blast across the land as they cleave a neat line through their centre. The Dusk fae cleave two more open spaces on either side of the first, splitting the thousands-strong army into four groups.

From the rear of the distinct lines, guards roll three wooden contraptions forward. To me, they look like giant spoons balancing on a point, but history and sense tell me they are catapults. The Dusk army will use them to send shards of iron — or melt it into a scalding liquid — over the battlements, or they will fill them with poison and send that careening through the air. Either way, it is an obvious threat to the Summer Court.

One Tohminic does not appreciate.

His magic gathers around him in a suffocating wave of intense heat. The taste of ash mixing with rot coats my parched tongue, the chirp of crickets and the screech of cicadas fills my ears, and my skin becomes sticky with a fine sheen of sweat. He holds a great deal of power in those torturous hands of his.

I should have known this would never be a siege. I should have known Tohminic would not allow his home to be surrounded or his freedom held in Vander's hands.

A flicker of flame appears in Tohminic's palm, growing steadily larger until he is holding a fireball the size of a large boulder with both hands. The crackling red and amber spins faster and faster until he launches it through the air, where it grows larger still as it travels.

If I thought he intended the blazing ball of fire for Vander and his army, I was so very wrong. All thoughts of the cage I am trapped in flee my mind, every stab of pain fades to nothing, and the sting of the iron beneath my palms is a mere tickle as I grip the bars and press my face close to the edge of the cage, watching as Tohminic's fire careens through the twilight on a trajectory for the Dawn ships.

What no one in the Summer Court expects, me least of all, is for each ship to be host to a Day fae. The water wielders balance precariously on the bowsprits, great orbs of glistening water growing in their palms, just as Tohminic's fire grew in his.

When the fiery ball is within range — almost scorching the sails of the first ships, now large enough to destroy two ships at once — the Day fae send their orbs of water crashing into the ball of fire. The hiss of steam rushing across the land is like a screeching blanket.

Tohminic snarls and kicks Wyn's cage in a fit of rage.

I peel my eyes from the fleet of ships for a mere heartbeat to ensure she is okay — she topples to the side, using a hand to catch herself on the iron bars, and though the metal sears through her palm, she does not utter a sound — and the moment she rights herself, I drag my gaze back to the armada.

Shadows speed through the water from every direction, tracking in a straight line for the closest ship. They dip and weave with and against the current, the sleek bodies of the seals cutting through the water with ease.

My blood runs cold. The selkies intend to board the ships and attack any fae who dares to get in their way.

Tohminic intends to fight his way to freedom.

It will be a blood bath.

I briefly wonder if the triplets or High Lord Jonik are on any of the ships. I cannot see the royal emblem of Dawn from here. The flag denoting the rising sun is impossible to see from such a distance, especially with the bursts of bright orange staining the sky beyond as the Mother Star sinks, her lower curve touching the ocean horizon.

Never mind the triplets left me alone in the middle of a forest with the threat of the Dullahan, Day's most feared creature, hanging over my head like a dark shadow. I am not so twisted that I wish them harm. In fact, I would mourn their deaths should the selkies succeed in their mission.

The pain in my palms becomes too much, and I snatch my hands away from the iron bars without taking my eyes from the ships in the distance.

Something dark oozes from the hulls of the ships and spreads through the water at a rapid pace, moved along by the Dusk and Day fae, the wind and water magic spreading it faster. When the selkies' shadows pierce the dark cloud, they freeze in their tracks, their shadows becoming smaller and smaller until they are gone completely.

"Your selkie army can't breach the armada." Vander's voice is a whisper on the wind, impossible to miss as it caresses my every sense. "You can't win this. Surrender the females."

From the rocky shore to the east, a ferocious snarl echoes towards us. Xaler has lost many of his soldiers without them so much as laying a finger on a single ship.

Tohminic whips an arm out and grips a guard by the neck of his tunic. "Take the females to Bria's chamber." He points to another guard without releasing the first. "Find Xaler. Have him meet me in the war chamber so we can reassess."

"Yes, My Lord," both males mutter as one.

The same two guards who dragged me onto the battlements grip the handles of my cage and pull me towards the corner tower.

Tohminic stands in front of them, halting their progress. "When you deliver them to her chamber, open the cages. Do not help them out, but do not hinder them, either. If the females wish to eat, they may make their own way to the dining hall. No. They *will* try to find food. You are not to touch them or help them. If you pass anyone in the halls, do not allow them to help the females. Though if my denizens wish to taunt or hinder, they have earned the right to do so."

"Yes, My Lord," the guard on the left says. "We understand. At what time do you require the females to be back in the chamber?"

"They have until the Mother Star has disappeared."

I cast a glance towards the horizon. It is not long enough. There is no chance of me climbing from this cage, making my way to the dining hall, finding something to eat, and making it back before the Mother Star is gone. Especially if a Summer fae comes across me along the way. This is another of Tohminic's games.

"Why?" I ask, unable to prevent the word from slipping past my lips.

Tohminic's eyes brighten. "You are no use to me if you cannot react. The short time free of the cage will allow your body to heal just enough." He moves aside, his yellow glare tracking me as the guards drag me across the battlement towards the steep descent of the corner tower.

The guards standing ready and waiting at the crenels do not take their eyes from the gathered Dusk army as I pass, each of them gripping their bows tightly in their hands. All I can think about is how this moment reflects the life I have lived.

Ignored, ordered to do as a male pleases, and used as a pawn in everyone's games. Bria of the Autumn Court, pawn and bastard.

My guards struggle to hold the cage steady as we begin the descent into the keep; the weight of the iron is too much with the steep decline.

The male on the right loses his grip, both hands slipping from the wooden handle he holds. "Blessed Mother Star!" he shouts, shoving his hands against the cage to keep it from rolling to the bottom. He screams in agony when his palms collide with the iron, then jerks them away.

It is too much for the second guard to take all the weight, and like his fellow Summer fae, he loses control of the cage.

It crashes against the sandstone wall, only to rebound and slam into the guard on the right, who is gingerly holding his hands to his chest. The collision sends him crashing to the ground — the rough bump from the wheel crushing the male beneath its substantial weight is something I will forever recall.

The huff of air rushing from fae lungs sends a shiver down my spine and knots my stomach, and I hope to never hear such a sound again.

But my mind cannot focus on the crushed male or the second guard scrambling to prevent the cage from crashing its way to the ground level. No, all I can think is I am going to die here tonight. I will be thrown in every direction as the cage smashes against the walls, I will endure the burning sting of iron against my flesh with every bump and roll, and I will scream from the pain, my voice carrying throughout Ad'Starrag and to the waiting armies beyond.

The last anyone will hear from Bria Sutherland will be the cries of pain and the sigh of breath deserting my lungs.

The Mother Star has other plans. The cage slams against the wall so hard, a wheel crumbles. It teeters for a moment before tilting to the side. The stars have blessed me with the tight corner of the tower, making it almost impossible for the cage to continue its destructive descent now it is on its side.

My body aches in an uncountable amount of places, muscles throbbing and spasming as a groan slips free and I push myself upright. The silk beneath my legs has come loose, and the iron bars burn new wounds into my flesh, but the sting is miniscule compared to the pulsing pain at the back of my head.

I touch a trembling hand to my knotted hair. It comes away slick with blood.

"Bria? Are you okay?" Wyn shouts from above.

"I think so," I moan.

Turning back, I am not surprised to see the guard who first lost his grip on the handles has succumbed to his injuries. The second guard has blisters on his palms, but appears otherwise unharmed. He calls for a replacement for his fallen comrade before shoving at my cage with his feet until the top faces the dip of the corner.

Together, he and the additional guard Tohminic sends down shove my cage to the very bottom. It takes them the entire time it takes for the Mother Star to disappear to make it to my chamber, and I do not know if I am relieved or disappointed I am not granted the opportunity to find food in this dreaded place.

The abuse I would have endured on my way to the dining hall would have been difficult, though the sustenance would have helped my body to heal and gain strength. Something I *need* if I wish to take any opportunity that may arise and escape.

The moment the guards step away from the cage — the hinges squeal as they open — I drag myself from the iron trap. The bars scorch my skin, the pain almost unbearable, yet I am determined to crawl to freedom.

I collapse in a heap, feeling the sturdy sandstone beneath my hands and knees at long last. If I was not so proud, I would kiss the beige stone. The relief is all-consuming, and the yearning to stand and stretch my legs threatens to overcome me. I push myself up. My arms wobble, my legs shake, and I crash back down. Any hope I had of silencing the guards and dashing for freedom disappears faster than my face dives for the floor.

I am too injured and too weak to do much else than lie here and thank the Mother Star for her mercy. *Gain strength first,* I tell myself. Then I can think about doing whatever I can to escape. Run or swim or fight. I do not care what it takes. I will flee beyond the wards, then I will fold to the front lines of Vander's army.

Wyn drags herself closer to me — I did not notice her crawling from her cage, too wrapped up in my freedom as I am — putting herself between me and the guards. "Bria, are you okay? Speak to me."

I must look worse than I feel. Perhaps I am too accustomed to the pain to know any different. Perhaps my mind and body are so ravaged I have lost all sense of awareness. The single word that haunts me flashes across my mind. *Red, red, red.*

I shove it away with a growl and heave myself up, determined to use the last of my strength to fight. I will not die here, where nightmares roam the day and unthinkable horrors invade my nights.

"How unfortunate you could not find food in the time I allowed," Tohminic says from the door, his tone laced with mocking. "Considering my first plan did not go as intended, Xaler and I have decided on another. Come."

"I am not going anywhere with you," I spit, finding my feet at last. My legs are weak and can only just hold my weight, but I force them to remain steady as I face Tohminic. "I hope you burn in the fiery pits of hell."

He only laughs and wields a gleaming dagger before lunging for me. I am so shocked, so weak, I cannot hope to fight back as he tightens his grip around my waist and presses the blade to my throat.

Wyn puts up a bigger fight, though the amount of blood soaking the front of her gown is concerning. She loses strength quickly and is soon in a similar predicament to me — trapped within the vicious embrace of a male.

"If Vander will not concede defeat after I gave him ample warning," says Tohminic, his tone demented, "then I will prove to him how serious I am. The entire Dusk Court will witness your death, Bria of Autumn. It will be one for those history books you love so much. You and the Dusk scum die tonight."

27

I DO NOT BELIEVE I have ever known such dread, such an intense feeling of powerlessness as I have in this very moment. The beads of sweat dancing along my spine tickle as if to remind me I will soon lose all feeling. The blood thrumming through my body deserts my fingers and toes, leaving them cold and numb, and gathers in the core of my being, my heart pounding harder and faster as if it, too, knows it will soon beat its last. It is nothing compared to the rattling breaths that have nothing to do with the blade at my throat.

There is a wordless whisper in the far reaches of my mind, buzzing with insistence. Whatever the whisper desires, I do not care to discover, not as I am dragged from my chamber for the last time.

Tohminic's hold is bruising. He is not gentle as he hauls me through Ad'Starrag, does not care to pause when I stumble on steps or when my body loses its will to remain upright. I am incapable of much more than struggling to draw air into my lungs.

"What do you think you are doing?" the guard trailing us sneers. The guard restraining Wyn.

I do not dare to try turning my head to see her, not with the cool kiss of metal against my throat.

Tohminic's determined steps falter as he turns. "Is she unconscious, then? From the blood loss?"

"I am not certain, My Lord. She was fine, then suddenly she was not."

I know different. It is in the way her eyes have rolled to the back, the way her hands have loosened by her sides. Wyn is sending an illusion to Vander and Torin, telling them of our predicament and warning them their reactions will have deadly consequences from now on.

My feet slip against the sandstone when Tohminic turns back and begins walking once more. "It is no matter," he says. "It will enrage Vander to see her in such a state."

Though I am thankful she has warned Vander and his court of what is coming, I cannot see the benefit in it. Yes, they know Wyn and I have blades to our throats. Yes, they are aware of how dire the situation is. It will not help. It cannot.

Every open arch we pass is host to a guard. They stand statue-still, the only movement coming from their assessing eyes; the fists gripping their outstretched spears and tridents do not so much as tremble from holding them upright.

I am dismayed at my minimal chances of escape, but through that panic is curiosity. I cannot fathom why Tohminic has ordered his guards to this part of the keep instead of sending them to the battlements or to surround the base of Ad'Starrag. Hope that the High Lord of Summer is as inexperienced as I believe him to be blossoms in my chest but struggles to reach full bloom through my seizing breaths.

As Tohminic steers me through the keep, all I can think is my life should not have led to this. My home court treats me like a pariah through no fault of my own, but because of my lineage. I am tormented purely for how I entered this cruel and unjust world. My father could have ordered the Autumn fae to treat me with kindness, yet he allowed them to ridicule his only daughter.

I did not help matters by feeding my rebellious nature, though I do not believe such acts warranted the abuse I have weathered here. A twinge of pain clenches my heart, a reminder of Nikolai that will follow me into death.

Although he is no longer lingering beside me, my mind still torments me with the reminder of my role in his suffering. If I had been smarter with my choices, if I had considered the consequences of my actions rather than acting as if nothing but sating my desire for excitement matters, Nikolai would have lived to find true love and happiness. My hands are red, red, red with his blood.

I will never forget that.

As we pass through the rotunda, I am surprised to see the Summer fae going about their usual full moon celebrations. I do not appreciate my last memories consisting of naked bodies, delighted moans, and the smack of skin against skin.

There are no guards patrolling the sex party; it would be easy to slip through the distracted crowd and out one of the open doorways.

Tohminic tightens his grip on my waist as if reading my thoughts. "Such a shame you will not experience the true pleasure of my court."

I am beyond thankful it has not come to that. My body is struggling, even with Tohminic's firm hold keeping me upright. If he were to force me to take part, I do not think I could have so much as begged the males not to touch me. The thought sends a shudder jerking down my spine.

We exit the rotunda through the eastern hallway. It takes us past the dining hall, then to one of the cylindrical towers. The tower in question is the only corner tower with stairs rather than a sloping ramp. It is difficult to command my feet to lift enough so they do not drag against the rough stone, and more often than not, my toes graze against the steps. It does not take long for the silk of my already worn slippers to wear away to nothing, and less time still for the skin of my toes to tear.

I whimper with every step, but it only serves to bring Tohminic pleasure. The simple sound of my pain delights him to no end, the evidence pressing against my lower back. Nausea builds in my stomach and bile burns the back of my throat. There is no doubt in my mind Tohminic is the most despicable fae I have had the displeasure of meeting.

The moment we step onto the battlement, all sound ceases to exist. Every guard within the keep, every fae whose echoes drift up from the rotunda, every breath... every sound evaporates. The silence only lasts a heartbeat — a mere blink in time for a fae — before chaos erupts throughout Ad'Starrag.

Any remnants of hope lingering in my weak body bursts. The hope that blossomed when I assumed the High Lord of Summer inexperienced with war, the hope of escape through the rotunda, the hope of a miracle getting me out of this... gone,

gone, gone. As panic claims my thoughts and fear threatens to break my mind, a single word filters through.

Red. Ad'Starrag will be bathed in it before long. Just as my hands are.

Because this court intends to fight. Tohminic intends to ruin Vander and the Dusk Court, starting with my death.

The booming thunder of thousands of fae moving through the stone keep is deafening. It would not surprise me if they could hear the sound as far west as the Night Islands, as far north as the Spring Court. I would not surprise me if the drum beat of the marching fae reaches Father in the Autumn Court or High Lord Ruith in his Winter Court in the north-west mountain ranges.

Tohminic forces me to move along the battlement, my feet slipping on the stone as he shoves me to the centre crenel. As we move, the guards and denizens of Summer take their commanded stances at the base of Ad'Starrag, along the battlement surrounding us, and at every window and balcony on the western side of the keep.

Guards push cannons to their stations and load them with glass orbs filled with a dark grey powder. The glass will explode upon contact with the Dusk army, the iron within coating their skin and clothes and filling their lungs. It is a brutal, disgusting form of attack. I remind myself it is no different to the catapults Vander has at his disposal, but I cannot shove the anger down.

Tohminic presses the blade harder against my throat the moment he steps up to the crenel. From beside us, a growl of anger rips from Wyn's throat. I do not know when she surfaced from her illusion, though I am glad she has returned.

It is a selfish thought to wish her here with me rather than with her brother and friends below. But history proves I am a selfish female — if I were not, I would have left Nikolai to his life instead of bringing him to ruin — and in my last moments, I will not allow myself to think negatively of myself. I am what I am, and now is not the time for shame or regret or guilt.

Now is the time to send my last prayers to the Mother Star, to beg her for mercy and a peaceful crossing to the afterlife. To wish for a happy life for Rennyn, a life without suffering for Father, and a life in which Fayeth may find peace with Father's betrayal.

As the Dusk Court falls silent, and the Summer fae settle in their new stations, I wonder if anyone from the Autumn Court will miss me.

Will my students forget me? Will the stable hands take care of Solana? Father and Rennyn and Fayeth... Will they go on, ignoring the seat I used to claim at the breakfast table, or will they mourn my death, their minds conflicted as they wonder what they could have done differently to prevent such a fate for me?

The whispers I have ignored grow more insistent. They speak of a cold kiss and taste of rust. They shout in my mind, urging me to bend and contort.

I will not allow my last moments to be filled with unknowns. These whispers are alien to my mind. I shove them back, replacing their demands with thoughts of the stars I so love, memories of the rare happy moments at the Autumn Court, and fight to recall how Solana smells after a long run.

My gaze lingers over the gathered Dusk fae, finding Vander as easily as if he were a beacon in the dark. I know if they give him the choice between me and Wyn, he will save his sister's life. I expect nothing less.

A wet heat trickles down my throat, tracking between my breasts where it seeps into the lavender silk of my gown. Fear would be a normal reaction. Panic and regret and sadness would all be understandable during such a moment. But the relief I feel at being freed from the world and its torment is not normal. Surely relief is the emotion of a broken mind under such circumstances.

Red, red, red. I will be covered in crimson soon enough. My blood will stain the sandstone, a lasting reminder of my existence.

"Vander of the Dusk Court," shouts Tohminic. "You have ignored all warnings to surrender and have refused to vacate my lands."

I wonder when he sent the message with his order for Vander and his army to leave, but the thought is fleeting. It matters not when, just that Vander refused.

Vander's voice carries on the breeze, a lone gust bringing the rough and commanding tone to our ears. "And you've refused to release the females. I think we're even."

"I think not!" screams Tohminic, a hint of hysteria tainting his tone. "This is the final warning I will offer. You have until the moon reaches its zenith to remove yourselves from *my* land. If you refuse once more, I will indeed return your sister and the Autumn bastard to you... without their heads."

A blast of icy wind slams into the keep, and Tohminic stumbles. The dagger at my throat slips, slicing deeper, and the dribble of blood grows to a steady stream.

The whispers in my mind fight for attention yet again, and this time I allow them presence in my thoughts. I feel their intention, hear their pleas, and smell the discerning differences between every weapon on the battlement.

Tohminic laughs. "Your magic is useless. It has done nothing but injure Bria further. Tell me, do you rejoice in the thought of her bleeding dry? Do you find pleasure in the sound of her cries?"

"Release her." Vander's command is one of deadly intention. Though he speaks only two words, the threat of retribution is clearer than the night sky, brighter than the silver moon high above.

"I will not." Tohminic's blade slices along the open wound of my throat as he turns towards the guard holding Wyn. "Kill her."

The world ripples. Disorienting in its intensity, the hazy film blanketing the land as far as the eye can see shimmers and pulses before everything I know disappears altogether. Replacing the scorching sands to the south, nothing but darkness. Instead of the rolling hills in the distance, nothing. A void.

Something inside me shatters. A pain so intense it causes my knees to buckle envelops my entire being, radiating from my very soul.

Radelea no longer exists. There is nothing but darkness. The darkness and the whispers and the red.

I drag the whispers to the forefront of my mind and clench my thoughts around them, reading them as if I speak the language of wordless voices. The darkness blazes with specks of star-like light, each taking the form of a weapon. Spears and tridents and swords and daggers, all in blinding silver.

I wrap my thoughts around the gleaming light at my throat and the shimmering blade at Wyn's and I *yank* with all my might. The dagger curls away from my skin, bending with a single thought.

Wyn's guard shouts in surprise as his blade curls like a wilted blade of grass. It is the catalyst for the mayhem that follows.

Guards shout, weapons clash, and grunts of pain echo through the still night as Dusk fae appear on the battlement. How they broke through the wards, I do not know. All I know is it is the perfect distraction.

Using what little strength remains in my body, I jab my elbow into Tohminic's ribs. The move is such a surprise for the Summer jerk, he loosens his grip, allowing me to twist from the cage of his arms.

A gentle hand wraps around my wrist, and Wyn screams, "Run!"

28

T HE WORLD BENDS TO Wyn's every command, the illusion of intense darkness fading enough that she has no trouble navigating the mayhem of the battlement. She drags me by the wrist through the throng of Summer and Dusk fae, twisting and turning the moment they move to avoid being captured again.

My feet protest at the rapid pace, my raw toes stabbing with pain with every step I take. My mind is too stunned to register the fact I am escaping, and I allow Wyn to drag me to safety, too numb to be much help. I used magic. Bria Sutherland, magicless bastard, not so magicless after all.

I have spent my life believing myself to be useless with only fae lights, weak shields, and folding to command. But the power to bend metal, the rarest gift an Autumn fae may wield? It is unthinkable.

I have always respected the metal bender in the Autumn Court. Fylson's rare gift of metal manipulation saved him from a life of squalor. For me to have that same magic coursing through my veins, a magic that is both feared and revered, it is... Only one metal bender is born every one thousand suns. I am rare. I am unique. It is more than I have ever been.

Why, though? Why did my magic choose now to make itself known?

"Bria," hisses Wyn, tugging on my wrist, "I need you to focus. We're at the top of the stairs. We can't risk either of us falling. Not now."

Shouts from the battlement grow closer. Paired with Wyn's urgent pleas, I am shaken from my thoughts. I can wonder about my magic another time, when I am safe and far from the Summer Court and its vicious fae.

"Can you lift the illusion so I can see clearly?" I ask, bracing a hand against the sandstone to steady myself. If I do not ground myself in the here and now, I am certain my thoughts will overcome me once more. Not to mention the weak body I am struggling to command.

"I'm not casting the illusion," she says, rushing her descent into the keep. "Vander is. If I disappear to tell him to lift it, I'll be leaving you here alone. I'm not okay with that."

The distinct boom of the cannons thunders through the clash of weapons and shouts, turning my blood to ice. My traitorous mind, determined to break me, conjures an image of the Dusk fae falling beneath the might of the iron powder.

My fault. It will be my fault they die. If I did not escape Tohminic's hold, he would not have given the order to fire the cannons, and Vander's army would be safe. My fault, my fault, my fault. All that blood will stain my hands right alongside Nikolai's. My palms, my knuckles, my fingers are all red, red, red.

My foot slips, and I crash into the stone stairs. Pain flares in my lower back at the impact, stabbing its way down my spine and through my legs. I do not let it deter me.

Trying my hardest to push back that single word screaming in my mind, I launch to my feet and leap the last four steps, landing harshly in the open hallway that leads to the rotunda.

Earlier, I had assumed every fae in Ad'Starrag had moved into position to be ready for a deadly battle. I was so very wrong.

I cringe away from the sword Wyn offers me, seeing nothing but slick blood dripping from the sharp point. More red.

"Where did you get that?"

Her eyes flick to two fallen guards.

"I-I can't."

"We have no choice but to fight our way out," she insists, waving the hilt of the sword in front of me. "Take it. I know you're hurting, but right now, it's kill or be killed. This will all have been for nothing if you don't fight. Do you understand?"

I take the offering with shaking hands, my lower lip trembling in time with the weapon. It feels alien. Deadly and heavy and everything I hate about the world. This blade has seen what horrors the fae can inflict, and it has enjoyed it to no end. The sick feeling of glee glides up my arm from the sword, making me cringe.

Wyn leads me through the rotunda. We barge through the fae still moaning in delight, slicing our swords through the air with no rhyme or reason. Splashes of red shine through the inky darkness, splattering on my ruined gown, on my arms and hands, on my face.

A sob crawls up my throat, passing tears as they stream from my eyes. More blood to add to the stains. It is all I can think as I stab and slice my way through the rotunda. *Red, red, red.* There is too much red.

A crack fractures my heart, a keening wail freeing itself from the trap of my body. I hate the red. I hate the red and the darkness and that Tohminic has made me endure such things. Red and red and red and hate.

The fracture runs from my heart to my mind, shredding me into thousands of pieces that I fear I will never have the strength to put back into place. I will never be the same after this night. I will never wish to see crimson or any of her cousins again.

The surrounding darkness is so dense, I can only make out Wyn's outline as she tears through the fae running in every direction. It is so dense I do not realise until the last moment that my flailing sword is tracking towards the neck of a naked female.

A scream tears from my throat when the blade cuts through her flesh as if it is nothing more than water. The crimson river cascading down her body is the brightest thing I have seen, bright enough to make me pause.

Why am I better than the fae here? Why are their lives worth less than mine? My sword just... No. *I* just killed another being for nothing more than to reach safety. I *murdered* her so I can escape, and all the blood, the red...

I hardly hear the clang of my sword crashing to the ground. I do not feel the pain of my knees colliding with the sandstone. My hands shake so terribly I cannot tell one finger from the other as I stare at all the red staining my skin.

"Red." The word moves from my mind to my mouth, my tongue curling around the letters of its own accord. "Red. It is all red, red, red."

"Bria!" Wyn screams, though I barely hear her cry through the buzzing in my ears.

"Red!" I shout the word so loud my throat tears, the tang of blood coating my tongue. The last sound does not appear, the word contorting into an anguished scream.

I am not better than the fae here. My life is not more important. I am not worthy of freedom.

Wyn's face swims before me, her silver eyes dripping with worry as they dart from side to side. She must see something written in the lines of my face or the emerald of my eyes because she throws an anxious glance behind her and shouts, "Fuck!"

All I hear is, "Red." The word slips from my mouth unbidden.

"What's red?" Wyn asks as she jerks me to my feet.

The tears lining my eyes are blinding, and I cannot see where she is leading me as she wields the sword like an extension of her arm. She cuts through the Summer fae — who are running in circles through the darkness, blind to where they are going — with ease.

More blood on my hands. They would not be injured and dying by Wyn's sword if the Dusk fae were not so intent on finding freedom for me. *Me.*

Red is all I know as Wyn drags me through the keep. Red is my constant as she hauls me through an open archway and into the cool night air. Red is my companion, my only friend, when I am forced to race across jagged rocks and into the ocean as Wyn creates a pocket of air around my head.

I know nothing of the water surrounding me, nothing of the pounding of my heart, and nothing of Wyn's constant pleas to push harder and faster. Red is all around me. It is in my mind and soul. It is me. I am red, and I cannot continue.

The decision comes with a wave of salt water crashing over me and trying to drag me into the depths of the ocean. I remember the serenity of almost drowning off the shore of the Dusk Court, and I believe it would be just as peaceful to let go right now, to leave such an unkind world and join the stars glittering above.

No matter how hard I try, how much force I use to shove at the bubble of air around my head, I cannot break through it. Wyn is determined to see me to safety. Yet... I am not sure I want to see another day.

I force my eyes to open and see the surrounding ocean — the water grows restless, the current pulling harder as Tohminic's emotions roil — but it is too dark to see much more than the darkest of blues. The longer I look, the more I see, and when my eyes have adjusted at last, they grow wide with fear. For that is an army of selkies speeding towards me, and if they catch me...

No. I will not go back.

The Summer Court may have broken my mind to the point of giving up, but I am not so lost to the pain that I am foolish enough to let the selkies drag me back into Ad'Starrag. Life would be one thousand times worse after this.

I thrash through the water, my body contorting as I twist and dip through the intense blue in search of Wyn. I could have sworn she was right in front of me. A quick glance at the shadows racing towards me and I know I am almost out of time.

A glint of silver wavers to my left — Wyn's stolen sword — and I twist in that direction, my arms and legs moving as fast as they can in my weakened state. Too slow, I move towards Wyn. Too slow, as she spins on the spot, searching for me.

Her mouth opens in warning, those bright eyes growing wide as they flick over my shoulder.

I follow her line of sight, a scream ripping free of my already torn throat at the proximity of hundreds of seals speeding towards me. For a moment, I forget I am in the ocean, with the Summer Court's wards so close I can feel the ripple of their magic, and frantically search for a weapon.

A rip in the current claws at what remains of my gown and drags me through the warmth of the water at such a rapid pace I lose all sense of time and space for a moment. At first, I resist the pull of the current. Then I realise Wyn is using her powers to influence the will of the water and drag me closer, so I command my body to relax and allow her to pull me through the wards.

Once I am close enough, we reach out to one another, each of us locking our hand around the wrist of the other. The world folds around me before I can so much as sigh in relief, cocooning me in a darkness so impossibly black it should not exist.

The void soothes the torment in my mind. It is as if nothing could harm me here, not my own thoughts or that one word.

Too soon, Wyn drags me away from the peace within the void and folds to the land bridge bisecting the sea. She releases her grip on my wrist the moment she steps onto the rough, slick rock and runs to the waiting arms of her brother.

Such love and care.

Rennyn could not bring himself to fight for my freedom, let alone be here when I am saved. My chest constricts at the thought.

My hands and knees sting when I collapse to the jagged rocks, though the pain is nothing compared to that in my heart and mind. The same single word continues to slip past my lips as I dig my fingers into the ground in reassurance.

"What's she saying?" a deep, soothing voice asks.

Wyn replies, "She's been saying it since we fled the battlement. Over and over: red."

A firm finger curls beneath my chin and forces me to look up. He is all I can see. His light brown skin, his dark hair, and the stubble lining his jaw.

Vander's eyes glow as bright as the moon when he says, "You're alright. You're safe." His fingers are soft as he brushes clumps of hair from my face. "I've got you, Princess."

29

W ITH JUST THAT MINISCULE point of contact — Vander's finger is hot against my chin — he folds through
the realm, stepping from the Summer Court into the void, then
taking another step onto a beach I do not recognise. The scents
of lavender and orange fill me with calm.

Even with the claws of night clinging to the land, I can tell
the sand is a brilliant white and the waves lapping at the shore a
welcoming lapis lazuli. A dense forest encroaches on the beach
to the south, the trees all larger than anything I have yet to see
in my five and seventy years.

The greenery calls to me with soothing tones. It is such a kind
contrast to the harsh reality of red that I stagger towards the
swaying branches of the nearest she-oak and run my shaking
fingers through the pendulous branches.

"Welcome to the Dusk Court," says Wyn as she steps up
beside me.

I do not pay any mind to the steadily growing crowd behind
us as fae fold onto the island before folding away to their homes.
I know Vander and Torin are watching me with apprehension,
yet I cannot pull my gaze from the rough needles of the she-oak,
even though my legs are shaking with the effort of remaining

upright. There is something grounding in the green, something that soothes the heartache tearing through me and calms the raging guilt.

"Come," says Wyn, curling an arm around my shoulders. "Let's get you to the infirmary. Me, too, if I'm being honest."

Indeed, her voice sounds weaker than I remember it. I peel my eyes from the branches and force myself to acknowledge her pain. She has seen better days — the wound to her stomach is still bleeding — and I am amazed she is still standing.

"I do not think..." I start, but my words trail off, replaced by a steady trickle of tears. How do I tell her I do not deserve this life she is giving me? How do I put my spiralling thoughts into words?

Wyn turns to her brother for help, but it is Torin who steps forward.

"I know." His dark eyes flick between my own. "I know what it is to discover your life is not what you thought it was. You've endured so much in such a short amount of time, and we understand you may not be quite yourself for a while. But standing on the beach and caressing the trees won't help you. Not in the long run. Take a branch with you if you want, though." He reaches an arm behind me and snaps a branch from the she-oak I was admiring and hands it to me.

"You do not understand. I do not think... I cannot go on like this. This is not who I am."

"What do you mean?" asks Wyn.

I lift my hands and stare at them. "They are red. There is so much red I cannot see any other colour. It's all red, red, red." My hands shake anew.

Torin clamps his tanned hands over mine. "We don't know what you went through in there, or why you believe your hands are red, but they're not. Your hands are clean."

I do not believe a word he says. Regardless, I allow him to steer me towards a narrow path in the forest where hundreds of Dusk fae are disappearing beyond the trees.

The she-oaks twist around the occasional swaying palm or towering pine, the tree plentiful so close to the beach. However, the farther into the forest we walk, the sparser the she-oaks become, and the more I run my fingers over the branch Torin handed me. The pines and palms in this part of the forest are lovely, but they are not as green. Their leaves are high above and out of reach, leaving only their trunks at eye level.

The bark wrapping around their trunks is brown. It is too close to red.

The Mother Star blesses me with the forest's exit sooner than I thought it would come, and the anxiety building in my chest eases a fraction. Through gaps in the trees, a grand building looms ahead.

Sitting atop a perfectly rounded hill, with a gravel path twisting up the slope and bisecting the bottle-green grass, the place is imposing. But as I walk closer — Torin still guiding me with a firm hand between my shoulder blades — I decide it is beautiful.

I have seen six of Radelea's primary court residences — the only court Father prohibited me from visiting is the Spring Court, but I have read of its grandeur — and they are all much grander than what lies before me.

I cannot call Dusk's centre of operations a castle or keep, and I cannot claim it to be a village hut. It lies somewhere between the two, and I have no name for the building, though I am not left wondering for long.

"This is Dusk Manor," says Wyn. "The ground floor is open to all. The terrace is a half level on the lower side of the hill and is where we're heading now. We warded the top level against entry."

"Why?"

"It is my home. Vander, Torin, and I live there."

I turn to her with my brow creased. "You allow the denizens to enter your home?"

She shrugs. "Father's hut is down the hill on the other side, but Vander and I decided we want to be more involved with our court and its fae, so we moved to the top level of the manor."

"You can explain it all to her later," says Torin. "I'm starving."

I do not aspire to be the one to belittle others and their issues, but Torin does not know the meaning of the word. *Starving.* The anger at his choice of word is brief, and fades when I remember he has given up days of his life for me.

"Then we best get you inside," I say, taking the first step onto the winding path to the manor.

My body has other ideas and refuses to cooperate as I navigate the twists and turns of the path and the slope of the hill. My aching feet slip on the loose gravel, my legs wobble, and my breaths come in harsh pants. A short walk through the forest is all I can manage.

When Torin offers to help, I shake my head. I will earn this freedom by forcing my legs to carry me into the manor. It is but an insignificant gesture to the Mother Star for a gift I do not deserve — the gift of life. Every day from now until my soul leaves this world, I will fight to earn the privilege of a mind not tortured by guilt and regret, of a body free of pain, and of a free life.

Although the hill is not all that large, it is enough to drain what remains of my strength. Not halfway up, I stumble and crash to the ground with a grunt. My arms shake with the effort of pushing myself back up. Locking my elbows does little to help. When I collapse once more, I scream in frustration.

A pulse of unrestrained magic caresses my back. It is soothing in its touch, cool in its tender kiss, and stronger than anything I have yet to feel.

"Just let us help you," says Wyn, trying to pull me up.

"No." I swipe at her hand. "I *have* to do this on my own."

She kneels in front of me, wincing when the move causes her pain. "You're injured, dehydrated, starved, and your mind is tortured." I snarl, but she goes on. "It's clear as day. You're not acting like yourself. The faster we heal, the faster we can make plans for what's coming. Let Torin or Vander carry you."

Perhaps I am being foolish. Deep down, I know the Mother Star would not grant me a second chance in this life if she does not believe I deserve it. Yet I cannot help but wonder if this is a test. This is my chance to prove to the stars and their mother that I am worthy.

Without letting go of the she-oak branch, I dig my elbows into the gravel and heave myself up the hill. Using my toes to push against the gravel path only adds to the pain coursing through my body — I cannot tell where one injury ends and the next begins; it is all rolled into one wound — but I persist, even through the cries of pain and flood of tears.

"Leave us." Vander's voice is a quiet command laced with poorly disguised fury that mixes with the magic pulsing around me.

Two sets of feet crunch over gravel, one a little slower than the other, the sound fading the farther Wyn and Torin walk.

"I won't pretend to understand what you're going through," Vander says, dropping to his hands and knees beside me. "You don't need that. What you need is to know you're not alone. You're in the Dusk Court now, and here, where the stars appear and the sun we worship shines its last rays, we stick together no matter the circumstances." He begins to crawl beside me. One hand and knee at a time, he moves in sync with me.

The High Lord of Dusk is crawling. For me.

The emotion such a simple act elicits threatens to drown me. I have never seen such kindness from anyone, let alone a male, and this... this is beyond anything the Mother Star can offer me.

"You're not alone," he repeats.

At this moment, I believe him. I know I will look back on this night many moons from now and remember the way Vander crawled beside me. I will remember he refused to walk, that his words pierced through my sorrow. Most of all, I will remember his companionship.

Vander is not better than his denizens. He is their equal. The knowledge gives me the strength to go on, and hand by hand, I make it up that small hill.

The moment we reach the open doors of Dusk Manor, I allow Vander to lift me into his arms and carry me to the downstairs infirmary. Not because I believe my trials with the Mother Star to be over, but because I do not think I can make it to the infirmary without succumbing to the darkness flirting with the edges of my vision.

He takes care to place his muscular arms around me, avoiding the more tender wounds as he lifts me from the dirt in front of the manor steps as if I weigh little more than a feather.

This close to him, his scent is overwhelming. It is the freshest of breezes, the ripest of apples, and the warmth of a summer's eve. It is the forest cedars and the salt of the beach. His scent is many things, but also... it is also just one. It is home.

I do not take note of my surroundings as he carries me through the ground floor of the manor. Nor do I notice the stairs or the long hallway. All I know is the feel of his body against my cheek, the scent of home, and the steady rise and fall of his chest as he breathes.

He pushes through swinging doors into a large chamber that is all white. "I don't think she'll be conscious much longer, Penna. She dragged herself up the hill."

"Why the fuck would you let her do that?" Wyn shouts, leaping from a bed.

"I won't force anything on her," says Vander, setting me on one of the many beds. "If it makes you feel better to know, instead of demanding she bend to my will, I crawled right alongside her."

His tone is enough to quiet Wyn's scathing words, though I imagine she will not let the topic rest for long.

The healer from the Dawn Court, Penna, pushes me against the bed when I try to rise and set Wyn straight — to tell her I did not wish to be carried, no matter how long it took me to climb that hill.

"Lie still so I can work," says Penna, her cobalt eyes flashing with both warmth and command. For a Dawn fae, a historically neutral party, she has a flair of rebellion about her. I like it.

"We'll leave you to it," says Vander, motioning for Torin to follow him out. "Wyn, as soon as you're able, I expect you in the war room. Tohminic won't let this slide for long."

The reminder of my captor brings a cold sweat to my forehead. I drag my eyes from the High Lord of Dusk as he walks through the door and train them on Penna, drinking in every detail to distract me from thoughts that are certain to plague my mind if I allow them.

Her silver hair has a tint of blue to it that is too bright to be natural. I wonder what kind of magic she used to colour it in such a way. Unable to determine the method myself, I throw all tact out the window and ask.

Penna laughs. "It's hair dye."

I look to Wyn in question — I have never heard of such a thing — but the seemingly normal moment fades when I catch sight of the scowl on her face. I turn away, unwilling to dive into *that* conversation.

"I saw it," she says. "When we were in the water, I saw you give up."

"Please, just leave it be."

"I'll do no such thing." Her tone supports her words. "Tell me why. When I went through so much — being forced into that cage and being run through with a sword — why would you just give up?"

Penna's eyes flick from me to Wyn, bright with curiosity while she sends pulses of healing magic into my body. The warmth of her power fills me, soothing away aches and knitting open wounds back together. Although she is healing the physical wounds covering my skin, there is nothing she can do for the demons haunting my mind, the crimson haunting my soul.

It is clear Wyn will not let the subject drop, no matter how much I beg her to.

With a sigh, I relent. "I am not a killer. I cannot just wear the guilt of Nikolai's death, shoulder the burden of those I slaughtered in the rotunda, and ignore the fact I am responsible for those injured when Tohminic gave the order to fire the cannons." My voice comes out like a whip. "Murder is not something I can live with, and there is so much red staining my hands."

"You were dealt this hand in life because you have the strength to bear it." She looks away after that, leaving me to ponder the truth to her words.

30

IT HAS BEEN FOURTEEN moons since I came to the Dusk Court, and during those fourteen moons, I have not left the infirmary. The white walls, so bright they chase away all thoughts of red, are my constant companion.

The walls and Penna, though I do not speak to her often. I prefer to bask in the brilliance of the white, knowing the red cannot creep into my mind if I focus on the walls for long enough.

Wyn's words are another constant, nagging at my mind during every waking hour. *You were dealt this hand in life because you have the strength to bear it.* I cannot decide if the words are true or false, whether they apply to me or are a mere sentence of comfort meant to drag me from the shadows weighing me down.

I often wonder if I have more to live for than I believed during those haunting moments in the ocean. Then, when I was wounded and scared with the selkies approaching, I thought myself useless and unworthy. I could not see past the red on my hands, could not so much as think of the other colours.

I could not see the blue of the water surrounding the island of Dusk, the blue of loyalty and freedom. Nor could I see the green of harmony and safety, the calming colour of nature. The yellow of the Mother Star, of happiness and warmth. The burnt orange sunset, the colour of fun and bravery. The purple mystery of dusk.

Worst of all, I could not see the grey. The colour is often overlooked, but it is the colour of love, the colour of the eyes that saved me and the hair that healed me. It is the middle ground of life, between black and white, where not all is so clean cut.

I am beginning to see the other colours now. Though the red still flashes in my mind more often than the others, and I wake in the middle of the night sweating, with crimson the only colour I can see. And the guilt and regret and heartache... They are twisting into something akin to fiery rage.

I am realising I owe nothing to the Mother Star, and I am left wondering whether spending my days pleasing her is the right way to live my life.

In my time in the Dusk Court, I have only seen Penna. Wyn left the moment she had healed enough to walk straight. She has not returned, and I wonder if my weak mind bothers her so much she regrets saving me from the Summer Court's clutches.

They have left me alone with my red thoughts and white walls, with only Penna to keep me up to date on everything that has occurred since the siege.

No one has seen hide nor hair of Tohminic or any of his denizens. When Vander folded me away from Ad'Starrag, his army of air and illusion wielders followed, leaving the Summer Court free to move to and from their keep. I cannot fathom why Tohminic would order his fae to remain within the sandstone walls.

Vander, Torin, and Wyn have spent every day debating their next move. Though Tohminic has not sent word of warning, and Torin has not heard whispers on the wind of a Summer attack, they wish to be prepared for anything.

Today, Zentha, Jonik, and the Dawn triplets will join them. My presence is required.

I do not know how to feel about entering a space that has always been off limits to me. Father never allowed females into the war chamber, believing them bad luck. So, as I tie the waist cincher tighter — the brown suede is soft, so soft it is distracting for a moment — and the eggshell white dress pulls together, I cannot help but think I will bring bad omens to Dusk's war efforts.

A soft knock on the infirmary door has me rushing to ensure the ruffled bust of the dress covers all it needs to — not that there is a single soul in the Dusk Court who has not seen my body after I arrived in the ruined scraps of fabric Tohminic had me dress in — and the off-the-shoulder sleeves are covering the worst of my scars. Shaped like the bars of the iron cage, they are brutal reminders of my time in Summer.

"Bria?" Wyn's voice filters into the infirmary. "I hope you're dressed, because I'm coming in."

I turn just as she enters, though I do not meet her eyes. "Well met."

She scoffs. "Enough with the formalities. How are you?"

"I am well, thank you. Penna has healed everything she can, though there is little she can do for the scars. Shall we make our way to the war chamber?"

"Look at me."

I hesitate before lifting my face. When I meet her gaze at last, there is nothing but kindness in her eyes.

She smiles and taps the side of her head. "I know you're still healing up here, but I meant what I said. You wouldn't be here if the Mother Star didn't think you could handle it. Smile, Bria. You deserve this life."

"I am not so certain." I collect the she-oak branch from the table beside my bed and clutch it in my fist. It has been a gift these past fourteen moons, soothing my spiralling thoughts when the nightmares wake me. "But thank you for saying that."

Wyn leads me down a short hallway towards a curling staircase, and we ascend to the ground level of Dusk Manor.

I have yet to explore the rest of the manor, and as much as I wish to, now is not the time. So, I settle for taking in as many details as possible. I note the cream walls and the gleaming sconces, the large kitchen on my right, and the many closed doors on my left. There is a sitting room beside the kitchen filled with light from the large windows looking over the north of the island.

We turn into a large space filled with shelves and tomes and scrolls and leather-bound books. I had not realised the Dusk Court had an archive of knowledge, but I am very glad to know it. I can see myself lounging in the bay window, being distracted from whatever I am reading, because that view... is marvellous.

Through the clear glass, I catch glimpses of glittering ocean, rolling hills, and a distant land mass that can only be the Spring Court. The thought makes me wonder what my birth mother thinks of how my life turned out, if the metal bending power I wielded on the battlements is the only magic I possess, and whether I inherited Spring's gifts of manipulating nature and reading the future.

The power to bend and contort metal has not shown itself again. Not for lack of trying on my part. Every night, once I am free of Penna's scrutiny, I fight to gain control of it once more. I have achieved nothing but the occasional aching skull.

Wyn drags me from my thoughts by walking straight through a statue of a fae male wielding a miniature tornado in his palm. An illusion, I suppose. She turns left and knocks on a wooden wall. There are carvings in the wood depicting a war scene — the civil war between Night and Dusk.

The wood, surprisingly, is a door. It swings open, revealing a large chamber decorated with tapestries of indigo, amethyst, and tangerine. In one corner, a raised platform supports a long wooden table and ten chairs, eight of them taken. In another, a small sitting area with tea and cakes laid out on the gleaming surface of a low table. The rest of the chamber holds plush rugs, stands filled with weapons, and crates filled with... I have no clue what lies within the wooden boxes.

"Glad you could join us for once," says Torin, smirking from his seat at the table. "Come. We have some questions."

My eyes travel past Torin and his golden halo of hair to the male beside him, and I dip into a curtsey. "Well met, High Lord Vander." I track my eyes to the rest of the fae, acknowledging Jonik, the triplets, and Lady Zentha. The last female, with hair the colour of pearls, I do not know.

Wyn snorts from behind me. "Enough with all that. In this room, we're friends and allies. Nothing more. Nothing less."

She sinks into the seat beside Vander. "There is no one fae more important than the rest."

I take the last remaining seat — between Torin and the stranger — flicking my eyes over the large parchment covering the table. There are dozens of wooden pieces placed over a map of Radelea, each court's piece painted a different colour. My eyes snag on the red flame that is the Summer Court and do not leave for some time.

"Bria?"

I do not know who the voice belongs to, only that it calls my name. Try as I might, the red flame demands my attention, as if it calls to my very soul.

"The poor dear. Her spirit knows nothing but torment." I can only suppose that is Zentha speaking. The High Lady of Day excels in the inner workings of spirit and soul.

Torin elbows me hard in the ribs. "Snap out of it."

I blink rapidly, at last able to pull my eyes from the wooden piece. "I am very sorry," I say, failing to hide the emotion straining my voice. "What was your question?"

The three males opposite are uncomfortable in my presence. The Dawn triplets avoid looking me in the eye, instead training their identical dark gazes on the female beside me.

Jonik, to their right and seated beside Zentha, clears his throat. He gives his sons a look that would make even my father wither. "Do you have anything you wish to say to Princess Bria?"

"I do not wish to hear anything from your sons, and please, do not refer to me as princess." It pleases me to hear my voice come out strong. "I have no claim to the title."

"But you wear the crown, Bria, no matter how jaded it once was, and no matter how despaired it currently is," says Zentha. "Your father took you in knowing what title you would demand."

I slam my hand down on the table. "My *father* would rather see me rot than lift a finger to defend my honour. I do not wear a crown. There is no title I deserve. Do not tell me otherwise." A sword on the rack in the corner creaks and bends. "My jaded crown only brought me torment and guilt, and the crown of despair will forever cut into my skull. I do not wish for a crown or title, Lady Zentha."

She dips her head in acknowledgement. "Very well. I apologise."

"Please," says Tasar from between his brothers, "let us apologise."

"I will not hear it." I am adamant. If it were not for the triplets leaving Wyn and me in that forest, I would not have suffered at the hands of the Summer fae.

Jonik sighs in a fatherly way. "Come now, Bria. They did not intend for you to be harmed. They are sorry for what you endured."

I look him in the eye, making sure he sees every ounce of hatred and betrayal in mine. "You gave the order. You commanded them home out of fear."

"We are here now," he says, as if it makes up for what I went through. "Dwelling on the past will do nothing but cause tension."

It is a shame for Lord Jonik I do not care for kindness any longer. For five and seventy years, I have accepted the rule of others without question and abided by the laws of Radelea. I will no longer be the kind — if not a little rebellious — daughter of High Lord Kerym of Autumn. I am Bria, metal bender and female who does not care for the opinions of others. Least of all the Mother Star, after everything she put me through.

"Kindness has not proved to benefit me in the past, and it will not do so now, Jonik. You are here as an ally to Dusk and enemy to Summer. Whatever forgiveness you were seeking from me, I do not give it."

"I like her," says the stranger beside me.

I turn to her, not at all impressed by her bright lavender eyes. "Who are you?"

Wyn's favoured snort sounds from the head of the table. "Bria, meet Nyree, leader of the Ill-fated."

The memory of Wyn explaining the Ill-fated is hazy, but I recall enough to know Nyree is taking advantage of Dusk's kindness.

I turn away, dismissing the Ill-fated leader. I do not like her.

"Before this turns into a fight to the death," says Torin, his tone laced with humour, "shall we get on with things?"

Vander watches Nyree and me carefully as he leans forward and asks, "How do we convince your father the Dusk Court is a worthy ally?"

I throw my head back and laugh. "Father will never support Dusk. Not after everything that has happened. Why?"

"If we have Autumn on our side, we will have fae at the southern, western, and northern borders of Summer, with the eastern border nothing but ocean. Lord Jonik has offered to keep his armada there, but we cannot risk Dawn's safety unless we are sure Ad'Starrag will fall."

"Why do we need to fight?" My question is simple, yet it elicits surprised gasps from around the table. I take a leaf out of Rennyn's book and arch an eyebrow. "I am safe, Summer has no hold over any other court, and there is no active warfare. Why anger Tohminic by surrounding him once more?"

"If we don't act, he will," says Wyn. "And if you think for one moment he'll show mercy —"

The door creaks open, a red-faced guard poking his head inside. "Excuse me, but there's a male here to see Bria. Shall I show him to the sitting room?"

"Who is it?" I ask, standing.

Everyone I know, other than my so-called family, is sitting in this very chamber.

The guard winces. "Says his name's Ren."

I push away from the table and shove past the guard. "Where is he?"

He stutters an answer, directing me to the stables outside.

Wyn hurries behind me, directing me through the manor to the double doors that exit onto the gravel out front. The stables are to my left, but I do not need her directions to find them.

Rennyn stands beside my beautiful Solana. He starts forward when he sees me approaching, my gown billowing behind me like a wraith on the wind.

"Do not come closer," I say as I stop four sword lengths away. "Why are you here?"

"Are you not happy to see me, sister?"

"No. I cannot say I am. What do you want?"

Vander and Torin stand on either side of me, and Wyn moves to Vander's right. Behind them, the triplets, Jonik, and Zentha make up our party.

"I brought Solana as a show of good faith," he says, handing the reins to a stable hand, who rushes to guide her into the stables.

Rennyn shifts his weight, his golden-brown eyes taking in those surrounding me. "Mother has fled the court. She…" He runs a hand through his hair. "She broke her mate bond with Father and has sought sanctuary in the Summer Court. You have to help me. As High Lord of the Autumn Court, I am begging for your aid and forgiveness. I am truly sorry for the ogre and for everything you have endured since."

Father's fate is not one I would wish upon any fae. Being the reluctant party of a broken bond, he will endure a lifetime of madness, while Fayeth will be free from the torment of the severed bond.

I ignore the mention of the ogre and scoff. "I owe you nothing."

"She has given Tohminic everything," Rennyn growls. "He knows our every plot, our every defence. *Everything*. We will fall without the help of the Dusk Court and its allies."

"You should have thought of that before you turned your back on me." I turn and walk away, only pausing to face Vander and say, "I do not accept an alliance with Autumn."

He dips his chin. "We'll find another way to bring Summer to its knees, Princess. You have my word."

A tear tracks down my cheek. War may be on the horizon, and we may have doomed this land to fall, but my hands are as red as the rage burning through me. I do not think I can survive a war. I am Bria Sutherland, and crimson haunts my soul.

About the
Author

Samara is a fantasy author from Melbourne, Australia, where she lives with her partner, three kids, and an English Staffy named Boots. Though she loves Melbourne, she grew up surrounded by a large family in north-west Tasmania and misses the quiet life.

Some of her hobbies include reading, a good ol' Netflix binge, camping, and playing Monopoly with her kids, but she can't do any of that without coffee.

You can follow her on TikTok for sneak peeks into up and coming works under the handle @samaradoesbooks or on Instagram under @samarasaward.author

Also by
Samara Saward

<u>The Opal Wolf</u>

<u>Helios Mage</u>
Heir of the Solstice
Prince of Persuasion
King of Deception

<u>Dragon's Oath</u>
Legacy
Enigma
Anarchy

www.ingramcontent.com/pod-product-compliance
Lightning Source LLC
Chambersburg PA
CBHW031937210726
48290CB00006BA/1643